LET'S GO GET 'EM

LET'S GO GET 'EM

TOM HARDING

Library of Congress Control Number:		2009908742
ISBN:	Hardcover	978-1-4415-6842-7
	Softcover	978-1-4415-6841-0

This book was printed in the United States of America.

To order additional copies of this book, contact:
Xlibris Corporation
1-888-795-4274
www.Xlibris.com
Orders@Xlibris.com
65024

DEDICATION

To my beautiful wife, Lillian, for all her patience and understanding while I spent many months writing this book. Thank you, Lillian. I love you.

INTRODUCTION

An adventurous, suspenseful, and irresistible read awaits readers as author Tom Harding releases his new book, *Let's Go Get 'em*. A story of the old times, this absorbing fiction depicts man's love, unique passion, significant hatred, and the power of luck in the lives of the sharpshooters.

Tinged with the right blend of characters, romance, and suspense, *Let's Go Get 'em* takes readers on a journey back to the year 1888 to learn the story of the bounty hunters and the daily dangers they had to face. It introduces readers to Dan Colt, a big, handsome bounty hunter of towering height, who has no fear of anyone, any time, anything, and anywhere. He is the nicest person one will ever meet, but some people make the mistake of riling him. He has the temper of a grizzly bear, but he has a soft spot for women and children. Of the bounty hunters during this era, Dan and his dog, Sammi, a 5 year old German Shepard are two of the best—and this is his and their adventure.

Let's Go Get 'em helps readers learn and understand the hunters' way of life through Dan's and the few others'. It relates about how Dan lived, his encounters and pursuit of the outlaws, how he loved, and how he helped others. It also tells how hunters use some of the cleverest ideas they can come up with to get the bad guys and keep themselves alive—only the best bounty hunters stay alive and those with very little or no experience usually don't live long. How did Dan manage to become one of the best hunters, face all the risks on his way, help others, love someone, and stay alive?

CHAPTER 1

There was an outlaw by the name of Butch Butcher; he went by the nickname the Snake. He and three other bandits ambushed three cowboys driving a small herd of cattle. The three cowboys got caught out in the wide open, with no place for cover. Snake and the other murderers were hiding behind large rocks. When they opened fire on the cowboys, a bloody battle erupted. All three cowboys were killed. Two of Snake's bandits were killed. Snake Butcher and Robert Sage were the only ones that survived the bloody battle. They were wanted for three murders and cattle rustling. Robert Sage was later caught and hanged in Texas where the crime was committed.

A bounty hunter by the name of Dan Colt went after Snake, but Snake eluded him for a couple of months. Dan, not being a quitter, stayed on his trail and finally caught Snake in a small town in mid-Arizona called Payson. Snake was in the saloon having, unknowingly, his last shot of whiskey. When Snake looked in the mirror, he saw Dan behind him. Snake froze for a second then grabbed for his gun. Dan grasped his wrist, squeezed it with a powerful grip that was so painful the Snake dropped to his knees. Dan said, "Your luck just ran out, Snake." Dan asked the rest of the bar patrons to stay back and out of the way.

Snake said, "You don't even know who I am."

"Oh yes, I do, you're the Snake."

Sammi let out a convincing bark and growl. She wanted to get Snake in the worst way, but Dan told her to stay back. Snake didn't want Sammi on him. He knew it was all over and didn't resist any further. Dan put the handcuffs on him, then picked him up and set him on a chair, and said, "Sit there, you son of a bitch."

Dan pulled a Wanted poster out of his pocket and unfolded it and handed it to one of the patrons and asked, "Does this look like the man sitting on that chair? Pass this around to everyone." After they all looked at the picture, Dan asked, "Is this him?" They all agreed that was him. He led Snake out to where Buck was tied. "I want to get everything clear," Dan said. "I will give you four choices if you try to run from me."

Snake asked, "What choices do I have?"

"Number one, I'll twist your head off with these ol' calloused hands." Dan showed his open hands. "Number two, I will cut your head off with this big bowie knife," he said, pointing to his knife, "number three, your throat ripped out by my dog, Sammi. That's her growlin'. And number four, a bullet from that .44 Magnum rifle you see sticking out of that saddle scabbard. Do you hear what I'm sayin'?"

"I hear you," replied Snake. Dan then took Snake to the jail, and the marshal locked him up for the night.

The next morning, Dan asked the marshal if he knew where he could buy a packhorse. The marshal thought for a second and then said, "You might try old man Jones. He has a few packhorses."

"Is that what they call him, old man Jones?"

"Yep, that's what they call him. If you want to go out to his place, you go down to that first street and turn left, then go about a mile. His place is on the right." Dan thanked the marshal. He saddled Buck, and he and Sammi headed out. When he figured he had ridden about a mile, he saw an old man in the front yard of a ranch house. Dan rode up and asked, "Are you old man Jones?"

"Yep, that's me. What can I do fer ya?"

"Well, I need a packhorse and a packsaddle. The marshal said you might sell me one."

"Well, I really don't have any for sale. What ya needin' 'em fer?"

Dan said, "My name is Dan Colt, and I'm a bounty hunter, and I caught Snake Butcher. He's wanted for murder."

"Oh ya, I've seen his Wanted posters," replied Jones. "So ya got him, huh?"

"Yep, I have to take him all the way back to Texas, and it's goin' to be hotter than hell ridin' all the way from Arizona to Texas. I need a packhorse real bad. I need to take extra water and food."

"Well," Jones said, "I'll tell ya what I'll do. You give me $25 and that big dog, and I'll sell ya a horse."

"No no no," Dan cut in. "I can't let you have my dog. Twenty-five dollars, ya, but not my dog. My dog's name is Sammi, and she saved my life a few times. She will be by my side until either she dies or I die, whatever comes first."

"Okay, if ya got ol' Snake, I'll sell ya one. Let's look at the horses."

Dan asked if he could buy one about the same size as the one he's riding. Dan tied Buck to the fence, and they walked by the barn where there were several corrals with about twenty or more horses in them.

Jones said, "There's ol' Claude." Claude was big, about fourteen hundred pounds. Sorrel with a full white blaze and four white stockings. Very flashy. Jones asked, "Is he big enough fer ya?"

Dan said, "Yep, he's big enough." Dan opened Claude's mouth and checked his teeth. "Ya, he's about nine or ten. He'll do."

"When ya goin' to need 'em?" asked Jones.

"Right now. I want to pull out tomorrow morning." So it was a deal. Dan, Claude, Buck, and Sammi headed back to town.

The next morning, Dan saddled all three horses. Then he walked down to the general store and asked the clerk if he had jerky. The clerk said he did. "How much do you need?"

"About five pounds and ten cans of beans and a couple sacks of the dried fruits."

The clerk put all the food in a burlap bag. Dan also bought four one-gallon canteens. He went back to the horses and led Claude to the livery barn and asked the man for two hundred pounds of oats in two burlap sacks. He strapped one on each side of the packsaddle then strapped the food and oats evenly to balance the weight. He took Claude to the water trough where the water pump was and filled the canteens. Dan was riding Buck. Snake's horse was tied to Buck's saddle, and Claude was tied to Snake's saddle. Snake was chained to his saddle. They were about fifteen days from reaching Texas to turn Snake over to the Texas Rangers and collect the two-thousand-dollar bounty. On the third day out, Dan could see at a long distance ahead what looked like Indian adobe huts, but he wasn't real concerned. The marshal told him before they pulled out that he would run into some Indians, but he thought that most of them were friendly although there were renegades. The renegades were either kicked out of the tribe or split away on their own. They lived by stealing; and they had no problem killing people for their money, their livestock, or anything else of value. They liked guns and would kill to get them. To be safe, if Dan saw anything at a distance that didn't look right, he would pull his telescope out from his saddlebags. The telescope had saved his life several times. But nothing looked suspicious at this time. The farther they rode, the more Dan could make out that it was an Indian tribe settlement consisting of adobe huts and a few tepees. No one seemed to pay much attention when they approached. Dan knew that water wouldn't be far from a tribe of Indians. Usually, they settle close to water. Dan noticed a field of corn. Now he knew water was near. He rode up to the Indian that was doing the least, figuring he would be the chief.

"Howdy," said Dan. The chief welcomed him. "Is there water here?" asked Dan

"Yep, there is water for the horses over there in the shade of those trees. There is water for the water cans there at the pump."

After watering the horses, Dan filled the canteens. The chief asked, "Are you and him the only two?" pointing at Snake and the big dog.

"Ya, just the three of us," replied Dan.

"Much danger," said the chief. "We call renegades." The chief held up seven fingers.

Dan asked, "Are they near here?"

"Don't know, sometime, ya. Sometime, no."

"I think maybe we should travel at night."

"By the way, my name's Dan Colt," Dan said, reaching his hand out. The chief shook Dan's hand.

"My name Chief Wild Horse." Dan asked the chief if they could rest there until sundown. The chief nodded his head.

Looking at the sun, Dan figured it was about four hours until sundown. They all rested in the shade. At sundown, the horses were saddled. Snake was chained to his saddle again. They traveled several nights with no problem. Dan was assured that they were past the area where the renegades were terrorizing and killing. They decided to travel by day again. It's hard to find water at night. Although, they did find one river and a couple small streams where there was enough water for the horses to drink. They were running short of water now. So they headed out early, hoping to find water for the horses. Otherwise, he would have to use the water from the canteens, which wouldn't last long.

They traveled several hours when they came across three covered wagons traveling west. They stopped, and Dan introduced himself. He asked if they had run across water.

One man said, "There's a small town about two hours back, and they have water."

Dan asked, "Do you have guns?"

"Yes, we do. Why?"

"There are about seven renegades that are looking for small wagon trains like the ones you have. They will kill you if you don't kill them first. They kill for your wagons, horses, and especially your guns. So whatever you do, keep a lookout for them. We traveled at night for several nights. The only thing is it's hard to find water traveling at night. But I see you have a few barrels of water, so you can travel farther between waterings than we can. So again, be careful and good luck." Dan headed out to get water for the horses. The guy was right. They pulled into this very small town, which didn't have a name. It consisted of a saloon and a store with very little merchandise. They were in pretty good shape for food. There was a blacksmith with a small barn but had enough room for the horses. They could get fed and watered. It being midafternoon would give the horses a good rest and get their bellies filled. Sammi also needed a little rest. Dan asked the blacksmith if there was a sheriff or marshal.

"No," answered the blacksmith. "The sheriff comes through about every two weeks."

Dan said, "I was hopin' you would have a jail."

"Oh ya, I built a jail cell for the sheriff so when he comes through with a prisoner, he could lock him up overnight."

"Do you mind if I locked Snake up overnight?"

"Is that the Snake that's wanted in Texas?"

"That's him."

"So you got the bastard? Good for you."

"Where can I get food for Sammi, Snake, and myself?" asked Dan.

The blacksmith said, "The saloon has sandwiches."

"Do they have good whiskey?"

"Ya, you can get mighty drunk on that stuff they sell."

Dan asked the blacksmith if he could put shoes on the big packhorse. He didn't have shoes when he bought him, and now he's getting some big chips.

"You bet," said the blacksmith. "He'll be ready for you in the mornin'."

Dan walked over to the saloon and asked for some whiskey and noticed a menu and asked the barkeep for three roast-beef sandwiches. He asked the barkeep if he could take a sandwich and some water to the prisoner in the jail cell. Dan noticed three shifty-looking guys sitting at a table. They seemed the kind that never made an honest dollar in their life.

When the barkeep returned from delivering the sandwich and water, he came in somewhat excited, talking loud, and asked Dan, "Is that prisoner the one they call Snake?" Dan was thinking, *What a question for him to ask in front of those shady-looking characters.*

"Ah, ya." Dan was thinking this could be bad. He was guessing he would find out. Dan had the other two sandwiches in front of him. He turned around and whistled for Sammi to come in and have her sandwich. When she came in, she was looking at the guys and was growling in a low, steady growl.

Dan said, "It's all right, Sammi. Here is your sandwich." Sammi gobbled down the sandwich, but she never took her eyes off the drifters. They felt uneasy with Sammi and her constant growl. So they drank up their beers and left. Everything else was taken care of for the night. The next morning, Dan was getting everything ready to move out. He asked the blacksmith if he had seen those drifters.

"No, not this morning."

Then Dan asked if there was any shelter ahead, in case those guys try to kill him and Sammi, take Snake for the bounty, and then take the horses and the guns too. That would make a good haul for 'em.

"Yes, headin' east, there are plenty places for shelter."

"Would you like me to send someone with you?"

"No, if I can find shelter, I'll be all right." Dan headed out, looking in every direction. After about two hours out, he saw dust about thirty minutes back heading his way. "Well, Snake, I think we better find a shelter and dig in. I think that's them."

Looking around, the only shelter he could see was a clump of trees. Dan thought they'd better take that. So they rode in far enough where he could still see the trail. Dan got the horses tied behind trees, and then he unchained Snake and told him to get down on his belly and stay there. "If you have any thoughts of running, Snake, remember Sammi is watching you."

Snake said, "Don't worry, I'll stay where you tell me."

"That's a good decision you made, Snake." Then Dan checked his rifle to be sure it was fully loaded. He then found a tree limb that was just right to steady his rifle over. Dan could see them coming before they could see him. He could see they had rifles in their hands. There was no doubt that they were after them to take Snake for the bounty. Dan figured if he could take one at about two hundred yards that would give him plenty time for the other two. As they got close enough, Dan steadied his rifle and squeezed the trigger.

Boom! Blowing one off his horse. The other two were now lifting their rifles to their shoulders. Dan squeezed the trigger. *Boom!* Number two down. The last one turned his horse and tried to get away, but Dan thought, *Don't take a chance.* He shoved another bullet in the chamber, aimed and squeezed the trigger, and *boom!* Three down.

Snake said, "That's damn good shootin'."

Dan answered, "In my business, you best be a good shot." Dan put Snake back on his horse then rounded up the outlaw's horses and tied them one after another. Dan went back to the dead outlaws, reached down, and unbuckled their guns and holsters. Dan told one of the dead outlaws, "You won't be needin' these guns anymore." Then he picked up their rifles and put them back in the scabbards. He hung the guns and holsters over the saddle horns. They were ready to pull out. Dan was riding Buck with the other horses in a string behind him. Dan turned around and had to grin. He said, "We look like a freight train, Snake."

Snake asked, "What are you goin' to do with the dead outlaws?"

Dan said, "I'm goin' to leave them for the coyotes." Dan asked Snake, "Do I look like the kind of a man that would let a poor coyote go hungry?" Then he grinned. Dan said, "Let's go, Buck. We need to find some water."

The string was on its way. Later that afternoon, they came across a small town in east New Mexico. Dan was happy to see there was a marshal's office and jail. They rode up to the jail and were met by the marshal.

"Howdy, neighbor," said the marshal. "Looks like you have the lizard in chains."

"No," said Dan, "this is Snake Butcher."

"Oh ya," replied the marshal. "I knew he was some kind of a slithery creature. It looks like you have quite a string of horses. Could I ask where you came across all of them?"

"Well," Dan said, "there were three outlaws that did something real stupid."

The marshal grinned and said, "Say no more. I'm glad ya got 'em."

Dan asked the marshal if he could leave Snake in his jail overnight.

"Sure. Bring him in, and I'll lock him up."

"Oh, by the way," Dan asked, "would you happen to have an extra bunk in there? I would like to sleep close by with my dog, Sammi."

The marshal looked at Sammi and said, "That is a mighty big dog. Is she friendly?"

"Only when I tell her to be."

"How much does she weigh?" asked the marshal.

"I think a little over a hundred pounds, and she is a light sleeper. No one will get past her. I had a couple months in trackin' Snake down, and I would hate to lose him now."

"Sure. The other cell is empty, and there is a blanket that you can roll up for a pillow. I don't think you will need it to cover up with in this scorching heat."

After getting Snake locked up, Snake started complaining about it being too hot in the cell. "Can't you chain me to the post out front?"

"No! I'm gonna sleep in there also. So quit complaining. Besides, where you're goin', it will be hotter than that cell. You might as well get used to it." Out the door, Dan took Buck and the other five horses to the livery barn and asked the man in charge if he would give the horses one gallon of oats and all the hay they could eat, and do the same thing in the morning. Dan asked if he could have them fed and watered by sunup. The livery man said that he would take good care of them, and they would be ready by sunup. Dan and Sammi walked back to the saloon and noticed a small café named Sally's café next door.

Dan stepped inside and asked, "Are you the owner?"

"Yes, I am," Sally answered. Then Dan asked if she could take Snake some supper and some cold water and asked if she could throw a beefsteak on for him. He then walked through the swinging doors of the saloon. He told Sammi to stay at the door. He sat down at the bar and asked the barkeep for a glass and some whiskey. The barkeep set a glass and a bottle of whiskey in front of him. The barkeep couldn't wait to ask Dan about Snake.

"I hear you have Snake Butcher in chains?"

"News travels fast," replied Dan.

"Sure does," said the barkeep. "This is a small town, and like ya say, news travels fast. It will be good to take that Wanted poster down so we don't have to look at his ol' Snake face anymore." The barkeep asked, "How did you catch him?"

"Well, that's a long story, about two months worth to be exact," answered Dan.

"Did he put up a fight?"

"Not after I gave him some choices if he tried to get away."

"Do you mind if I ask what his choices were?" asked the barkeep.

"Well," Dan said, "I told him that I or my dog would kill him. He's been pretty good ever since."

"Where do you have to take him to collect the bounty?"

"Well, I would rather not talk about that."

"Oh ya, I understand," replied the barkeep.

Dan paid for his drinks and went to Sally's café and had his supper. He then moseyed back to the marshal's office and sat on the bench out front. A kid about sixteen or seventeen years old came over and sat down beside Dan on the bench.

"Hi, mister, are you the one that caught ol' Snake?"

"Yep, I reckon I am."

"Don't you know that you can take him in dead or alive?"

"Ya, I know that," said Dan.

"So why don't you shoot him and take him in dead, then you won't take a chance of him gettin' away?"

"No," said Dan. "I'll take him in and let the Texas Rangers hang him or whatever they want to do with him."

The boy said, "I'll kill him for ya if you want me to. I'll get my dad's shotgun."

"No no no, I don't want you to kill him."

"But you don't understand," said the kid. "You can lay him across his saddle and chain his head to one stirrup and his feet to the other stirrup, and you won't have to feed him or take a chance of him gettin' away. If you want, I'll shoot him between the eyes."

"Wouldn't that be great?" said Dan. "If you blow his face off, then when I take him to the Texas Rangers, they can't recognize him. Then I get no bounty."

The boy said that he would shoot him in the belly. Dan thought for a minute and then said, "Okay, go get your dad's shotgun." The boy took off, running as fast as he could to get the shotgun.

Dan stepped in the marshal's office and asked the marshal, "What the hell is wrong with that kid?"

"I think he's a few cows short of havin' a full herd." The marshal laughed and said, "That's dumb Goober."

"Is that his name?" asked Dan.

"I don't know. That's all I've ever heard him called," answered the marshal. "He and his parents moved here about four or five years ago. We think his mother dropped him on his head shortly after birth."

Dan turned around, and here comes the kid with his dad's shotgun. He ran up to Dan, and Dan said, "Here, Goober, let me see the gun." Goober handed the double-barreled shotgun to Dan. Dan opened the breach. Sure enough, both barrels were loaded. Dan turned to the marshal and asked if he would please take the gun and lock it up until he was gone out of there tomorrow.

"This kid is goin' to kill somebody with this damn shotgun." Then he turned to the kid. "I'll tell you why I don't want him dead."

Dan asked, "Have you ever smelled a dead body after a few days on the trail? He smells bad enough as it is."

"Oh ya, I didn't think about that," said Goober.

The next morning, Dan and Sammi were up early. The man from the livery barn came over and told Dan that the horses were fed and watered about an hour ago. They were in good shape and ready to go.

"Would you like some pancakes before you head out?"

"Well, I'd like that, but the only thing is that I would have to feed Snake too."

Then he said, "I'll have my wife fix plenty for you, Snake, and some for Sammi." "I'll be happy to pay for the breakfast. By the way, what's your name?"

The livery man said, "My name is Jake, and no, you can't pay for your breakfast."

Then Jake said, "I'll tell my wife, and she will have 'em ready in a few minutes."

After they ate, Dan asked Jake how far it was to water and food headin' east. Jake thought for a few seconds and then said, "There is a small river about five hours' ride from here, and there's plenty of grass along the river if you want the horses to graze for a while."

Dan asked how far it was from the river to the Texas border.

"About another five hours from here. You're lookin' at nine or ten hours. Dan, do you have enough food along?"

"No, Jake, I don't have enough to get there."

Jake asked, "Do you want to buy enough jerky to get you there? Ted, the owner of the market down the street, has jerky. He keeps plenty dried ahead for people coming through. They stock up before pullin' out."

"What time does he open?" asked Dan.

"He should be open in a few minutes."

When the store opened, Dan stopped in to pick up five pounds of jerky. He saw some canteens hanging on the wall. He asked Ted if he could tell him how much water it would take to get him, Snake, and Sammi to the next town.

"How many canteens do you have with you?"

"I have four that hold one gallon each."

"That should get you to a little town called Lariat, that's just across the border in Texas, with no problem."

Dan filled the canteens at the water pump that was in front of the saloon at the water trough. The horses and Sammi took on a little more water, as if they knew they were heading out on a long hot trail. They headed out for the river five hours away.

It was another hot day, but the horses could make it to the river where they could take on another good drink and get on the trail again. Dan was wanting to get to Lariat, Texas, and turn Snake over to the rangers and get rid of him. Late that afternoon, they did pull into Lariat.

They covered the ten-hour ride in a little over eight hours. Dan turned Snake over to the marshal. Dan and the marshal had a conversation. The marshal told Dan that it could take eight to ten days for the bounty money to get there. Dan then took the six horses to the livery and put them away. He rented a room at the hotel that was over the saloon. The trip was over.

"Thank you, God," he said as he headed for his room.

Chapter 2

Dan was awake early the next morning. He took the outside stairs down because the saloon hadn't opened yet. Dan just walked around town, stopping, mostly killing time. The thing that caught his eye was the little café. The name of it was Silly Lilly the Hillbilly Chili Queen Café. Dan had to laugh. He stepped in and asked the lady, "Are you Silly Lilly?"

"Yes, I am."

Dan asked, "Do you serve breakfast or just hillbilly chili?"

"Yes, we do serve breakfast." Dan ordered and had his breakfast.

When Dan left the café, he could see the saloon was open. He had met Maggie the night before, when he rented a hotel room over the saloon. Dan stopped in the bar for a couple of swigs of whiskey before going to the room. Maggie was the owner of the Wagon Wheel Saloon and Hotel. She is the day barkeep. At night her barkeep is Howard, a big guy that has no trouble taking care of drunken cowboys. So he stopped in to pass the time. Maggie welcomed Dan and asked how everything was and if the room was okay.

"It was absolutely great for a good nights' sleep and a good hot bath."

"What would you like, Dan? Whiskey or coffee?"

"I'll have some coffee." So they sat at a table, talking. "I'm curious, Maggie, how did you come to own a saloon? I don't think I've ever seen a saloon that was owned by a woman. Not that there is anything wrong with it."

"Well, Dan, it was about five years ago when my husband, Harold, was trying to stop a fight between two drunken cowboys. He stepped in between them, and one cowboy had pulled his gun to shoot the other drunk. Harold got the bullet instead. He was shot in the heart and was dead when he hit the floor. So I kept the saloon, just trying to make a living."

"I'm sorry, Maggie, that you lost your husband. It's too bad that a two-bit drunken cowboy can take a good man's life. I hope that someone killed him." Dan changed the subject as he could see Maggie was reminded of that horrible day. "Maggie, tell me, what's around the outlying area of this town?"

She never got to answer him as, at that time, a young blond-haired blue-eyed boy ten or twelve years old came in the back door. He had a broom and dustpan in his hands. He began sweeping the floor.

"Is that your boy, Maggie?"

"No, Dan." Maggie then asked Billy to come and meet Dan. "Billy, this is Dan." Billy stuck his hand out, and they shook hands.

"It's nice to meet you, Billy."

"It's nice to meet you too, Mr. Dan." Billy went back to sweeping the floor. Maggie and Dan continued their conversation. Maggie explained the situation about what happened to Billy.

"Billy and his mother, Madeline, were home. His father, Ben, was away that day. His mother heard something outside. She went to the window and saw several renegades. She grabbed the rifle that Ben left for her, just in case something like this were to happen. There were just too many of them. When she first saw them, she told Billy to run out the back door and run deep in the trees. Billy did what his mother had told him. On the way out, he grabbed his little .22 rifle that his father bought for him, but he never had a chance to shoot at the renegades. Best he didn't. He wouldn't have stood a chance. Ben was teaching Billy to shoot and the dos and don'ts of handling a gun. Billy was back in the trees when he heard several gunshots. When Billy heard the renegade's horses running away, he raced back to the house and discovered his mother lying in a puddle of blood. She was dead. Billy looked out the window and saw two renegades dead on the ground. Billy was ten years old at that time. He jumped on his horse and rode to town as fast as he could. When Billy got to town, he was crying hysterically. Billy loved his parents very, very much. There were at least a dozen or more townspeople that went looking for the renegades. They hunted for them the rest of the day until sundown, but they never found them. Several of the men went out to the farm to bury Madeline. So I put Billy up until his father got home. They were seriously wondering if something had happened to Ben also. After two days, the people were worried about Ben. Some of the townsmen decided to ride out to the farm to see if Ben was home yet.

"When they reached the farm, Ben's horse was standing in an open corral with the saddle and bridle still on her. They were going to unsaddle her. They noticed blood spatters on the saddle, which led them to believe that Ben was either wounded or dead. Now Billy was faced with losing his father as well. The townspeople, nearly all the men, started looking for him, following the tracks that his horse had left. They tracked her for several miles until they came to a creek, and then they lost the tracks. They fanned out, trying to find the tracks again. No such luck. They never found the trail again. They spent two days searching before they called the search off. That was two years ago. The townspeople got together trying to figure out what to do with Billy. So I told them that I would keep him for the time being. I had a room in the back of the saloon. Two of the men came over and helped me clean it, and we found a little bed. We had Billy taken care of. Billy helps me for taking care of him. Billy's mom, Madeline, never knew that Ben was, supposedly, dead, and Ben never knew that Madeline was killed. Strange thing."

"That is a strange thing, Maggie. What is the future for Billy?"

"Well, Dan, nobody knows what his future will be."

"Does he go to school?"

"No, Dan, the closest school is a four-hour ride each way. His parents tried to teach him, but they had very little schooling themselves. I've been trying to help him with his reading, but only for the last couple months."

"This is a sad story, Maggie. It's not fair for the young boy's unknown future. He has a lot to face. Maybe we can come up with something. He needs a helping hand of some kind." Dan was going for a ride in the country just to look around. "I'll be thinking about the boy and his future also."

"Thank you, Dan, I can tell you have a big heart." Billy must have heard what Dan said. He came over and asked, "Mr. Dan, would you mind if I saddle my horse and ride with you?"

"Well, I guess so, if it's all right with Maggie."

Maggie said, "Sure, it's all right with me."

So Dan, Billy, and Sammi headed for the stable to get their horses and saddle up and be on their way.

"That's a beautiful black mare you have, Billy, is she yours?"

"Ya, she was my dad's horse. She can run faster than any horse around here. My dad would enter her in the races at the county fair every year, and she would always win."

"Well, Billy, she is one beautiful horse. What's her name?"

"Her name is Cricket."

"She looks like a racehorse, Billy." As they rode out a ways, they came across hundreds of corrals big enough for thousands of cattle or horses.

"What are all these corrals used for, Billy?"

"When a cattle drive comes through, they give the cattle and their horses two or three day's rest. Earl Burns owns the corrals. He also owns the feed store. One time, two drives came in one day apart. There was almost a gunfight between the two cattle companies. After that, Earl added some more corrals so that wouldn't happen again. Earl feeds and waters the cattle. I don't know how much he charges, but he is always happy when he knows they're comin'. Earl is cockeyed."

"What do you mean, Billy?"

"Well, when he looks at you with one eye, the other eye is lookin' at that barn over there, so I don't know if he's lookin' at me or the barn over there."

"How many drives come through each year?"

"I don't know, Mr. Dan, but it is a lot. There's a drive comin' through not today, not tomorrow, but I think the next day. They're headin' for Lubbock or Amarillo. Sometimes the cowboys get drunk and want to fight."

"Well, Billy, sometimes cowboys are out there for many days, chasin' cattle. When they get to town for a couple days, they like to get a jug of whiskey and kick a little dust off their boots."

"I know, Mr. Dan, but sometimes they like to kick the dust off some other cowboys' boots too."

"Billy, what else do you do in the saloon besides sweeping the floors?"

"Well, I take the trash out, and sometimes, Ms. Maggie sends me to the store to buy things for her."

Dan asked, "You don't sample the liquor, do you?"

"I did once. One day, a cowboy left a full glass of beer. He hadn't taken a drink of it, so I took it and put it behind the barrel that sat on the bar. After that, when I would walk past it, I would take a little swig of the beer until I drank it all. It made me walk funny. Wahooo! Ms. Maggie got real mad at me, so I won't do that anymore."

Dan, with a grin, asked, "So you've been on the wagon ever since, huh?"

"What does 'on a wagon' mean, Mr. Dan?"

"On the wagon means you quit drinking booze."

"Ya, I quit drinking booze, Mr. Dan. I'm on a wagon. Mr. Dan, do you think I could be a bounty hunter like you?"

Dan thought for a minute and then said, "Billy, if that's what you want for your future, there is no reason why you can't be a hunter. But you should know that it is a very dangerous profession. Bounty hunters get killed quite often. You need to make sure that is what you want. It will be a while before you will be big enough to take on a job like that."

"Mr. Dan, I wish you could start teachin' me now."

"Well, Billy, there is no such thing as teaching you. Every hunter has their own way of catching the bad guys."

"Would you maybe take me with you? I could do odd jobs when we travel. I can take care of the horses and other jobs."

"Billy, you never know when you might not come back alive."

"I won't be scared, Mr. Dan. I'm a perty tough kid, and I'm a good shot with my rifle." About then, Dan noticed something on the edge of a thick clump of trees. Dan told Billy to get down and stand behind his horse and stay there until he told him to come out.

"What's wrong, Mr. Dan?"

"Just do as I say, Billy." So Billy did what Dan said. Dan stepped down from Buck, reached into his saddlebags and pulled out his telescope, and looked at some movement at the edge of the trees. Sure enough, there were two Indians watching them. *They must be renegades*, Dan thought. Dan was studying them through the telescope. It looked like a woman's necklace on one of the renegades.

Dan asked Billy, "Did your mama have a necklace?"

"Ya, Mr. Dan, she did."

"What did it look like, Billy?"

"It was made of little balls about the size of marbles."

"What color was it, Billy?"

"It was white, Mr. Dan."

"Billy, I want you to look through the telescope and look at the Indian on the left. Look what he has around his neck."

When Billy looked, he said, "Mr. Dan, that's my mama's necklace."

"Are you sure, Billy?"

"Ya, I'm sure, Mr. Dan." Dan pulled his rifle out of the scabbard and laid it across a rail on the corral and aimed carefully. He squeezed the trigger. *Boom!* It blew the renegade off his horse. The other one vanished back into the trees. Dan waited for a few minutes before going after the necklace. He knew there was at least one in the trees, but he didn't know how many more. Dan told Billy to stay there.

"Billy, if you see any renegades come out of the trees headed your way, get on Cricket and head for town as fast as she can run. You shouldn't have any trouble outrunnin' 'em. Now, do as I say, Billy."

"I will, Mr. Dan."

Dan told Sammi, "Let's go get that necklace." They started closing in on the trees. The renegade rode out of the trees, heading away. Dan stopped Buck and told Sammi to stay back. Sammi wanted to go after the renegade, but Dan said, "No, Sammi!" Dan aimed his rifle and squeezed the trigger. *Boom!* The renegade slumped forward on his horse.

"I don't think he's going very far, do you, Sammi?" Sammi's little bark told him she agreed. He knew she would see it the same way. Then Dan sent Sammi to check in the trees. Sammi went in the trees as fast as she could run. A few minutes later, she returned, and everything was clear. Dan rode over to the dead Indian and took the necklace off the sleazy renegade's neck and rode back to where Billy was waiting. Dan rode up and asked Billy, "Is this for sure your mother's?"

"Yep, Mr. Dan, that's it."

"We'll take it back to town and ask Maggie to wash it for you. No tellin' what it might have on it with that scum wearin' it for the last two years. Then you keep it in memory of your mother."

"Thank you very much, Mr. Dan." They rode back to town.

When they walked into the saloon, Billy said, "Ms. Maggie, look at this."

"What is it, Billy? That looks like the necklace your mother wore when she went to church every Sunday. Where did you find it, Billy?"

"On a renegade's neck. Dan shot him dead and wounded another. Dan said the other one wouldn't go very far."

"Billy, I am so excited for you." Maggie patted Dan on the arm. "Thank you, Dan, for doing this for Billy."

"I'm happy that I had the chance to do it for Billy."

Billy asked Maggie if she would clean it for him.

"Sure, Billy, you bet I will clean it for you." After the necklace was cleaned, Billy saw one of the townsmen named Wally come in to have a little snort of whiskey. Billy ran over to show Wally the necklace. "Where did you find it, Billy?"

Billy began telling Wally how it happened.

Maggie said, "By the way, Dan, the marshal wants to talk to you about something."

"Oh thank you, Maggie." Dan and Sammi walked down to the marshal's office and stepped inside. The marshal shook Dan's hand. "I've heard that you are one of the best hunters there is. I want to show you some Wanted posters. He reached down under the counter and pulled out some posters. This is Robert Colter. As you can see, he has a $25,000 tag on his head."

Dan's eyes took a first and then a second and then a third look at that $25,000 tag. "But I must tell you, he has a big gang of outlaw followers. Some say there are thirty to forty bandits that run with him. They are all wanted with bounties on their heads. They are some of the most wanted murderers, bank robbers, train robbers, and kidnappers. You name it, and they are wanted for it. Now before we go too far into this, I have to ask if you know of some big canyons somewhere in the Nebraska and South Dakota territories. There are some rugged canyons. They live back in there. No one knows how many there are. Some people say that there are between twenty, and as many as fifty, of them. It will probably be hard to find 'em, but if you could get 'em, you could have enough money to do you the rest of your life. There are no bounty hunters so far that will attempt goin' after them."

"Why do you suppose that is, Marshal?"

"Well, Dan, they are afraid, that's why."

"I don't blame them," said Dan.

"I want to say it one more time, they can be deadly. The bounties range from $2,000 to $25,000. I have nine posters here, but there are a lot more than that."

Dan said, "Let me think about it for a few days."

"Sure, there is no hurry," said the marshal.

"I'll stop back, and we can discuss it some more." Dan went back to the saloon. There were at least a dozen men there waiting to shake his hand and show how much they appreciated what he had done for Billy. After several handshakes, Dan sat down at a table where several of the townsmen were sitting. Before he knew it, there were four glasses of whiskey sitting in front of him. The way everyone was laughing, slapping shoulders, and swigging a little whiskey, it showed that they loved Billy very much. Why the townspeople were celebrating was just knowing that the killer of Billy's mother was dead, and that Billy had his mama's necklace. That will mean a lot to Billy through life. The next thing they knew, Howard, the barkeep, came over to the table with Billy. He picked Billy up and stood him in the middle of the table. All the people were cheering. Billy stood on the table holding his mama's necklace as high as he could hold it over his head as he turned around and around, shaking the necklace. Billy had happy tears in his eyes. It was not just Billy with happy tears; some of the grown men had tears also. Maggie was no exception. She had happy tears too. She said that she had never seen a happier crowd in the saloon. Dan was pleased to see the people of Lariat like one big family. No matter if something good happens or something bad, they all stick together.

Dan thought about the outlaw gang for a couple of days. Then he stopped in to see the marshal. The marshal invited Dan to sit down at the table. The marshal walked over to a cabinet and returned with nine posters. He spread them out on the table. The one that kept drawing Dan's interest was the $25,000 one, but the other eight posters would sweeten the pie. The largest poster was $25,000, two at $5,000, two at $3,000, four at $2,000.

"Marshal, the way I figure it, that would come to $49,000. Marshal, do you have any way of finding out how much the total is for all the gang?"

"I can find out about some of the others, but no one knows for sure how many there are back in there. The governor said that no matter how many there is, they all had a bounty on their heads, and there will be a minimum of $2,000 for each one."

"Ya know, Marshal, if I could find another good hunter to go with me, I would be interested in the job."

The marshal asked Dan if he knew Joseph Cobb.

"No, I don't think I do. What can you tell me about him?"

"I don't know the name of the town he lives in, but it's just on this side of Amarillo. Everyone up there knows him."

Dan turned around and asked Sammi, "What do you think, Sammi, should we go meet Joseph Cobb?"

Sammi gave a little bark.

The marshal asked, "What did her bark mean?"

"She said, 'Let's go, Dan.' So you're convinced that Joseph Cobb is a top-notch hunter?"

"Well, Dan, he's still alive, ain't he?"

"Ya, that's true," nodded Dan. "Let's go, Sammi, and meet Mr. Cobb. Oh, by the way, Marshal, if you know anyone that's needin' horses. I have three horses with saddles plus Snake's horse and saddle. He won't be needin' it anymore. Each horse with a saddle is worth $40."

Dan and Sammi went back to the saloon and told Maggie that they were going to be gone for a few days on a business trip. Billy heard Dan and Maggie's conversation. Along came Billy. "Mr. Dan, can I go with you?"

Dan said, "No, Billy, you have to do your chores for Maggie."

"Ms. Maggie, could I do twice as many chores when I get back to make up for when I'm gone?"

"It would be all right with me, Billy. But Dan's going on a business trip, and he probably doesn't want you tagging along."

Dan grinned and said, "Well, Maggie, it's okay with me as long as it's okay with you." Maggie nodded her head with her approval. "It's a hard ride, Billy. We'll ride from sunup until sundown. Are you sure you can handle it, Billy?"

"I can handle it, Mr. Dan. Believe me, Mr. Dan, I'm a perty tough kid."

"Then we better go tell Frank at the livery barn that we need our horses fed and watered so they are ready to go at sunup."

"Do you want me to go tell him, Mr. Dan?"

"If you want to, Billy, tell him to feed and water both our horses. Also the packhorse." Billy left on the run through the swinging doors and almost knocked the marshal down as he was walking by.

"I'm very sorry, Mr. Marshal."

"That's okay, Billy. What happened that you're so excited about?"

"I get to go with Mr. Dan to meet Joseph Cobb."

"Well, I'm happy for you, Billy."

When Billy returned to the saloon, Dan asked him if he would run down to the market and pick up a few cans of beans and five pounds of jerky. He handed Billy a $10 gold coin. Billy got a burlap sack and shot out the door headed for the market. Maggie said she would pack up a bunk roll for Billy.

"Dan, how many days do you think it will take? I will send some clean clothes for Billy."

"I would like to think five days. Two days going, one day convincing Mr. Cobb to join me, and two days coming back. But there is no way of knowing what might be lurking out there to slow us down." Dan asked Maggie if she would store all the guns that he got from the bandits.

"Sure, Dan, we can put them back in Billy's room where no one can see them." When Billy came back from the store with the sack of groceries, Dan asked Billy about his saddle. "It seems a little too big for you, and as much riding on this trip as we are going to do, you're going to get a sore butt. Go take a look at the saddles I got from the bandits. Maybe you can find one a little smaller, maybe one with a padded seat."

"Thank you, Mr. Dan, I'll go see if there is a better one 'cause mine does make my butt sore when I ride a lot." Billy came back and told Dan there was a saddle that he liked. It had a soft seat.

"Well, Billy, it's yours."

"Thank you very much, Mr. Dan. I'll take good care of it so when we get back, you can sell it."

"Billy, I'm not loaning it to you. I'm giving it to you."

"You mean I can have it forever?"

"That's what I mean, Billy."

"Wow," Billy said. "I'm goin' to get the saddle soap and clean it really good." Billy shot out the door on his way to the livery barn. Dan and Maggie sat at a table, talking about the trip.

"You know, Dan, it seems that I've known you forever even though you have only been here a few days. You have the whole town as your friends. You will never know how much the people in this town think of you, and that includes me."

"Well, Maggie, I'm happy to hear that. From all the people I've met in Lariat, they are all very special people. I like this town a lot. Someday, I might come back and retire here."

"Oh, Dan, that would be wonderful."

"I might buy a little farm and raise a few cattle and a few horses."

"You know, Dan, that place that Billy and his parents lived before all hell happened, I don't know who owns it. But maybe Billy has some interest or may have some ties to it. There is a box full of papers that some of the townsmen found. This was after they determined that most likely Ben was dead. In fact, the box is under Billy's bed. You're welcome to look through it if you want to. I don't think anyone has looked in it yet."

"Maggie, when we get back from meeting with Joseph Cobb, maybe we can look into it. Maybe Billy has something coming."

"I believe, Dan, that Billy's parents were buying the farm. They had some cows but not many. Just a few. They had four or five horses. I don't know what all else they had. I don't talk about that with Billy. So I don't know for sure. Some of the townsmen, I'm sure, will know."

"Maggie, let's wait until I get back from the trip, and we will take a look at them."

CHAPTER 3

The next morning, Dan and Billy were up early and got the horses saddled and the packhorse loaded and headed out. Billy had hung a saddle scabbard to his saddle with his little .22 rifle to take along.

Maggie was waving and said, "Hurry back, you guys." Billy was smiling and waving to Maggie. Billy was looking so proud of himself and his new saddle. But most of all, he was proud that he was riding beside the world's best bounty hunter. They rode for about three hours. They came to a small creek where Dan decided to let the horses take on some water and rest for a little while. There were some big cottonwood trees for shade for the horses and Sammi.

Billy asked Dan if he could shoot his rifle for practice. Dan said, "Sure, if you want to." Dan walked over to a tree and placed a small stick on a limb. Billy took his rifle about one hundred feet from the tree, aimed, and *pop!* He shot the stick off the limb.

Dan was surprised and said, "Billy, that was a very good shot. Your father taught you well." Billy asked Dan if he could shoot from farther away. Dan walked over to the tree and put the stick on the limb and walked away. Billy walked back about twice as far; then he carefully aimed and then another *pop!* He shot the stick off the limb.

Dan said, "Billy, that was a very, very good shot."

Billy asked Dan if he could shoot Dan's big gun. Dan said, "Billy, that big gun kicks like a mule. It might knock you to the ground."

"But, Mr. Dan, I'm a perty tough kid."

Dan said, "Well, I guess if you're sure you want to, but don't blame me if you get knocked to the ground."

Billy ran over to Dan's horse and pulled the big gun from the scabbard and walked back about a hundred feet. Dan put the stick on the limb and got behind Billy. He wasn't sure what was going to happen. Billy aimed the big gun and squeezed the trigger and *boom!* Billy took four steps backward. Dan caught him.

Billy looked at Dan with big eyes and said, "That dang thing kicks perty hard."

"I told you it was going to kick hard. Do you want to try it again?"

"Ya, Mr. Dan, I think I can do better this time."

Dan said, "I don't have to put the stick up, it's already there. In other wards, you missed your target."

"I might have shot a bird in the top of the tree." Dan and Billy both had a good laugh at that.

"Okay, Billy, this time I want you to lean into it. Put your shoulder up tight against the butt of the gun. Are you ready?"

Billy said, "I'm ready, Mr. Dan."

"Now, don't think about what's going to happen when you pull that trigger. Think that you're eating an ice cream cone and keep your mind off the kick, okay?"

"It's kinda hard thinking about eating ice cream when I know what's goin' to happen, but I'll try." So Billy pressed the gun tight against his shoulder and leaned forward, and Billy said, "Yummy ice cream," and squeezed the trigger. *Boom!*

"I missed, Mr. Dan."

"Billy, you missed, but you took the bark off of the limb about three inches from the stick. That was very good for only the second time you shot the big gun. By the way, Billy, how did the ice cream taste?"

"I'll have to admit, Mr. Dan, I didn't taste the ice cream. I was too busy thinking how hard that dang mule was goin' to kick." They both had another laugh. "Mr. Dan, I think I can hit the stick this time."

"Okay, one more shot." This time Billy knelt down on one knee and aimed very carefully. *Boom!* Billy jumped up and said, "I hit the stick, Mr. Dan, I hit the stick."

"You sure did, Billy. You sure did. You now are considered a sharpshooter. You can't get any better than that, Billy. Well, Billy, we better get movin'.

We have a long way to go, so we need to saddle up and get on the road again."

"Thank you, Mr. Dan, for letting me shoot the big gun."

"You're welcome, Billy. Are you ready to shoot it again?"

"Oh ya, Mr. Dan, I like shooting it."

"But it kicked you pretty hard, didn't it?"

"Ya, but I'm a perty tough kid, Mr. Dan."

"That you are, Billy, that you are. You're a pretty tough kid."

As they moved on, late afternoon, Dan spotted a cottontail. Dan asked Billy, "Do you think you can hit that rabbit with your little rifle from here?"

"Sure, Mr. Dan." Billy pulled his rifle out and aimed very carefully and *pop!* The rabbit dropped.

"Good shot, Billy, now we will have rabbit for supper." Billy picked up the rabbit and tied it to the back of his saddle. They traveled on until the sun was about to set.

"Well, Billy, I think we better stop for the day. We need to cook that rabbit for supper." So they set up camp, built a fire, and started cooking the rabbit. Dan picked up his saddlebags to get some utensils and discovered two bottles. He pulled one out. It was a bottle of whiskey. "What the world." Then he pulled out the other one, yet another bottle of whiskey. "That Maggie, she is so thoughtful."

About that time, Billy said, "Look here, Mr. Dan. Ms. Maggie sent a bunch of bottles of sarsaparilla for me in my bunk roll. You know, Mr. Dan, I love Ms. Maggie as if she was my mother."

Dan said, "She is a very special lady, Billy. She will probably always be your second mother." The rabbit was cooked, and Dan opened a can of beans.

Billy said, "Mr. Dan, do you know how to get the lid off this sarsparilla?"

"Sure, hand it to me." Dan pulled out his knife and popped the lid off. Dan had a couple of swigs off the whiskey bottle, and Billy drank a sarsaparilla, and they had some of the rabbit, and Sammi got the leftovers. They turned in for the night. The next morning, they broke camp and headed out. About two hours later, they came upon a ranch with a large herd of draft horses and draft mules.

Billy stopped his horse and said, "Holy mackerel, look at those big horses and mules, Mr. Dan. I've never seen horses that big before."

"They are called draft horses and draft mules. Some of them weigh well over two thousand pounds. You know, Billy, seeing those big horses and mules, this just might be exactly what I am lookin' for. Let's stop in and talk to the man that's raisin' these big animals."

They rode in by the barns and saw a young man putting shoes on one of the big horses. Dan rode up and said, "Howdy."

The young man said, "Howdy, what can I do fer ya?"

Dan asked, "Do these horses and mules belong to you?"

"They belong to my dad."

"Is your dad here?" asked Dan.

The young man said, "He's in the house. Do you want me to get him fer ya?"

"Thanks, I would like to talk to him," said Dan. So he stopped what he was doing and went to get his father. When he returned with his father, Dan could see that he was a very old man. Dan stuck his hand out and said, "My name is Dan Colt, and that's my boy, Billy, and my dog, Sammi." They shook hands.

The old man said, "My name is Arnold West, and that's my son David. What can I do fer ya?"

Dan asked, "Are these horses and mules for sale?"

"Yep, they are. What you needin' 'em fer?"

"In a couple of weeks, we are pullin' out for the Nebraska and South Dakota territory, and we need to take feed and water for the animals because we are not sure how far it will be between water and feed for the stock."

"That's good thinking. So many people strike out with very few provisions, thinking that every day they will find all the food and water they will need. They get out there and thirst or starve to death." Arnold asked, "What you wantin', horses or mules?"

Dan asked, "Are these mules weighin' about 1,700 to 1,800 pounds?"

"Ya, that's real close. Do you need harness?"

"Yes, I do," said Dan.

"Well, a pair of the mules with harness will cost you $120."

Dan asked, "Do you have a heavy-duty wagon that you would sell?"

"No, Dan, I don't. I have one, but we keep it for our own use."

"David uses it when he's breakin' the mules and horses."

"You know, Dan, there is a widow woman a couple of miles up the road. Her name is Katy St. John. Her husband died a few years back. She has a lot of farm machinery that just lays there and rusts. I think she has two wagons sitting there. She might sell one of 'em. Do you need the mules and wagon today?"

"No, but we will need them three or four days from now. I'll come back through."

"Do you want David or me to ride up there and ask her?"

"If you would, I'll be happy to pay you for your time."

"No, Dan, I don't want pay for it. How much you willing to pay for a good wagon, Dan?"

"If she has one with four-inch wheels, in good shape, I'd be willing to pay her up to $40."

"Well, Dan, I'll see what I can do."

"I'll pay you for the team now."

"No, just pay me when you come back."

"By the way, Arnold, would you happen to know a man by the name of Joseph Cobb? He lives up north of here."

"Why yes, I know Joe. He's a cattle rancher. About a four-hour ride from here."

Dan thought for a moment then said, "No, the Joseph Cobb I'm looking for is a bounty hunter."

Arnold said, "That is Joe. He is a bounty hunter, and he also has a large cattle ranch."

Dan asked, "Why would he want to be a bounty hunter? He must be worth a lot of money."

"Yes, Dan, Joe is a very rich man. People ask him why he is a bounty hunter. He just grins and says somebody has to bring in the bad guys. People think it is just a challenge for Joe. Joe is quite a scrapper too. He's a perty tough ol' boy," said Arnold. "If you want to go to Joe's ranch, you stay on this trail, like I say about four hours. Then watch for a sign that says Cobb Cattle Company. Turn left at the sign. It's about a mile to the ranch house."

"Thanks, Arnold, you are very helpful. Well, we best get on the trail."

"In the meantime, Dan, you take good care of your boy and that good-lookin' Sammi dog. She's a dandy."

Dan, grinning, said, "That's why I brought Billy and Sammi along. Billy can shoot the ears off most of the bad guys, and Sammi can take care of the rest. See you in a few days, Arnold."

"We'll see ya when you get back, Dan." They headed north.

Dan said, "Well, Billy, what do you think? Maybe Joe, being a rich man, might not be ready to go after he finds out how long it could take to catch the whole gang."

Billy said, "You know, Mr. Dan, I think Joe will want to go with us to get the outlaws."

"What is this 'us' stuff, Billy?"

"Oh, I forgot to tell you, Mr. Dan. I was thinkin' that you need me to help with the chores and things. Don't you think, Mr. Dan?"

"Billy, don't you remember how dangerous it is? If Joe goes with me, there will be two of us and about twenty to fifty outlaws against us. If you want to be a hunter when you grow up, you don't want to get killed when you're twelve years old, do you?"

"Well, Mr. Dan, I was thinkin' that I can be learnin' while I'm growin' up, and I'm a perty tough kid. Remember, Mr. Dan, I'm a very good shot with my rifle, and if I can earn some money, I'll buy a big gun like yours."

Late that afternoon, it was getting dark. They decided to camp for the night. Dan asked Billy if he was ready for a can of beans.

"Yes, sir, Mr. Dan. I'm gettin' kinda hungry." So they undressed the horses and hobbled them so they could mosey around grazing grass.

Next morning, they saddled up and headed out, and an hour later, they came to the sign that said Cobb Cattle Company.

"Well, Billy, we are about there."

"You know, Mr. Dan, maybe if we treat Joe real nice, he will go with us."

"Well, Billy, I wasn't intendin' to get in a fight with him. Were you?"

"Oh no, not me 'cause Arnold said Joe is a perty tough guy."

"Look, Billy, that looks like Joe's place up ahead. Looks like he has a nice setup there. All the buildings are nicely painted and all. I think Arnold is right about Joe. Looks as if he has lots of money."

"Wow, it looks like it," answered Billy.

"I don't know, Billy. A man with this much money, I'd be surprised if he would walk away from this setup to catch some outlaws."

"I know," said Billy. They rode up to the house and tied their horses to the hitching post. Dan walked to the door and knocked on it, and a lady came to the door and asked if she could help them.

Dan asked, "Is Mr. Cobb here?"

"No," she said. "Mr. Cobb went to town for supplies."

"Can I ask if you are Mrs. Cobb?"

"No, I'm the housekeeper. Mr. Cobb doesn't have a wife."

Dan asked if she knew what time Mr. Cobb would be coming home.

"No. When he goes to town, he doesn't get home until late afternoon."

"How far is it to town?"

"It's not far, maybe a little less than an hour."

"Could you tell me how to get to town?"

"You ride back to the front gate and turn left, and that will take you to a town called Dawn. Mr. Cobb will be there."

"Thank you very much, ma'am."

"You're welcome," she said and closed the door.

"Well, Billy and Sammi, let's go to town."

She was right; it was less than an hour's ride. They rode into town and found a water trough. The horses and Sammi needed a good drink of water. While they were drinking, Dan noticed two old-timers sitting on a bench.

Dan said, "How are you fellas today?"

One of the old guys said, "Doin' good."

Then Dan asked if they knew a man by the name of Joseph Cobb.

"Why yes, he is at the saloon just four buildings down."

"Thank you very kindly." Dan walked down to the saloon and pushed through the swinging doors. There were five men sitting at a table, sipping whiskey.

Dan asked, "Is one of you Joseph Cobb?"

"Yes," one big man stood up and said. "That's my name. Can I help you?"

"Dan Colt is my name."

"I know you're a hunter by the size of your knife," said Joe. Joe was a big man, close to Dan's size. He also carries a holstered .45 and also a large bowie knife.

Joe said, "I've heard of you. I hear you brought Snake Butcher in."

"Yes, I did, but how in the hell did you hear that all the way up here?"

Joe laughed and said, "We have old Art. He has large freight wagons. He comes through here once a week. He's a nosy old fart. He brings all the news from Amarillo to Lariat and back. I'm pleased to meet you." They shook hands. "Anyway, how can I help ya?"

"I'd like to talk to you about business, but I see you're busy now."

"No, no, we were just sitting here, tellin' lies to each other," Joe said. "We can talk in the back room."

So they walked in, and Dan said, "I'll be right back. I need to get some posters."

Dan hollered from the doorway for Billy to bring the posters from his saddlebags. Then he walked back in and sat down at the table. In a few seconds, Billy came in with Sammi following. Billy handed Dan the posters. Dan told Billy to take Sammi and wait out front.

"Is that your dog, Dan?"

"Yes, her name is Sammi, and she has saved my life a few times."

"Well, Dan, that is one beautiful dog. Do you take her with you when you're huntin' the bad guys?"

"She goes with me everywhere I go, especially when I'm after the bad guys. Joe, I want to show you these nine posters. This is the one I want you to see to start with. Robert Colter for $25,000."

"That, Dan, is a mighty hefty tag on Mr. Colter's head."

Dan said, "Look at the rest, then I'll tell you the rest of the story."

Joe looked through the other eight, one by one, then asked Dan to tell him about them.

Dan started out with where the outlaws were located. He said they are all somewhere between the south side of the Dakota territory and the north side of Nebraska. They are in some canyons with one way in and one way out. That the people that live in that area say that there are somewhere between twenty to fifty of them, and they all live back in that canyon, and they all have a bounty on their heads. He also told Joe that he asked the marshal if he knew if there were any other hunters after 'em. Dan told Joe that the marshal said no, that he approached several hunters but nobody was interested because they were afraid.

"The marshal is trying to get as many posters as he can for me by the time I get back. He is saying that there are many of them that have no posters on them, but there will be at a minimum of $2,000 on any one of them that hangs out with Colter.

"So, Joe, what is your thought so far?"

"Well, I don't know what to think just yet."

Dan said, "I'll tell you some things that you might think negative. I'm probably goin' to end up takin' Billy, the boy that's with me. He's an orphan. His mother was killed by some renegades, and his father left one morning on some kinda business and never came back. That's been two years ago. I don't know how much time it will take to bring the Colter gang in.

"We are goin' to get into some cold weather, and it could be severe cold weather. We're going to need a team and wagon to carry supplies and a few extra guns and ammunition. I have plenty of guns that we can use as we could run into more things that we don't foresee. On my way up here, I ran into Arnold, an old-timer who raises draft horses and mules. They weigh about 1,700 to 1,800 pounds. Arnold is checking on a heavy-duty wagon for me down the road, a couple miles from his place, but I won't know until I get back from here if he found one. Well, Joe, I know you need to think about this, and I don't blame you. This isn't going to be the average 'go get the bad guy, turn him in, and collect the bounty.' What I would like is for you to think about it for a few days then let me know."

"I can write a note and have old Art drop it off on his way through Lariat."

"That will be good, Joe. Billy and I will go ahead and head back to Lariat. Let me know what you decide, Joe."

CHAPTER 4

Dan, Billy, and Sammi put things together and headed back to Lariat. It was midafternoon.

"Well, Billy, maybe we can get a few miles down the road before sundown."

"Yep, Mr. Dan, we should do that."

"What do you think, Sammi?" Sammi let out her little bark.

Billy said, "Sammi says let's go."

"So you're learning Sammi language, huh, Billy?"

"Yep, Mr. Dan, I know what she's sayin'."

They rode until it started getting dark. They decided to stop for the night. "Well, Billy, it's jerky and beans for supper."

"We should have shot a rabbit, Mr. Dan."

"I thought that was your job, Billy."

"Okay, Mr. Dan. Tomorrow night, we'll have rabbit."

The next morning, they loaded the horses and headed out. They knew there was a little creek coming up. They needed to get some water in the horses then they could put some miles behind them today. Shortly after, they came to the creek and let the horses and Sammi take on a big drink. They headed on down the trail. Two hours later, they came to an unexpected sight. Dan pulled out his telescope and could see two men standing and one hanging.

"Billy, maybe you should stay back a ways. You might not like seeing what's ahead."

"What is it, Mr. Dan?"

"Well, Billy, it appears there's been a lynching, and that is never a pretty sight."

"Mr. Dan, I'm not afraid, I'm a perty tough kid."

"I know, Billy. Okay, we'll see how tough you are."

They rode up to the lynching. Dan kept an eye on Billy. He looked a little pale. Dan asked the two guys, "Is everything all right?"

"Well, it is now that we hanged this horse thief."

"How do you know if you hanged the right guy?"

One of the guys said, "He drove off a few of our horses, and we caught him and hanged him."

"Ya, I can see that," said Dan.

"I'll get the horse he was ridin' and show you the brand on him. Then take a look at the two horses we're ridin', and you can see it's the same brand."

Dan said, "It looks like he had it comin'. You guys take life easy now, ya hear?"

As they rode on, Dan looked at Billy and asked, "How was that, Billy? Are you all right? You look a little pale."

"Well, Mr. Dan, I felt a little funny inside, but when I saw his tongue and eyes hangin' out, it gave me the willies."

"Well, Billy, you're wanting to learn to be a bounty hunter. You just experienced lesson number one," Dan said with a grin. "You're going to see things in your future that will make this look like a Sunday picnic. We are off to see Arnold about the mules, and I hope he found us a wagon. Is that a good plan, Billy?"

"Yes, Mr. Dan."

"How about you, Sammi?" Sammi let out her little bark.

"Sammi said, 'Let's go to Arnold's,'" said Billy.

Two hours down the road, they came to Arnold's farm. Dan noticed a large wagon that wasn't there when they came through. "I think Arnold found a wagon for us. What do you think, Billy?"

"Yep, I think he did, Mr. Dan."

Arnold saw them coming, so he met them at the wagon and shook Dan's and Billy's hands and gave Sammi a pat on her head. "Well, Dan, I think you might like this wagon. This is the one that I told you about. The lady said she knew the wagon needed some repairs, so she would sell it for $30. The neck yoke and double trees were in the wagon, so I asked her if they went with the wagon. She said yes, they did go with the wagon.' David greased the wheels for you."

Dan said, "I do thank you and David for all the help. I think it's well worth $30. The seat and some of the side boards need replacing. We can do that when we get back to Lariat, huh, Billy?"

"Yes, sir, Mr. Dan, we can do that."

Dan asked, "Arnold, these mules are well broke to drive, aren't they?"

"Ya, Dan, they are well broke. David breaks all the mules and horses, and he does a good job of it. When David harnesses them, you'll see they are well broke."

"That's good enough for me," said Dan. "I'll pay you, and we can get down the road a ways."

Arnold hollered for David to get the team of mules harnessed and hitch them to the wagon. When they were getting ready, Billy asked what the mules' names were.

Arnold said, "The one on the left is James, and the one on the right is John. They are good mules, and they are very gentle." David finished hitching the mules. He jumped in the wagon and drove them around the barnyard a few rounds and then asked Dan if they looked all right.

"They look good to me." Dan went to the house with Arnold and settled his debt. When they returned to the wagon, Dan said, "Billy, bring Claude and Buck and tie them to the back of the wagon, and we'll be on our way."

The mules stepped out with a faster pace than most, which was good. It will make for less time on the road. They made it two hours before sunset. They pulled off the trail on a bare spot and unharnessed the mules and unsaddled the horses. They all got fed and turned in for the night.

The next morning, Dan got up and woke Billy and said, "We better get the mules and horses dressed and ready to go. We should reach Lariat by midafternoon."

Billy started to saddle the horses while Dan was harnessing the mules. Billy said, "Ol' Claude and Buck, I can hardly get the saddle on them, they are so big."

"Oh, Billy, I'll throw the saddles on them, then you can cinch 'em up and bridle 'em."

"Okay, Mr. Dan, I can do the rest."

Soon they got on the trail headed for Lariat. Time went pretty fast, getting them to Lariat early. Dan stopped the mules and asked Billy if he thought he could drive 'em.

Billy answered, "Sure, Mr. Dan, I can handle 'em."

"Okay, Billy, you get down and tie Cricket to the back of the wagon and bring Buck for me. Now when you get to town, start yelling at the mules like you're an old mule skinner."

Billy climbed up on the wagon and took the reins. Dan was riding Buck. As they entered the main street, Billy started yelling at the mules, "*Haaa haaa*, get up you blasted lame brains."

Several of the people came out of their stores, standing along the sidewalks, watching what was going on. They started clapping and whistling and carrying on. Billy continued yelling at the mules, "Haaa haaa, get up ya lop-eared canaries."

Some of the townspeople were saying things like "goin' good, Billy, Lariat's new mule skinner" and "hey, Billy, you're doin' good." Billy pulled up in front of the saloon and said, "Whoa, mule, whoa."

Maggie came running out and said, "What in the world, Billy, are you doing driving those big mules? They are huge."

"Well, Ms. Maggie, it's like this. It helps to be a good mule skinner if you're going to be a bounty hunter."

Maggie said, "I've never seen anything like this."

Dan stepped down off Buck. Maggie walked over and gave Dan a big hug and patted him on the arm, saying, "Thank you for doing all these nice things for Billy. You will have to tell me what all happened on your trip. But first, Billy has to give me a ride on the wagon."

"Is it all right, Mr. Dan?"

"Sure, Billy, I'll ride beside you." Dan helped Maggie climb up the wagon. Dan didn't want anything to go wrong with Billy and the mules, so he jumped on Buck and rode beside the wagon close enough so he could jump in if he needed to. When there's nearly two tons of mule, you don't want to do something stupid. Billy gave Maggie a ride around town. The townspeople were still clapping, and one of the men asked Billy, "Who's that beautiful lady you're escorting around town, Billy?"

"Oh, this is Ms. Maggie." Billy pulled up in front of the saloon. Billy was saying, "Whoa, mule, whoa."

Dan helped Maggie down and told her, as soon as they got the horses and mules put away, they would be back to the saloon. "Billy, drive 'em over to the livery barn, and we'll put 'em away."

Billy asked, "Did I do a'right, Mr. Dan?"

"You did an excellent job, Billy. By the way, Billy, where did you come up with all those mule calls such as the one 'get up, ya lop-eared canaries'?"

"Well, Mr. Dan, one of our neighbors farmed with mules, and we could hear him yellin' at the mules all day long. Some of his mule calls were kinda nasty, so I don't call those."

"Oh okay, Billy, that makes sense." Dan asked Frank, the livery man, if he had a corral they could keep the mules in.

Frank said, "We have plenty of room." When the animals were put away, Dan, Billy, and Sammi walked back to the saloon.

Maggie welcomed Dan and Billy back and had a glass of whiskey and a bottle of sarsaparilla for them. "This is a welcome-home drink," said Maggie.

"Well, Maggie, I thank you. That is very nice of you."

Billy said, "I thank you too, Ms. Maggie."

"Oh, by the way, Maggie, someone stuck a couple bottles of whiskey in my saddlebags. Do you have any idea who did that?"

"Why no, I don't have any idea," answered Maggie.

Billy said, "Someone put a few bottles of sarsparilla in my bunk roll too."

"Well, I can't imagine," she said with a little grin. Howard came in and took over the night shift. Maggie then went over and sat at the table with Dan and Billy. "It's good to see you guys are back."

"It's good to be back, Maggie."

Maggie asked, "How was your trip?"

Billy spoke up, "We saw a lynchin'."

"You saw a lynching?" asked Maggie.

"Ya, there was a horse thief that got caught by two men, and they hanged him."

"My God, that's awful."

"Did it make you sick to see something like that, Billy?"

"Well, Ms. Maggie, it didn't make me sick. But when we got close enough, I saw his eyes and his tongue hangin' out. It sure gave me a real creepy feelin'."

"I can imagine," said Maggie. "I'm sure if I seen something like that, I would probably faint."

"Well, Maggie, Billy doesn't know how pale he was, but he was as white as a ghost. I wasn't sure whether he was going to faint or not, but he did okay. I can tell you right now he's goin' to be a real tough bounty hunter, huh, Billy?"

"Yes, sir, Mr. Dan."

"So, Dan, did everything turn out okay, and did you get a chance to talk to Joseph Cobb?"

"Yes, Maggie, I did. Oh, by the way, Maggie, what day does Art, the freight hauler, come through Lariat?"

"He comes on Wednesdays."

"What day is this?" Dan asked.

"This is Saturday," answered Maggie. "He'll stop here on his way through. I have a liquor order coming." Maggie said, "Billy, I need some things from the market. I'll give you a list. You can get some money from the cash drawer." After Billy went out the door, he turned and asked Dan if it was all right if Sammi went with him.

"Sure, Billy, she can go." Dan then filled Maggie in on everything that had happened on the trip and about Billy shooting the big gun. "That boy is goin' to be a sharpshooter. That kid is good. And he's smart and very witty."

"Dan, let me ask you about Billy's future. I know if you try to leave without him, we'll have to hog-tie him. That boy is counting on going with you. I know it's a dangerous job, but I know, Dan, that you will protect him the best way you know how."

"You know, Maggie, I will take the best care of Billy that I know how. And who knows? I might need to use his sharpshooting skills someday. But if things go bad, I'll step in front of Billy and take the bullet rather than Billy gettin' it. But you know, Maggie, sometimes we can be in harm's way and don't know it."

"Yes, Dan, I understand."

"I think we need to know how the rest of the town thinks about it."

"Dan, do you mean like a vote from the townspeople?"

"I guess that would be the best, Maggie. Because if anything happened to that boy, I wouldn't be able to live with that the rest of my life."

"I know," said Maggie, "but when would you want to meet with the town?"

"I guess the sooner, the better, Maggie. I'm goin' to have to make a decision on gettin' ready."

"Well, Dan, what about tomorrow after church? I can put the word out, and I can guarantee you they will all be here."

"Maggie, I need to go over and talk with Frank about some repairs on the wagon. Then when I get back, let's look at the papers under Billy's bed."

"Yes, Dan, let's do that."

Dan walked over to the blacksmith shop. Frank was shoeing a horse. He looked up and said, "Hi, Dan, how are ya?"

"I'm doin' good. How are you doin', Frank?"

"I'm good. What can I do for ya, Dan?"

"After you finish shoein' that horse, I'd like to talk to you about doin' some work on the wagon that I brought back with the mules."

"Okay, let me finish clinching these nails, and I'll be right with ya."

After letting the foot down, Frank stretched and said, "This damned ol' back doesn't hold up as good as it used to. What ya needin' done, Dan?"

"I would like to see if you could build something to hold water barrels on both sides and replace all the wood that needs it. The seat needs some boards replaced and a couple side boards, and the wheels need to be checked good. We will be haulin' some heavy loads."

"I was lookin' at the wagon, Dan, and that's a heavy-duty wagon with four-inch wheels. It's built to carry mighty heavy loads. Okay, Dan, I'll figure out what it will cost, and I'll let you know."

"No," said Dan, "just fix it. I know you will be fair."

"I'll be closed tomorrow, but I can start on it Monday mornin'. Oh, by the way, Dan, Marshal Bert came by a while ago and said, if I see you, to let you know that he wants you to stop off at his office."

"Well, thank you, Frank. I'll go see what he wants."

Dan stopped in to see the marshal. The marshal said, "Come on in, Dan. Grab a chair and sit down."

"Thank you, Marshal."

"I have some good news, Dan. To start with, we received the bounty money from Snake's bounty. I had it put in the bank vault." The marshal asked Dan if he knew Bob that runs the bank.

"Yes, I did meet Bob."

"You can ask Bob for the money anytime you want. Now, I did get a few more posters. These and the nine you have total more than $70,000."

"Lordy, Lordy," said Dan. The marshal mentioned that no one knows how many unknown bandits are back in there. "By god, Marshal, this is gettin' more interesting every day. Thank you, Marshal. I expect we will be leaving here in a few days."

"I take it, Dan, that you met with Joseph Cobb."

"Yes, I did, Bert."

"If you don't mind me askin', is Joe goin' to jump in with ya?"

"I don't know yet. Joe is goin' to send me a note with Art, the freight driver, with his answer when Art comes through Wednesday. Marshal, can I get copies of all the posters?"

"Sure, Dan, I'll get them copied at the newspaper office. They should be ready Monday afternoon. They are closed tomorrow."

"Bert, I need to ask you if you would keep the dollar amount quiet. There is no reason for anyone else to know."

"You bet, Dan. Nothing will be said."

"Thank you, Marshal."

Dan went back to the saloon and sat up at the bar. Maggie was tending bar, and she asked, "Do you want a drink, Dan?"

"Ya, Maggie, I do."

While bringing Dan some whiskey, Maggie told him, "The word is out, and I expect it has covered most of the town, about the meeting here tomorrow after church. By the way, Dan, Billy is so afraid that he might not get to go with you and Joe."

"Well, Maggie, I'm 99 percent sure that he will be able to go, but I need to hear it from the town."

"Yes, I understand, Dan. If that is all that's holding him up, I might as well start packing Billy's clothes. I've been talking to some of the townspeople, they think this is the best chance for Billy to get more out of life. You saw the way the townspeople celebrated when you shot and killed the renegade that killed Billy's mother and got the necklace back for Billy."

"Well, Maggie, we'll see what happens after the meeting tomorrow. Maggie, could I have the privilege of escorting you to church tomorrow?"

"Why, of course, that would be nice," answered Maggie. Sunday morning, Dan went down to meet Maggie. She was wearing the same green gown as when he met her. She is an absolutely beautiful woman. Dan took Maggie's arm, and they walked with Sammi trailing behind. Dan pointed to the porch of the church and told Sammi to stay there until church was over. They were welcomed at the door by two little old ladies, and of course, Maggie knew both of them. She gave both a big hug. One of the ladies looked at Dan and asked, "Do I get a hug from you, big fella?"

"You sure do," said Dan. So Dan gave both ladies big hugs. Maggie introduced Minnie and Sarah to Dan. They handed Maggie and Dan the weekly bulletins that gave the names of the hymns and what the sermon was about.

Tom Harding

There was a little old lady playing the organ. Dan was thinking how sweet the music was, coming from the keys and the precision and accuracy of the little old lady's fingers. Absolutely beautiful. After the sermon was over, they went back to the saloon. Maggie asked Dan if he attends church services often.

"Not as often as I should, but when I'm about to go on a bounty hunt, I like to talk to God. This time I asked God to keep Maggie, Billy, and all the special people of Lariat, and Sammi, and all my livestock on the right path and out of harm's way."

"How nice, Dan. You are a very thoughtful person. Oh no, Dan, look at the townspeople waiting in front of the saloon." Maggie unlocked the doors and let the people in.

"I think you're right, Maggie, about the whole town showing up."

Howard, the night barkeep, came in and told Maggie he would take over the bar. "Thank you, Howard." Maggie started by thanking everyone for showing up and told them they needed to make a decision on Billy's future."

"Dan, do you want to explain your position in this?"

"Yes, Maggie, I would. I think you people know what the meeting is all about. It's a decision whether Billy stays in Lariat or goes with me bounty hunting. You all know how dangerous my job is." About that time, Billy and Sammi worked their way through the crowd and stood beside Dan. "I don't know how you want to come up with a decision. Does any one of you have anything to say?"

One man said, "Well, Dan, I think I can speak for most everybody here. Billy has no future here. Everybody today knows that you are like a father to Billy, and he needs a father at this time. We know that Billy is like a son to you."

Maggie stepped up by Dan and said, "Does anyone else have anything to say?" Nobody answered. "So let's take a vote. All in favor of Billy staying in Lariat, raise your hand."

Everything was quiet.

"No hands. Everybody in favor of Billy going with Dan, raise your hands." Everybody in the saloon raised their hands, including Billy and Maggie. Dan said, "Thanks to each and every one of you. Sammi and I will take the best care possible of that boy."

CHAPTER 5

Several of the townspeople stayed to see what was in the box that Ben and Madeline left behind. Maggie asked anybody interested in seeing what's in the box or anybody who knows anything about their financial affairs to please let her know. Dan said, "Thank you. Billy, would you get the box that's under your bed?"

"Sure, Mr. Dan, I'll go get it."

When Billy returned with the box, they poured everything on the table. A few people stayed to see what was in the box. They opened a large envelope. There were three birth certificates—Ben's, Madeline's, and Billy's. Billy's read March 5, 1876. They continued opening envelopes. Some cattle sales, lumber for repairs, purchase of seed corn for planting. After a couple dozen envelopes, they came across some paperwork that was on the farm. There was a title with some receipts on payments made to Marvin Banks, with an address in Amarillo, Texas. In the envelope was a paid receipt for an annual payment of two hundred dollars. The last payment being paid the fall of 1886, two years past, and the first payment made was the fall of 1874.

Dan said, "That $4,000 would be the full amount, $200 annual for twelve years would be $2,400 paid. That would leave $1,600 balance. Meaning, Billy owns a large portion of the farm. Does anyone know if a Mr. Banks ever came looking for Ben or Madeline, wondering about the last two years' payments? If so, let me know. Something is strange about the payments."

Dan suggested that they send a telegraph to Amarillo and try to get in touch with Marvin Banks. Maybe they could get things worked out. If Billy has something coming, let's get it for him.

"Maggie, would you write a note explaining to Buddy at the telegraph office to get in touch with the office in Amarillo and see if they can find this Marvin Banks and have him contact someone here. Maggie, would you agree for Mr. Banks to contact you?"

"Sure, Dan, that I'd be happy to."

Dan turned to see who all was still there, asking what they thought. "If you are in favor, hold your hand up." All hands went up. "I guess everyone is in favor. Maggie, can you handle it from here?"

"I'll handle it from here," answered Maggie.

Monday morning, Maggie sent Billy to the telegraph office with a note asking Buddy to send the information to the telegraph office in Amarillo, asking for all the information on Marvin Banks. Dan came in the saloon and told Maggie that he was going to ride out to Billy's parents' farm.

"That might be a good idea, Dan. You might run across something that might be helpful." Billy came back from the telegraph office and asked Dan if he could ride out to the farm with him. "I haven't been there since my mom was killed."

"Well, Billy, I was just talking to Maggie about going out there. But, Billy, if you want to go there, it might bring back some awful memories. You have the right to go if you want to, and I'll go with you."

"Mr. Dan, I want to go."

"Well, Billy, we better saddle up and get on our way."

They saddled up. Dan, Billy, and Sammi were on their way to the farm. It was a short ride to the farm. Dan was keeping a close eye on Billy for fear that he might fall apart. Billy looked around and mentioned that the place needed a good cleaning and the weeds pulled.

Dan said, "It's been two years now that the weeds have grown."

"I know, Mr. Dan." Billy turned and started for the house. The front door was open, and Billy looked in and saw that the stain of his mother's blood was still there. Dan noticed that Billy was holding back tears for the moment. He stepped in and walked a long ways around the stain. He walked back to his bedroom and walked in. There was a small picture that had been taken of his parents at their wedding. It was sitting on an apple box. That was what Billy used for a nightstand. Now the tears were getting harder to hold back.

Dan asked, "Are you okay, Billy?"

Billy started sobbing, tears running down his cheeks. Dan knelt down and said to Billy, "It's okay to cry. You need to just cry it all out."

Billy was wiping his tears with his shirtsleeve when he walked outside and saw his mama's grave. Someone had made a plaque and nailed it to a wooden cross. Billy asked Mr. Dan if he would read what it said.

"Sure, Billy. It says, 'Madeline, may God be with you, and he has a special place in heaven for you. We will always love you and miss you.'"

After a few minutes, Dan asked Billy, "Are you feeling a little better, Billy?"

"Ya, Mr. Dan, I do. Let's look in the barn, Mr. Dan."

They were checking the barn; in the feed room, there were four wooden barrels with lots of grain in them. The next room they used for the tack room, there were harnesses, two old saddles, halters, ropes, bridles, bottles of ointments, rakes, shovels, many small tools.

"You know, Billy, we better bring the wagon back and pick up these things and find a place to store it."

"Ya, we should do that, Mr. Dan."

"When Frank gets the wagon repaired, we'll hook up the mules and come back after it. I'm surprised the renegades didn't come back and steal all of your dad's belongings." Dan asked Billy if it would be all right if he looked around the house for more information on how much of the farm he might own.

"Sure, Mr. Dan, I can show you where things are."

"Do you think you'll be all right, Billy, or would you rather not go back in the house?"

"No, Mr. Dan, I'll be okay."

So they looked through the house and didn't find much. Billy remembered that there was a broken piece of a log up on the loft where his parents' bedroom was. Billy said, "Sometimes they would keep things in there that they didn't want people to see."

"Billy, would you want to crawl up on the loft and see what was in there?"

"Sure, Mr. Dan."

Billy crawled up the ladder and squeezed between the bed and the wall until he reached the broken log. He pulled the broken piece out and felt back in the cavity. He felt something and pulled it out and said, "Mr. Dan, it's a little canvas sack."

"Feel in there real good, Billy, to make sure you have everything."

"That's all, Mr. Dan."

"Okay, bring it down, Billy."

Billy tossed the sack down to Dan. Then Billy crawled back down.

"Let's take it back to the saloon and open it there. Is that okay with you, Billy?"

"Okay, Mr. Dan."

Dan put the sack in his saddlebags. They headed back to town.

"I guess I was a sissy back there, Mr. Dan."

"Billy, you were not a sissy. I'll tell you something that happened when my mama died. I cried every day for many days. I just couldn't get over losing her, and to this day, I still say a prayer for my mama and get tears in my eyes."

"Mr. Dan, could I ask you to not tell anybody that I cried?"

"Billy, let me ask you, if you saw a boy your age that didn't cry when his mother got killed and then you saw another boy your age that cried when his mother got killed, which one do you think loved their mother the most?"

"I think the one that cried, Mr. Dan."

"So, Billy, do you want all the people in town to think you didn't love your mama as much as they thought you did?"

"I want them to know that I loved my mama with all my heart."

"You know, Billy, when I lost my mama, I cried all the way through my mama's funeral. All the people, one by one, gave me a hug and would say, 'I'm so, so sorry, Danny.' They knew that I loved my mama with all my heart."

"Maybe I'll tell Ms. Maggie, huh, Mr. Dan?"

"I would if I were you, but if you don't want me to tell, I won't."

They reached town and stopped to put their horses in the livery barn. They made their way to the saloon.

Maggie asked, "So you made it back? How did things go?"

"Ms. Maggie, when I went in my bedroom, I saw my parent's wedding picture on my stand. I had to cry, but Mr. Dan said it's okay to cry."

"Oh, Billy, it's definitely okay to cry. I'm glad you did. You've been holding all of your emotions bottled up inside for two years. It's time you let it all out."

"I want you to know, Maggie, that Billy is one hell of a tough kid. Maggie, we found this in the house."

"What is it?" asked Maggie.

"We don't know yet. We decided to wait until we got back here to open it."

"So, Dan, do you want to open it on the table?"

"Yes, Maggie."

Jack, one of the townsmen who was sitting at the bar, was asked by Maggie to be seated at the table. Jack did move to the table. Dan turned the canvas sack over on the table. There were some envelopes and ten $20 gold coins with a note wrapped around the coins. Dan unfolded the paper and read, "Mr. Marvin Banks, this is a payment for the year of 1884."

Everyone looked at each other, wondering what this was all about. There must be a reason why the payment wasn't made. So they opened another envelope, and it also had ten $20 gold coins in it with a note that read, "Mr. Marvin Banks, this is a payment for the year of 1885."

Billy spoke up and said he remembered that Mr. Banks would come by once a year. "My mom would give him an envelope."

"Billy, are you sure?"

"Yes, sir, Mr. Dan, I'm sure."

That means something has happened to Mr. Banks. "Billy, would you run down to the telegraph office and see if Buddy has gotten an answer from Amarillo."

"Yes, sir, Mr. Dan."

"Come on, Sammi, you can go with me. We'll be right back."

"What do you think, Maggie and Jack?"

Jack said, "I'm thinking like you. I think Mr. Banks is dead."

"What do you think, Maggie?"

"I think the same way. Something has happened to Mr. Banks."

"Maggie, would you get a glass of whiskey for me and one for you and Jack also while we wait for Billy to come back."

"Thank you, Dan, but I'll wait until Howard comes in, and then I'll have one with you guys. But I'll get one for you and Jack."

A few minutes later, Billy came in with a note from Amarillo. Dan opened the note and started to read it out loud:

> This is the answer to your question about Marvin Banks. I went to our bank and asked our banker if Mr. Banks has a bank account. The answer was, yes he does, but his account has not been accessed for a long period of time. Then he came out with his books that

went back to 1883. Then he checked all the way back, and the last time his account was accessed was October 18, 1883. I asked how much his account had in it. He said that he couldn't reveal that figure. I checked with the city courthouse, and according to the records, there is no Marvin Banks or there is no other person in the city of Amarillo by the name of Banks. I seen two older men sitting on a bench across the street, so I went across and asked them if they ever knew a man by the name of Marvin Banks. One of the old fellas said he knew him but said he has been dead for quite some time. I asked if he had any idea how long. He said it's been probably two or three years or more, and if he needed anymore information, just let him know.

After reading the note, Dan said, "It looks to me like the $400 belongs to Billy." They all agreed that the money belongs to Billy.

"So you mean all that money is mine, Mr. Dan?"

"I think so, Billy."

It was five o'clock, and several guys stopped in for a drink on their way home. Dan showed each one the note and asked them to read it. Then he asked them what they thought. After all the customers read the note, they all agreed that the money belonged to Billy.

Dan said, "Billy, I think we better put the money in the bank for now and see what happens, don't you?"

"Yes, sir, Mr. Dan, I think so too." Dan and Billy walked to the bank. Robert Williams, the owner of the bank, was just closing it for the day. Dan told Robert that they would come back tomorrow.

"No, Dan, what do you need?"

Dan said, "We were going to open an account for Billy, but we can come back later."

Robert unlocked the door and asked them to come in. "How much do you want to deposit, Billy?"

Billy said, "I have $400," as he pulled out of his pocket all the gold coins and laid them on the counter.

Robert asked Billy, "Do you always walk around with that much money in your pocket?"

"No, sir, Mr. Robert, this is the most money I've ever had."

Robert counted the coins and said, "Yep, you have $400. Is that right?"

"Yes, sir, Mr. Robert."

"Here, Billy, you need to fill out this form and sign your name at the bottom."

"Mr. Robert, I don't know how to write."

Dan asked Robert if they could take the form to Maggie to fill out. She knew Billy's past history, and he didn't.

"Sure, Dan, that's fine." Dan, Billy, and Sammi went back to the saloon. Frank, the blacksmith, was waiting for Dan. "Well, Dan, I think your wagon is ready to haul some heavy loads. I want you to take a look to see if I forgot anything."

"Let me ask you a question, Frank. Would you be afraid to take the wagon across country with a heavy load?"

"No, Dan, I wouldn't be afraid at all."

"Well, then neither am I, Frank. Billy and I are goin' to take the mules and wagon out to the farm and pick up what's left out there. I was surprised that there's a lot of things out there."

Frank said, "I guess we assumed the renegades stole everything."

"I'll be over in the morning to hitch the mules, and I'll pay you for the repairs. Thank you, Frank, for getting the wagon repaired this soon."

"I'm glad I could get it fixed for ya, Dan."

"I'll see you in the morning, Frank."

Maggie saw Dan was finished talking to Frank. "Dan, I have the form filled out, but Billy is supposed to sign it, and he don't know how to write."

"Maggie, I think you should sign it for Billy."

"But what if something happens to me?"

"Robert, from the bank, will know who that money belongs to, and all the people in this town will know. Besides, nothing is going to happen to you, and that's an order because I'm starting to like you a lot."

"Oh, Dan, do you mean that?"

"Sure I mean that. Do I look like a man that would fib about something like that?"

"Dan, that makes me feel like a schoolgirl that was just asked out on her first date. I guess I should tell you, Dan, that I started liking you the first day you came to town."

"Why, Maggie, you should of told me before."

Maggie said, "I guess I'm from the old school. The man is suppose to make the first move." The rest of the evening, Maggie and Dan had lots to talk about, and they talked until the wee hours of the morning.

The next morning, Dan, Billy, and Sammi went to the livery barn and harnessed the mules and hitched them to the wagon. Dan stepped in and asked Frank how much he owed for the repairs.

"How about $4, Dan?"

"No, Frank, that's not enough. You have spent a lot of time workin' on it."

"No, Dan, all I want is $4."

"Oh, by the way, Frank, those barrel brackets look very heavy-duty. They will carry the heavy barrels of water."

Frank motioned for Dan to follow him. They walked out to the wagon, and Frank showed Dan how the brackets would fold up when they were not carrying barrels.

"That is perfect, Frank." So Dan paid him, and they were about to pull out for the farm. Dan grinned and asked, "Billy, are you going to drive these lop-eared canaries?"

"Yes, sir, Mr. Dan. These ol' canaries know when this ol' kid takes the reins, they better behave themselves."

Dan had a big laugh at that. Sammi jumped in the wagon, and they were on their way. Twenty minutes later, they reached the farm.

"Where do you want me to put the mules and wagon, Mr. Dan?"

"Just pull them up and tie 'em to that tree. Billy, do you want something from the house?"

"Yes, sir, Mr. Dan. I want that picture of my mom and dad and the box that it sits on."

"Is there anything else?"

"No, Mr. Dan, that's all."

"Do you want me to get them for you, Billy?"

"Would you do that for me, Mr. Dan? I don't want to go in there anymore."

"I'll go get them for you, Billy."

"Thank you, Mr. Dan."

While Dan went to the house to get the picture and the box, Billy started to load the wagon with all the things that had been left in the barn. When Dan returned, he went to get the harness and noticed four wooden barrels with wooden lids that Billy's father used to store feed in for the animals. "Billy, those wooden barrels are just what we need for water barrels on the wagon."

"Sure, Mr. Dan, we can use them."

"We'll have to soak the barrels. They are all dried out. We can tighten the metal straps before we soak 'em. Billy, what do you think about giving

Frank the grain in the barrels, seein' how Frank has been taking care of your horse? There's a lot of grain in those barrels."

"Ya, Mr. Dan, that's a good idea."

After loading the wagon heaping full, they headed back to town. Billy had the reins again, and he felt very important when he was driving the big mules. When he pulled into town, Billy started talking to the mules loud so everyone could hear him. He kinda likes a little attention. They pulled in front of the livery barn.

Frank came out and said, "It looks like you have a wagon full." When Billy had a chance, he asked Frank to see what was in the barrels. Frank took the lids off and looked in the barrels.

Frank asked, "Were these barrels of grain your father's?"

"Yes, Mr. Frank. Can you use the grain, Mr. Frank?"

"Yes, I can. How much do you want for all of it, Billy?"

"No, Mr. Frank, I don't want to sell it to you. I want to give it to you. You've been good to me, and you take good care of my horse."

"That's nice, Billy, but I would be happy to pay you for it."

Dan told Frank, "Billy will feel bad if you don't accept it."

"Well, I thank you, Billy. You're a very good boy."

So Billy drove the team around the back of the barn where Frank keeps the grain tanks. After they unloaded the grain, they unhitched the team and put them away. Dan, Billy, and Sammi headed for the saloon. Billy was carrying the picture and the apple box.

When they walked in, Maggie had a big smile and hug for Billy and Dan. She then brought a glass of whiskey for Dan and a sarsaparilla for Billy. Maggie sat down at the table. Billy showed Maggie the picture of his mother and father.

"How nice for you to have that picture. Are you going to put it next to your bed?"

"Ya, I'm goin' to put it in there right now."

"Come on, Sammi, you can help me." Billy set the picture of his mom and dad on the apple box then put his mother's necklace around the picture. Maggie asked what all they brought back.

"A wagon full." said Dan.

When Billy and Sammi came back, Dan asked, "What do you want to do with all the stuff in the wagon?"

"What do you think I should do with it, Mr. Dan?"

"I don't know, Billy, whether you want to sell it, or do you want to keep it?"

"What do you think I should do with it, Ms. Maggie?"

"Billy, why don't you keep it for now, and then when you guys get back from the big hunt, you can decide then. When I went to the bank today to sign on your bank account, I was telling Robert down at the bank that you guys were out to the farm, picking up all the stuff that was still there. Robert said if you need a place to store it, he had a small building in the back of the bank. He'd never used it. And if Billy needs a place to store it, he's welcome to use it."

The next morning being Wednesday, they moved the wagon around to the building that Robert so generously offered. By the time they unloaded the wagon, it was getting near to the time for Art to come by with the note from Joe Cobb. Dan, Billy, and Sammi went back to the saloon; and Maggie sat down with the boys and asked, "What will you do if Joe doesn't go, Dan?"

"I have no choice, Maggie. I'm already halfway across that river. I can't turn back now."

"So, Dan, are you saying that you will still go even if Joe doesn't go?"

"I've made too many preparations and bought the mules and wagon. I hope Joe goes. But if he doesn't, Billy, Sammi, and I will still go get 'em."

"I kinda hate to see you go by yourselves. Like I told you, Dan, I've gotten very fond of you. More so than you know."

Shortly that afternoon, Art showed up and had a letter for Dan. "What do you think, Maggie? Will Joe go or not?"

Billy and Sammi went to the bank to thank Robert for letting him use his building.

"Well, let's open that note."

As Dan opened the letter, everything was quiet. Dan started to read the letter.

Dan Colt,

You should receive this letter on Wednesday. I'm leaving here on Friday morning. I should reach Lariat late Saturday.

Your best regards,

Joseph Cobb

Billy and Sammi returned from the bank.

"Do you want to hear what Joe had to say, Billy?"

"Yes, sir, Mr. Dan."

"Well, Billy, Joe will be here late Saturday." Billy jumped up and shouted "yahoo!" and Sammi gave her little bark.

"So, Billy, we better start gettin' things ready."

"What do we need to do first, Mr. Dan?"

"We need to get three of those barrels soaked so they will expand so they will hold water. Get them and submerge them in the horse trough out front then pump the trough full. Turn them every two hours. After you get them soaked, stand them on the barrel shelves that Frank made for us. Put one on each side of the wagon, then put the third one in the back of the wagon, then get a bucket and grab hold of that pump handle. And that will keep you busy for a while. After you finish, get a rag from Maggie and wipe all the dust out of the fourth barrel so we can use it for storage."

"Okay, Mr. Dan, I'll get started right away."

Dan hitched the mules and pulled the wagon around in front of the water trough. Billy hopped in the wagon and handed the barrels to Dan. He set them by the trough. "Okay, Billy, I'm goin' to put the mules away, and you can start soakin' 'em."

After Dan had put the mules up, he walked to the market and asked Ted to put together a box of medical supplies. He needed a large bottle of iodine, gauze, cotton, tape, and anything he had that's medicine.

"You said a large iodine?" asked Ted.

"Yep, that is for if someone takes a bullet. We pour the wound full of iodine to keep infection from settin' in. I won't need the order until sometime Saturday."

"Okay, Dan, I'll put it together for ya."

Later that afternoon, Dan stopped in the saloon for a glass of whiskey. Billy had been turning barrels all day, and Marshal Bert had stopped and asked Billy why he was tryin' to drown the barrels.

"Mr. Bert, these dad-burn barrels will hold water when ol' Billy gets through with 'em."

Earl Burns stopped and said to Bert, "We have a cattle drive comin' through, and it's the Colburn Cattle Company."

"I know, Bert. They get drunk and cause more trouble than any of the other drives that come through. Maybe we should get our guns ready."

Billy heard the conversation between Bert and Earl. Billy went in the saloon and said, "There's a cattle drive comin' through in a couple days."

Maggie asked which company it was.

"It's the Colburn Cattle Company."

"Oh boy," said Maggie, "they are the worst ones that come through."

Dan asked, "Is there anything I can do, Maggie?"

"I don't know, Dan, but maybe if you asked Bert."

"I'll walk over and see what Bert says." Dan met with the marshal and asked about this particular cattle company. Maggie is a little nervous about them comin' through.

"Dan, the last time they came through, they broke two of Maggie's tables and broke the big mirror behind the bar. They did some other damage too. I can't remember what all they did. I couldn't control 'em at all."

"Bert, can you swear me in as a deputy?"

"The pay isn't much, Dan."

"I don't care about the pay. I just want to help keep Maggie's place in one piece."

"Well, in that case, you're on." Bert opened the desk drawer and pulled out a badge and handed it to Dan.

"Do I start tonight?"

"You might as well, Dan."

"I guess you have to swear me in, huh, Bert?"

"I already did when you weren't lookin'. So that's a job already done."

Dan pinned the badge on and asked, "Do I get a pair of handcuffs?"

"There are several pairs hangin' on that hook. Help yourself."

"So I'm an official deputy." Dan went back to the saloon and went over to where Maggie and Billy were sitting and told Billy, "I have to arrest you, young feller."

"What did I do?" asked Billy.

"Do you see this badge?"

"But I didn't do anything, Mr. Dan."

"The marshal said you were trying to drown some barrels out here by the water trough today."

"Oh, Mr. Dan, you're kiddin' me."

"Ya, Billy, I'm teasin' you."

"Where did you get that badge, Mr. Dan?"

"Marshal Bert deputized me until the rowdy cattle drivers leave town."

"I need to ask you, Mr. Dan, do you think Marshal Bert would deputize me? I have my rifle, and I heard that if you want a bad guy to go down, you shoot 'em in the knee. They'll go down real fast."

"I don't think that would work, Billy. If you shoot all the rowdy cowboys in the knee, who is goin' to chase the cattle?"

"They could still chase the cows, Mr. Dan. They would just have a sore knee, but so what?"

"I don't think Marshal Bert is goin' to buy that."

Maggie came over to the table. "What are you doing wearing that badge?"

"I'm a deputy, Maggie. Only while the drunken cowboys are in town." Dan took the badge off and put it in his pocket.

CHAPTER 6

Saturday morning, everything was going good. Townspeople could see the dust from the cattle coming toward Lariat. The townspeople were nervous about the cattle drive coming to town. They haven't forgotten the last time they came to Lariat and destroyed a lot of property. "We are goin' to see if we can't stop some of this damage," said Dan.

The cattle started coming through town at 3:30 p.m. It took about two hours to herd all the cattle into the corrals. But it didn't take long for the cowboys to get to the saloon. Dan had his badge pinned on. They started out kinda quiet for the first couple of hours. Dan was in the saloon, keeping an eye on things.

Billy came in and said, "Mr. Dan, Joe Cobb just rode in. He's puttin' his horse away now."

"Billy, go tell Joe that I'm here in the saloon."

"I'll go tell him, Mr. Dan."

A few minutes later, Joe came in and shook Dan's hand.

Joe asked, "Where did all these cowboys come from?" Dan explained to Joe about the cattle drive and all the damage they did the last time they came through. "I see you're wearin' a badge, where's mine?"

"Billy, run over to the marshal's office and tell Bert that Joe Cobb needs a badge also."

"I'm on my way, Mr. Dan." Billy didn't take long to get a badge and a pair of handcuffs. Joe pinned the badge on. Dan and Joe sat at a table. Dan had a chance to explain about these cowboys. Billy was sitting at the table, listening to Joe and Dan discussing what they could be like after a few more drinks.

Billy said, "Mr. Dan, see the one with the black hat and the red kerchief? He's the one that broke the tables and the mirror behind the bar."

"Are you sure, Billy?"

"I'm sure, Mr. Dan."

"Billy, go upstairs and ask Maggie how much the repairs cost her the last time these cowboys came through last year."

"I'll be right back, Mr. Dan."

"Oh, Billy, ask Maggie to stay in her room for now. We'll let her know when it's safe. We might run into some minor problems."

When Billy came back, he brought with him a note from Maggie that read two tables, $6, and the mirror, $6, total $12.

"Okay, Joe, I'm goin' to get either $12 from that drunken bastard or kill him."

Joe said, "I'll take the six on the left, and you take the six on the right."

"Sounds good, Joe."

"First, Billy, I want you to go to you room and stay there until I tell you."

"Okay, Mr. Dan." Billy did what he was told and went to his room.

"Are you ready, Joe?"

"Yep, I'm ready." The two big guys walked over, and Joe stood close behind half the cowboys on the left, and Dan did the same on the right. Sammi was right behind Dan with her steady growl. Dan told the guy that Billy had pointed out, "Cowboy, I need to get $12 from you for the damage you did the last time you came through."

"Nope, I ain't goin' to pay anythin'."

"You have a choice. You can take me or my dog, Sammi."

He turned and reached for his gun. Dan pulled his knife and grabbed his arm with his other hand, and with a powerful swing and the blunt edge of the heavy knife, he hit him across his arm. The cowboy screamed and fell to the floor. Joe saw one of his six cowboys turn to go after him; he knocked the cowboy's hat off and grabbed his hair, pulling his head down. And with a powerful uppercut, the cowboy hit the floor with blood gushing from his nose and from his mouth.

Joe asked, "Does anybody else want to try their luck?"

The cowboy that tried his luck with Dan was screaming and said, "You broke my God damned arm."

Dan said, "Sir, that was my full intention."

Another one of Joe's half wanted to be a hero. He jumped off his stool and took a swing at Joe. Joe caught the cowboy's fist in midair and hit him so hard the cowboy flew backward and hit the edge of the bar with his head. One more down.

"Are there any more takers?"

The others seemed that they had no intention to test their fighting abilities at this time. Dan asked the rest if they were willing to give up their weapons.

One cowboy asked, "Why do you want our guns?"

Dan's answer was, "So you don't do something stupid like trying to shoot it out with Joe or me."

"Put your elbows on the bar and keep 'em there."

The rest of the cowboys that were still sitting on a barstool finally did as they were told. Dan and Joe picked the cowboys' guns out of their holsters one at a time.

Dan asked the rest, "Do you think you can have a few drinks without causin' any more trouble?"

They all agreed. Dan was looking toward the back of the room. He noticed what looked like a big bore rifle sticking out the crack of the door of Billy's room. Dan hollered at Billy, "What are you doin', Billy?"

"I was just backin' you and Mr. Joe up, just in case."

Marshal Bert walked in and looked around then asked, "What the hell happened, Dan?"

"We had three cowboys that weren't thinkin' right, Marshal."

Bert asked, "Is everybody okay?"

"No shots fired," answered Dan.

"Well, Marshal, the three on the floor are under arrest. That one has a broken arm, the one lyin' in the puddle of blood, I don't think he's breathin'. The third one is breathin', he's just sleepin'."

"I didn't know, Dan, that anything was goin' on, or I would have been here to help you guys."

"We didn't need ya, Marshal," said Joe.

"I can see that. You guys handled the problem well."

Dan told the one with the broken arm to get up.

"My arm is broke and hurts like hell."

Dan said, "Shut up or I'll break the other one. Bert, you can take this one over to the jail and lock him up. He owes Maggie $12, and we need to hold him until it's paid."

Joe checked the one lying in the blood. "He has no pulse."

Dan hollered at Billy to get the mop and get the blood mopped up. Bert went to the funeral parlor and asked them to pick up the dead cowboy.

"After they get the dead cowboy out of here, Billy, you can tell Maggie she can come down."

Marshal Bert said, "I need four of you cowboys to each grab either an arm or leg and carry him over to the jail."

Four of the cowboys stepped down and picked him off the floor and carried him to the jail. The marshal followed them. He unlocked the cell door. They laid him on the bunk. The marshal thanked them. Later, after everything was cleaned up and straightened up, Maggie came down. She didn't know what had happened, but she was pretty sure somebody drew blood.

Dan took Maggie's hand and led her to the bar and explained to the cowboys. "This lady is the owner of the saloon. And I ask you, why do you bunch of rowdy cowboys want to come in and cause trouble and do damage? This lady is just tryin' to make a living. She has never done anything bad to you guys or to anybody else. The one with a broken arm will never be allowed to come in here again. The dead one, well, he won't be back either. Now you other nine that chose not to do damage and get in trouble, go sit at the bar."

Then Dan asked Howard to give the nine cowboys a drink, also one for Maggie, Joe, and himself, and Billy, a sarsaparilla. Dan tossed a $10 gold piece on the bar. After the cowboys got their drinks, they all stood up and thanked Dan for the drinks and told Maggie they were sorry there was trouble, and the big guy said, "I will see to it, when we come through next year, there will be no trouble. By the way, my name is Buck."

"Hi, Buck, my name is Maggie, and I'm happy to meet you, Buck."

And Buck said, "When we come in, we will turn our guns over to the barkeep."

Maggie said, "Whenever you come in and turn your guns over to the barkeeper, the first round of drinks will be on me."

Back at the table, Dan asked, "What the blazes were you doin', Billy, with that big bore rifle?"

"Well, Mr. Dan, I was just backin' up you and Mr. Joe. Remember, we are three bounty hunters workin' together."

"Was that rifle one I collected from the outlaws?"

"Yes, sir, Mr. Dan. You guys did a good job. You didn't need me, but if you had needed me to help, I was there."

"What do you think, Joe? Do you think Billy's going to be a top-notch bounty hunter?"

"Absolutely, Dan."

Just then, Marshal Bert came in and said, "The second one is still sleeping."

"Is he still breathin'?" asked Joe.

"Ya, he's still breathin'." Bert asked, "Who hit that cowboy?"

Dan pointed and said, "Mr. Cobb there had that privilege."

"When he wakes up, he's goin' to wonder which one of your mules kicked him in the mouth. He has the fattest lips that I've ever seen." Bert walked over and asked if one of them would ride out and ask the trail boss to come to town because he needed to talk to him. One cowboy said he would go get him.

An hour later, the cowboy and the trail boss came into the saloon and asked, "Where's the marshal?"

Billy said, "I'll go get him." Billy ran down to the marshal's office and told Bert that the trail boss was at the saloon. Dan asked the trail boss to sit down and have a drink.

Dan held his hand out and said, "My name is Dan Colt. And this is Joe Cobb." The trail boss said, "I'm happy to meet ya. My name is Carl Abbott."

Bert came in and sat at the table. Dan introduced Carl to Bert.

"What did you want to talk about, Marshal?"

"Well, Carl, we had a little problem with three of your cowboys."

"What happened?" asked Carl.

"The trouble started on your last year's drive. One of your cowboys that's in my jail now busted some tables and threw a whiskey glass and shattered the mirror behind the bar. We need to collect for the owner of the saloon."

"How much does he owe?"

"He owes $12 for damages and a $5 fine for causin' trouble. And the other one has to pay a $5 fine for causin' trouble. Total is $22. We can't release them until the bills are paid. The one that always causes trouble has a broken arm. We have one dead, and we have one with the fattest lips I've ever seen."

"Well, Marshal, what happened to the one that was killed?"

Bert said, "He made the mistake of taken a swing at Mr. Cobb." Dan pointed at Joe.

"So what happened to the one with the fat lips?"

"Well, he made the mistake of tryin' to fight with Mr. Cobb." Dan pointed at Joe.

"So what happened the one with the broken arm?"

"He made the mistake of tryin' to pull his gun on Mr. Colt." Joe pointed at Dan.

Maggie came down to the bar. Dan introduced Maggie to Carl Abbott. Carl stood up and took Maggie's hand and put his other hand on top, patting her hand. He apologized for what his men had done. "I'll pay the damages and fines. Then I'll hold the money out of their wages."

"Thank you, Mr. Abbott."

"How about the ones at the bar?"

"They haven't caused any problems. The big guy at the other end of the bar said he would see to it they wouldn't cause any problems or do any damage from now on."

Carl said, "That's Buck, he's the toughest one of all the herders. If he is on your side, he'll keep the rest of 'em in line." Carl paid for the damages and fines. The cowboy with the fat lips, his name is Dude, is now awake. He's complaining of a severe headache and a hurtin' mouth and a broken nose.

Carl brought Dude and Jack to the saloon. "I want you two to apologize to Maggie."

They did say, "Ma'am, we are sorry for what we did."

Maggie accepted their apology.

Carl said, "I recommend that you, Dude and Jack, should stick to chasin' cattle, and let the big boys do the fightin'. You're lucky they didn't kill all three of ya, although you both look like leftover death."

The cowboy Dude with the messed-up face said, "I've never been hit that hard in all my life."

The next morning, Dan, Joe, Billy, and Sammi were getting things put together; and Dan noticed Carl was taking the two cowpunchers back to the herd.

Dan asked, "When are you movin' the herd out, Carl?"

"We're pullin' out early Monday mornin'."

"Thank you, Carl. I hope the rest of the trip goes good for ya. Oh, by the way, Carl, you might want to explain to Dude and Jack that drinkin' and fightin' don't go good together."

Carl said, "I think they found that out the hard way."

Back to preparing for the trip, the wagon had three barrels of water; one barrel full of jerky, cans of beans, dried fruits, and several other foods, plus medical supplies; a large tarp; four bottles of whiskey; ten bottles of sarsaparilla; three extra rifles, loaded; six extra boxes of ammunition; four hundred pounds of oats for the livestock; and many other supplies.

Dan asked Billy if he had his little .22 rifle loaded in the wagon to take along.

"Yes, sir, Mr. Dan."

"How many bullets do you have?"

"I have about a half a box."

"Run across the street, and get two more boxes, and tell Ted to put them on my bill. And tell him that I'll be over to pay for all the supplies before we pull out. Do you have a hat, Billy?"

"No, Mr. Dan, I don't."

"Okay, Billy, while you're in there, get you a hat and some new boots. Your old ones are getting a little shabby."

"Thank you, Mr. Dan."

"The reason for the extra bullets, Billy, you're going to be in charge of bringin' in at least two rabbits a day."

"I'll get 'em, Mr. Dan. I'm ol' Billy, the sharpshooter."

"Oh, that's right," said Dan.

"What do you think, Joe? Can you think of anything else we need?"

Joe said, "I can't think of anything else."

Billy asked Dan if he could borrow one of the guns and holsters that was in his room.

"Well, Billy, you can take one of them along, but we'll have to do some schooling along the way before you can carry it. I don't think any of them will fit you."

"Oh ya, Mr. Dan, that one fits real good if I poke a couple of holes in the belt. Frank at the livery barn has a hole puncher."

"Well, bring the gun and put it in the wagon. Then take the holster up and ask Frank to punch some holes in it."

"Okay, Mr. Dan, I'll be right back."

Joe asked Dan if he was ready for a drink at Maggie's.

"I was thinkin' the same thing, Joe." So they made their way to the saloon. Maggie brought a bottle of whiskey and two glasses.

"You might as well bring Billy a sarsparilla too."

"Where is Billy?" asked Maggie.

"He's gettin' fitted for a holster up at Frank's."

Maggie asked, "Do you mean a gun holster?"

"Ya, he's goin' to be packin' a pistol."

"Dan, do you think that's a good idea?"

"Well, Maggie, he will have to shoot several boxes of ammunition through that gun before he can wear it."

"That makes me feel a little better. When I saw him driving them big ol' mules, it scared me, and now he'll be carrying a pistol. But I know you will take good care of Billy. Are you guys leaving tomorrow morning?"

"Ya, Maggie, we need to get on the road. In fact, I need to talk to Bert."

"Joe, let's walk over and talk to him."

"Okay," said Joe. They met with Bert at his office.

Dan asked, "What's the best way out of here goin' north?"

"Do you know any good trails or bad trails? Do you know of any problems with outlaws or Indians?"

"Well, there is no way to know for sure. Ever so often, we hear of some trouble on the trails, but the trail headin' north is well traveled. And we don't hear of much trouble, but you guys bein' bounty hunters, I know you watch out in every direction at all times. I know that you guys would be hard to take down, but it doesn't hurt to be careful all the time."

"So, Bert, you suggest we stay on the north trail as far as we can before we have to turn, and then we have to angle to the northeast. Thank you, Bert, we're pullin' out in the morning."

"Oh, by the way," said Bert, "there is a stretch about forty miles from here. A ten-mile stretch that has no shelter, no trees. You might want to keep an eye out goin' through there. That's about all I can tell ya."

"Thanks, Bert."

Bert asked them to be careful. "We want you guys and Sammi to come back safe."

Billy came in wearing the holster. Bert looked at Billy and said, "Why are you wearin' that holster? Are you goin' to start packin' a gun?"

"Yep, as soon as Mr. Dan says I can."

CHAPTER 7

The hunters were making last-minute preparation before pulling out for the big hunt. Dan, Joe, Billy, and Sammi all went back to the saloon. They were trying to think if there was anything they were forgetting.

Maggie said, "I know something you're forgetting."

Dan asked, "What is it?"

Maggie said, "Me."

"Maggie, we can't take you along. This is goin' to be a tough trip, and I don't want you to get hurt."

Maggie said, "I know, I was just thinking it would be fun to make a trip like this. I guess I better wash some glasses before I run out."

Billy asked Dan if he could get some money from his bank account.

"What did you need money for, Billy?"

"Well, Mr. Dan, I want to buy a bowie knife like yours."

"What are you goin' to use it for, Billy?"

"Well, Mr. Dan, one thing, it seems like it would be kinda handy for breakin' somebody's arm when you're mad at 'em."

Dan and Joe busted out laughing.

Dan said, "Billy, I guess you were watchin' closer than I thought. Billy, if you want a knife, then you should get one. You will need to ask Maggie to go with you to the bank."

Maggie was washing glasses behind the bar. Billy went over and asked her if she would go with him to the bank to get some money.

"Did you ask Dan if that was all right with him?"

"Yes, Ms. Maggie, he said that it was okay."

So after she finished washing glasses, Maggie said, "Okay, Billy, are you ready to go now?" They went to the bank and met with Robert Williams, the banker.

Maggie told Robert that Billy wanted to withdraw some money.

"How much do you need, Billy?"

"I would like a $20 gold coin."

Robert asked Maggie if she would sign on the line at the bottom before he handed Billy the coin. "Okay, Billy, here is your $20 gold coin."

"Thank you, Mr. Robert, and thank you, Ms. Maggie."

Robert told Billy to be sure not to lose it.

"I won't," said Billy. Maggie and Billy went back to the saloon. Billy went over to the table where Dan and Joe were sitting. Billy sat down at the table and asked Dan, "Am I drivin' the mules tomorrow?"

"Yep, you and Sammi."

"Oh boy," said Billy, "Sammi gets to ride with me."

Dan said, "Ya know, Joe, I was thinking, Billy has those harness. What if we took our ridin' horses and break 'em to drive as we go. If we get into some tough goin', we could harness them and hitch them in front of the mules. I know the wagon is full, but we can hang the harness over the wagon racks. Billy, would you loan us the harness?"

"Sure, Mr. Dan and Mr. Joe."

Joe said, "We can swing around the back of the bank and pick them up on the way out." Several of the townsmen stopped in the saloon to have a drink and to tell Billy good-bye and to wish them all good luck on their venture. Everyone asked Joe and Dan to watch out for Billy. Howard took over the night shift. Maggie came over and sat down with Dan, Joe, and Billy. Maggie had a sad look on her face.

Dan asked, "What's the matter, Maggie?"

"Oh, I just hate to see you guys leave. You will probably be gone for a long time."

"Well, Maggie, it probably won't be as long as you think. We will try to get it over with as fast as we can, and we will be headed back to Lariat. I will send a telegraph to Buddy, and he can give you a note from us when we get there to let you know everything is all right. I will give numbers such as 'we got two coyotes yesterday.' Meaning, that's how many outlaws we caught. The reason for that is we don't want all the telegraph operators to know what we are doin'. It's okay for Buddy to know, but he needs to keep it under his hat. You can explain it to him."

The next morning, they were getting the mules harnessed and the horses saddled. It was finally time to pull out. Maggie was there to see them off.

Billy gave Maggie a big hug and said, "We will be back, Ms. Maggie, I promise." Maggie and Billy both had teary eyes. Then it was time to say good-bye to Dan. Maggie had a difficult time to keep from breaking down and crying. Maggie wrapped her arms around Dan. With tears running down her cheeks, she asked, "Dan, please promise me that you will come back."

Dan said, "I promise, Maggie, that I will be back as soon as possible."

Some more of the townspeople came by to wish them a good and safe trip. Billy and Sammi jumped up on the wagon and were ready to go.

Billy said, "Sammi, you and ol' Billy can handle these darn ol' mules." Billy pulled around the back of the bank. Dan and Joe hopped down and got the harness from the shed and threw them over the racks on the wagon. Dan and Joe were on their horses and ready to pull out. Billy said, swinging his arm in motion, "Mr. Dan and Mr. Joe, come on, let's go get 'em."

Dan said, "Let's go get 'em, Billy and Joe."

Joe said, "Let's go get 'em, Billy and Dan."

Billy felt like he was ten feet tall. As they rounded the bank and on their way, Maggie was still waving and said, "You guys hurry back as soon as you can."

"We'll be back soon," said Dan. They were heading north out of town. "We have about a thousand miles ahead of us," said Dan. The mules seemed to be handling the weight of the wagon, and everything in it without any problem. They had a good, fast gait so that will make for less time on the trail. Billy and Sammi had the mules moving along. Dan and Joe both agreed their saddle horses were working hard to keep up.

Joe said, "All I can say, Billy, is that you're a natural-born mule skinner."

"Ya, I know it, Mr. Joe."

Billy asked, "How do I look with my new hat and boots?"

"You look like a top-notch bounty hunter, Billy," said Dan. The trail was well traveled and smooth going, and that made it easier for the animals. It was midsummer, and the weather was hotter than hell. About four hours out, they decided to pull over where there were trees to give the horses and mules some shade and a few minutes' rest. They gave the mules and horses and Sammi a drink of water. The twelve one-gallon canteens were for the guys. The reason for the extra canteens of water was if it was too far between water holes and the barrels run empty, they may have to give the extra water from the canteens to the animals. Dan and Joe are not concerned about running out of water with them carrying that much along.

Joe asked, "Billy, how ya doin' in this heat?"

Billy said, "I'm okay. I'm a perty tough kid, Mr. Joe."

After a few minutes' rest and everyone got a drink of water, they pulled out, hoping to get a few more miles behind them for the day. But they knew that the mules needed to take it easy for the first few days. They just came off pasture and had very little work. They needed to get legged up and build up some muscles. The hot weather didn't help either.

Midday Dan said to Billy, "Start cuttin' across to that clump of trees, and we will settle in for the night. That will give you plenty of time to get some rabbits or anything edible." When they got to the trees, Billy pulled the mules up and got down, unhitched them, and pulled the harnesses off. They watered the livestock and put the hobbles on the rest of the animals, except Cricket. Billy had to ride her, looking for some rabbits for supper.

Billy was saddling Cricket when Dan said, "While you are out there, see if you can find a dead tree. Throw your lasso on it and drag it back or find whatever else to burn for cookin' supper."

Billy asked Dan if he could use one of the big guns to shoot the rabbits.

Dan said, "Billy, if you shoot a rabbit with one of the big guns, all that would be left would be his ears and tail."

"Ya, that wouldn't be good, huh, Mr. Dan?"

"Billy, whenever you are out lookin' for rabbits and you see any riders, you turn Cricket and come back to the wagon as fast as you can."

Billy hopped on Cricket and went looking for rabbits. About thirty minutes later, they heard Billy's little gun go *pop!*

Dan said, "I think Billy got one."

"Sounds like it," answered Joe. It was only about five minutes and *pop!* again. Joe said, "It sounds like he got number two." Soon they saw Billy dragging part of a dead tree with his rope dallied to the saddle horn.

"Well hell, look, Joe. Billy's bringin' a wild turkey tied to one side, and a rabbit tied to the other side."

"I see supper comin'," said Joe.

Dan said, "Ya know somethin', Joe, if you give that boy a job to do, he's goin' to do it no matter what."

"Yep, he's a good boy," agreed Joe.

"Well, Mr. Dan and Mr. Joe, did ol' Billy bring in our supper or not?"

Dan said, "Yep, ol' Billy brought in our supper."

Joe said, "We only heard two shots."

"That's all there was, Mr. Joe. You're talkin' to ol' Billy, the sharpshooter."

Joe asked Billy, "How did you get close enough to the turkeys to get a shot at 'em."

"I was ridin' over by those trees, and when I got close enough, I could hear them gobblin'. So I tied Cricket to a tree, and I snuck around the trees until I could see one out in the open. I had to shoot the turkey first. I knew as soon as I shot, those turkeys were goin' to be on the fly. The rabbits just stood there, lookin' around."

"I see you shot the turkey through the head, Billy,"

"Yes, sir, Mr. Joe. I always shoot them through the head so the bullet don't damage any of the meat. My father taught me that."

"Well, Billy, your father taught you real well. Ya know somethin', you are ol' Billy, the sharpshooter." Dan asked Billy to feed the stock their oats and give them a drink of water.

"Yes, sir, Mr. Dan. Ol' Billy can take care of that job."

Dan pulled the cork out of a bottle of whiskey and handed it to Joe, and Joe took a generous swig and said, "This is to our upcomin' hunt," and handed the bottle back to Dan. And Dan said, "Here's to our safety on this hunt, and that we all go home alive." Then Dan took a big pull off the bottle. "Damn, that's good stuff," Dan emphasized. Dan and Joe were cookin' the turkey and the rabbit over a big fire. Billy and Sammi came back from feeding and watering all the stock.

Billy said, "That supper is smellin' mighty good. Me and Sammi are gettin' hungry."

"It won't be long now, Billy," said Dan.

After they filled their bellies, they sat around the fire. Billy was having a sarsaparilla while Dan and Joe were having just a little sip. Although they drink very little whiskey when they are on the trail of outlaws, they needed to have a clear mind, and their equilibrium must be in perfect condition. That helps to stay alive.

The next morning, Dan made a panful of biscuits and asked Billy if he would get the pail of sorghum from the wagon for the biscuits. Dan, Joe, Billy, and Sammi had their biscuits. After breakfast, they did their regular chores—feeding and watering the stock, harnessing, and saddling, etc. They all mounted and were on the road again. Billy was on the wagon, drivin' the mules. Claude and Cricket were tied behind the wagon. Sammi decided to run alongside for a while. Dan and Joe rode alongside as well. All of the stock had a good night's rest, so they were steppin' out at a pretty fast pace.

Each day, the mules would get stronger and would perform a little better. After a couple hours out, they could see a wagon coming toward them. It looked like there were about four people in the wagon. Dan checked with his telescope and decided there was nothing to fear. Finally, they met each other.

Dan said, "Howdy, neighbor. Where ya headed?"

"Howdy to you too, and we are goin' to Amarillo."

The older man asked Dan what they had to look forward to down the trail. Dan said, "We're comin' from Lariat, and we didn't have any trouble."

The older man said, "We didn't have any trouble either, but we were warned at the town of Vega. They said that there had been a band of outlaws that rob and kill people for their money and other valuables along that stretch. About two hours back, there was a Mennonite family that was murdered last week. The Mennonites don't carry guns. Their religion doesn't believe in firearms. So they didn't stand a chance."

"Did someone give them a buryin'?" asked Dan.

The older man said, "A man in the town of Vega said that the Mennonite church members picked them up and buried them in a little cemetery behind their church. But we came prepared. We all have rifles and pistols, but it still makes ya kinda uneasy comin' through there."

Dan said, "Thank you for the information. We'll keep our eyes open as we travel, and you do the same."

"Well, you heard what he said, so I guess we better be prepared for anything," said Dan. They pulled out with all three of them knowing that it could get ugly. Dan said to Billy, "If it should happen, you get behind the water barrels and get down as far as you can."

"But, Mr. Dan, I need to help. We should work together. We are all sharpshooters, and we can pick them off before they know what hit 'em."

"Well, Billy, I promised Maggie and the townspeople that I would try to keep you out of harm's way."

"I know," said Billy, "but we are in harm's way, and there's nothin' we can do about that. So please let me help, Mr. Dan."

"Okay, Billy, if there are more than four of them, you can help. But if there are four or less, then you do as I said. Joe and I will have plenty of time to take care of four or so of 'em. Okay, Billy?"

"Okay, Mr. Dan."

"Now we need to make plans," said Dan. "I think we can assume that they will be coming from the east, and they will try to catch us out in the open. They will think that they are catchin' us by surprise. They won't know that we will be ready for 'em. We need to keep an eye on all four sides. I think we should make a plan where we will each take our positions. What do you think, Joe?"

"Ya, Dan," said Joe. "Let's put Billy behind a full barrel to protect him. I'll take the rear wheel, and you take the front, depending, of course, on which side they come from. What do you think, Dan?"

"That sounds good, Joe."

"Now, Billy, when you jump down, you grab the bridle of the mule on the left and pull them around as far as you can without movin' the wagon. That will give 'em less exposure. Joe and I can keep the horses behind us for their less exposure. Now do you know what to do, Billy?"

"Yes, Mr. Dan. If we see them comin', we jump down, and I grab a mule, turn 'em sideways, but not to move the wagon. Then I stand behind the water barrel and shoot from beside the barrel. Joe will be to my right side, and you, Mr. Dan, will be on my left, and don't shoot until you say go."

Dan said, "We need to take them out at a fair distance. We don't want them gettin' close enough to shoot our livestock."

Joe said, "I'll take the ones on the right. Billy, you take the ones in the center, and Dan, you take the ones on the left."

"Okay, I think we are ready for 'em," Dan said. "The one thing that they won't think of is, when their ridin' a horse at full speed, tryin' to take aim with their rifles or their revolvers, it is nearly impossible. We will be restin' our rifles over the side board of the wagon. The only way they can be equal is if they could hit us with a surprise attack, but we are not goin' to let that happen."

Billy asked, "Mr. Dan, what if they snuck up on us while we were sleepin' at night?"

"Well, Billy, that's Sammi's job, and she won't let that happen."

"Oh ya, Mr. Dan. I didn't think about Sammi."

"Ya know, Billy, Sammi is on duty twenty-four hours a day, and she will never let us down." They continued on down the trail with all four watching every direction. Sammi also realized that something was wrong. About two hours later, they came upon the Mennonite wagon that the old man told them about. The wagon was tipped over on its side. They pulled over and stopped and were looking at the wagon. Blood covered almost the entire wagon. They shook their heads in disbelief.

Billy said, "There is somthin' under the wagon box. It looks like a book."

Dan and Joe took hold of the wagon and sat it up. There was a book. The Bible. It was also spattered with blood. Dan opened the cover. On the first page were names of the family. The names were

Jonathan William Yoder, born April 16, 1846
Martha Mildred Yoder, born May 2, 1848
Samuel William Yoder, born January 10, 1869
Issiah Richard Yoder, born September 4, 1871
Samantha Ann Yoder, born, June 1, 1874
Wilma Jane Yoder, born May 10, 1876

Dan stood there for a few minutes, shaking his head, and turned sideways so Joe and Billy couldn't see the tears in his eyes. Dan gets a little emotional when something bad happens to women and children. Billy then walked around the wagon so Joe and Dan couldn't see his eyes either.

Joe said, "Those dirty sons of bitches killed the whole family."

Dan said, "Those bastards! I wonder if there are posters on 'em so we can get their pictures."

"We need to go after 'em," said Joe. "Let's go to the town the old fella said. I think he called it Vega. Let's see how much the town people know about this massacre."

"Let's go," said Billy. They all got aboard and headed for Vega. Billy was acting differently. He had a flashback of his mother's slaughter. Billy was mad, and it wasn't going away easily. He is serious that he wants to see them killed. All of them. If they're wanted dead or alive, Billy would choose to take them in dead.

Dan asked, "Are you all right, Billy?"

"Ya', I'm all right, Mr. Dan."

Dan noticed that Joe was quiet too. *Well,* Dan thought under his breath, *I guess I'm bein' quiet too.*

Billy was pushing the mules to speed them up so they could get there faster. Billy won't be happy now until the whole gang is dead.

Joe asked Dan, "What are we goin' to do if there are no posters or pictures out on them? Do you want to go after them anyway?"

Dan said, "I'm for it, Joe. How about you, Billy?"

"Let's go get 'em," Billy answered.

"This is goin' to slow down our big hunt, said Dan, but they will still be there when we get there."

Joe said, "Maybe this will give us some practice." They rolled into town about 4:00 p.m. They rode directly to the sheriff's office. They tied the mules and horses to the hitching post and went in to meet the sheriff.

"Hi, Sheriff, my name is Dan Colt. And this is Joe Cobb, and this is Billy Priest."

The sheriff said, "Hi, I'm John Cord, and it's nice to meet you guys. What can I do for ya?"

Dan started off with, "We hear you have a big problem with some outlaw killers livin' somewhere in this vicinity."

"Yes, we do," answered John. "We have some ruthless killers. Just last week, they killed a whole family of Mennonites."

"We heard a little bit about it," said Dan. "Could you tell us more about what happened? Do you have posters on them?"

"Do you mean a tag on their heads?" asked John.

"We need pictures to identify them," asked Dan.

"No," said John. "Tell me, what's your interest in them?"

"We want to bring them in," answered Joe.

"Is there just the two of you?" asked John.

"There are four of us. There is Joe, Billy, and this one by my side is Sammi, and I."

"I hope you know what you're doin'," said John.

"How can we find out if you or any of the townspeople can't tell us anything about the massacre?" asked Dan.

John asked, "Are you bounty hunters?"

"Yes, we are, but we would appreciate it if this goes no further than here," said Joe.

"This won't go any further than here," said John.

Joe said, "To be honest with you, we are going after them bounty or not. We want to see them dead—not dead or alive, just dead."

John said, "What I can do is telegraph the governor and ask if he would warrant a bounty on their heads."

Joe said, "John, like I said, if there is no bounty, we don't care. We are going to stay until we take the gang down. All of them. There is no room in this world for this bunch of cutthroat murdering bastards. We need the posters with their pictures, if available, just for identification."

"Okay," said John. "I'll get all the information from the people here in town, and what the governor will be willin' to pay for them dead or alive. If there is a bounty, you might as well get it. No one else seems to want to tackle that kind of job.

"We have a big bell at the church. When we need to talk to the whole community, we ring the bell five times. One member from each family will drop what they're doin' and come to town as quick as they can. I'm goin' down to the church and ring the bell now. So in the morning, come by about ten o'clock, and I'll see what we can do. Is it okay if I tell the governor about you guys bein' hunters?"

"That will be all right, answered Joe, and we will be here at ten."

Dan, Joe, Billy, and Sammi pulled to the outskirts of Vega and set up camp. While they did the chores, they were thinking of how and when this all took place. The worst kind of hatred had set into all four of them. Even Sammi knew something was not right. *We need to come down on every member of the gang that massacred the Mennonite family. They all have to die.*

The three were quiet, but one could tell what they were thinking. Joe said to Dan, "We have to get that gang and take 'em in dead. No alive ones."

Dan agreed. Billy said, "Don't forget me, Mr. Joe."

Dan said, "Billy, this could be one hell of a fight."

"I know, said Billy, but we need to kill one for Jonathon, one for Martha, one for Samuel, one for Issiah, one for Samantha, and one for Wilma. Okay, Mr. Dan?"

"We will see what information Sheriff John has for us in the morning."

They decided to get some sleep and see what tomorrow would bring.

The next morning, they did the chores and had their biscuits.

Dan said to Joe, "Why don't you and I ride in to see what the sheriff found out so we can start makin' plans."

Joe agreed.

"Billy, will you and Sammi stay and watch the animals?"

"Okay, Mr. Dan, we'll watch 'em."

"Billy, we're only goin' to be a half a mile away, but if you think something is wrong, or if you see any bunch ridin' to this area, just jump on Cricket and you and Sammi come directly to the sheriff's office."

"Okay, Mr. Dan, I will."

So Joe and Dan rode to see the sheriff. They stepped in the sheriff's office. John welcomed them in and said, "I think I have some good news. The governor said there will be a reward, but without definite proof, it might just be a small amount, such as $500 per head. But if you get definite proof, it could be in the thousands per head.

"If we can prove that they murdered the Yoder family, the bounty will go up tremendously," said John.

"That is what the governor said. There was one of the townspeople who rode upon the massacre and stopped quickly and rode back into the trees so he wouldn't be seen. He had heard gunshots before he came upon them. He said they were all dead at that time. He rode to the Mennonite community and told some of the men what had happened. Some of the Mennonite men hitched up their horses and wagons to get the dead family and bring them back for burial. Then he came to me to report what happened. He asked to be anonymous for fear that the gang would come and kill him for what he had seen. I don't know why, but they tipped the wagon on its side. There was about eight or maybe ten of them. One was riding a gray horse, and one was riding a black, the rest were riding bays. They took the Mennonite's team and harness and a large sack full of something. The team of horses they took, one was black with a white star on her forehead, the other one was also black with a stripe on her head, and she also had two white socks on her back legs. They rode about a half a mile north. Then they turned to the east, and that was the last he could see of them from the trees. But when I rode by where they turned, there was a trail. I could see back in there quite a long distance, but I could not see them. They had vanished."

Dan asked, "Do they ever come to town for supplies?"

John thought for a second and said, "There are some men that come to town and stop at the saloon, but nobody knows who they are. They caused trouble a few times, but nothin' real bad. They kinda stay to themselves. They have a few drinks, and then each buy a jug of whiskey before they leave. Then they stop at the general store for groceries and other supplies, and then they are gone."

John said, "Ed, who is the owner of the saloon, said he thinks that they are part of the gang, but he has no proof of that. Nobody seems to know what they look like. As of now, as far as I know, there are no Wanted posters on them."

Dan said, "John, you have been a big help. This gives us something to go on."

"I hope you get 'em," said John.

Dan and Joe rode back to the campsite and started making plans to take the gang out.

Dan said, "Listen to what I think might work, Joe. Let's make a sign that says, 'Want to buy a working team of horses.'"

Joe asked, "So we might get some sellers of the Mennonite team?"

"Or, Joe, do you have any better plan to go on?"

"No," said Joe, "that sounds like a good place to start."

"Let's do it," said Billy. Sammi let out her little bark as if to give her approval. So they went back to town and asked the sheriff for a large paper and a pencil. Dan sat at the sheriff's desk and made the sign. Dan asked John if Ed, the owner of the saloon, could be trusted.

"Ya, Dan, Ed is very trustworthy. If you want to include him, he'll work with you."

"I think we better include Ed, don't you think, Joe?"

"Ya, we need to talk to him and get things worked out," agreed Joe.

So they went to the saloon and introduced themselves to Ed. They shook hands, and Ed asked them to sit at the table. Dan and Joe explained to Ed what was going on.

"We need to get them, and we think this might bring them out in the open. Those bastards killed all six of the Yoder family, and they need a one-way ticket to hell."

Joe asked Ed, "Have you ever noticed the colors of the horses they were ridin'?"

Ed said, "I never paid that much attention to their horses. They normally stop in on Mondays." Then Joe asked if they stopped in at any particular time. "Normally, they come in midafternoon. They are usually here about an hour or two. Never more than that, but each of them buys a jug to take with them."

Dan asked, "How many come in?"

"Sometimes three, and sometimes it seems like there is as many as nine or ten." Dan then asked Ed about hanging the sign where it could be seen easily. "Sure, hang it on that post." Dan asked Ed to not let anyone know that he knew them or what they do. "No, I won't, answered Ed. Ed then asked, "How can I let you know if they come in?"

Dan said, "We will probably be watching but, if we aren't here, ask Sheriff John to let us know. He can ride out to our camp and inform us."

Dan and Joe rode back to their camp to discuss the strategy of every move that they had to make. There was no room for mistakes. They agreed to not take them on in Ed's saloon. That way, no innocent people would get hurt.

Dan said, "We need to wait until Monday to see what happens." He asked, "Oh, by the way, Billy, do you still want to buy a big knife like Joe and I wear?"

"Yes, sir, Mr. Dan. As soon as I can find one."

"Well, Billy, I saw some knives in the window at the general store as Joe and I walked by."

"Hot dog!" said Billy. "I'm goin' to ride into town now and buy me one."

Dan said, "No, Billy, I don't want you ridin' out there by yourself as long as this gang is runnin' loose. We can go in tomorrow and buy one."

Joe looked at Dan and said, "Tomorrow is Sunday, and they will be closed."

Billy said, "I need to get it so I can start practicin'."

Joe said, "I'll ride in with Billy. I need to stop at Ed's to pick up a couple jugs. We are gettin' a little low."

"Thank you very much, Mr. Joe," said Billy. He asked Dan if Sammi could go with them.

"Sure, Billy, she can go with you."

They saddled up and rode to town to buy a knife. When they rode up to the general store, Billy hopped down and saw the knives in the window. His eyes about popped out of his head. "Mr. Joe, I think I want that big one with the leather sheath."

"That's a big knife," answered Joe.

"That's the one," said Billy. They walked in, and Billy told the clerk that he wanted to buy the big knife in the window.

The clerk said, "Young man, that's a mighty big knife. Are you sure that's the one you want?"

"Yes, sir, that's the one. You see, sir, I will grow bigger, and the knife won't grow anymore."

"Well, I guess you know what you want," the clerk said. "You owe $1.50."

Billy pulled out his $20 gold coin and laid it on the counter. The clerk looked at the gold coin and asked, "Do you always carry that much money on you all the time?"

Billy said, "Yes, sir, I have a lot of money in the bank."

"Well, good for you, young man."

CHAPTER 8

Billy got his new big knife; he felt like he was as tough as any bounty hunter in the world. Billy unbuckled his belt and ran it through the sheath. He had the biggest smile on his face that he ever had. Billy had that knife hanging on his hip.

"How does it look, Mr. Joe?"

"Well, Billy, you look like a bounty hunter, and a tough one at that. You look like a perty tough kid."

They rode over to Ed's to get a couple bottles of whiskey and a few bottles of sarsaparillas. Joe did his shopping and put the bottles in his saddlebags.

"Are you ready, Mr. Joe?"

"Ya, Billy, I'm ready."

Billy said, "Come on, Sammi," and they headed back to camp. Billy couldn't keep his eyes off that big knife hanging on his hip. "Ya know, Mr. Joe, I'm thinkin' if Mr. Dan would let me wear that .45 revolver on my other hip, I think I would look like a perty tough kid."

"You will have to talk to Dan about that."

They reached the camp, and Billy said, "Mr. Dan, take a look at this." Billy jumped down and turned sideways so Dan could see his big knife.

"By golly, Billy, that ought to bring in some outlaws."

"Ya know, Mr. Dan, I was thinkin' if I could wear that holster that Mr. Frank fixed to fit me, and that .45 revolver on my other hip, I would be a perty tough kid."

Dan said, "Billy, you haven't even shot it yet. I'll tell you what." Dan walked to the wagon and pulled out two boxes of .45 shells. "There is one hundred shells in these boxes. After you shoot all of these, maybe you can carry the .45, but you have to handle it real good. This thing is going to kick like a mule. Tomorrow morning, we'll see what you can do. You need to fire a few a rounds through that big gun. Not your little rifle, but that .44 big gun you brought with you."

"Okay, Mr. Dan. I'm ready."

"Billy, you go and find some of the bean cans or whatever else you can find to shoot." He had them all piled up.

Sunday morning, they had their biscuits, and fed and watered the stock. It was time for Billy to shoot some cans. Dan told Billy to tack the bean cans out a far distance and stand them up. Billy did what he was told. Dan loaded the .45 then told Billy, "I want you to hold it in both hands for a few shots."

Billy asked, "Should I whip it out of the holster like I'm drawin' against an outlaw?"

No, no, no, no, Billy, you just hold it in your hands very carefully. Aim at the target and fire. I want you to know that it's goin' to kick like hell. So make sure you hang on to it. It's goin' to try to jump right out of your hands. You got it, Billy?"

"Yes, sir, Mr. Dan. I'm ready."

"Okay, Billy, go!" Billy raised the gun and slowly squeezed the trigger and *boom*. Billy had a strange look on his face, but he hung on to the gun.

"How was that, Mr. Dan?"

"Well, Billy, you did good. Now hold it the same way, only close one eye, and look down the sights. Just like you do when you shoot your little rifle. Now do it again."

Billy looked down the sights with one eye closed and *boom*.

Dan said, "You made the dust fly close to the cans. Now does it scare you, Billy?"

"Oh no, Mr. Dan, it takes a lot to scare this ol' kid."

"I know that, Billy," Dan said. "Why don't you shoot twelve rounds then get the .44 rifle, the big gun, and shoot a few rounds through it."

Billy did what Dan said. Billy practiced a few rounds with the .45. Then a few shots with the .44 rifle, back and forth between the two guns. Billy hit the can almost every shot with the rifle. The .45 was a little tougher for Billy, but Billy wouldn't give up. After a few shooting sessions, Billy was getting a little better feel with the revolver and showed a lot of improvement.

It was Monday, and about time to watch Ed's saloon. Dan looked at the sun and said, "It must be about noon, and maybe we should go to town and have some dinner at the café."

They watched the saloon for the bad boys. After dinner, Dan said, "I'm goin' to talk to Ed at the saloon. Joe, you and Billy wait across the street on the bench and watch the saloon. I'll be right back." Dan went to the saloon and met with Ed. They shook hands. Then Dan told Ed, "If the gang shows up and happens to ask about the team, and if they want to talk to me, I'll be across the street. If you wave at me, I'll come in by myself. Billy and Joe will be waiting across the street. I want them to think I'm a farmer, and that's what I need the team for, farming."

Ed asked, "Do you want to give a name?"

"Just call me Buck. They don't know the difference. We won't take 'em today. We want them to think that they have a sale on the team of horses."

Ed said, "I'll see what I can do to help you get 'em."

Dan left the saloon and met back up with Billy and Joe. Dan explained what he and Ed talked about. "If they do show up, I want you, Billy, to take care of my knife. I'll wear my gun, but if they see the knife, they might suspect me of being a hunter. We don't want that until it's time."

Dan, Joe, Billy, and Sammi waited a couple hours. Their wait might pay off. Six of the gang rode in. One was riding a gray, and one was riding a black plus four other riders. Dan unbuckled his knife and handed it to Billy. "Now, I want you, Billy, to stay back just in case something goes wrong. Joe, if you would stay outside the saloon, close by but out of sight."

Ed stepped outside and waved to Dan. Dan walked across the street and into the saloon and ordered a glass of whiskey. Ed poured the whiskey and brought the drink to the table where Dan was sitting. Ed was talking loud enough so they could hear what he was saying.

Ed told Dan, "The guy at the bar wants to talk to you about a team of horses."

Dan stood up and asked, "Which one wants to talk to me?"

A big guy stood up and said, "Hi, my name is Maggot. At least that's what my friends call me."

Dan said, "My name is Buck." They shook hands.

Dan was thinking under his breath that this filthy maggot son of a bitch was going to die very soon if everything goes right. Maggot asked if Dan needed to buy a team of workhorses.

"Yep," Dan said. "I do need a pair of good horses."

Maggot said, "I have a nice pair."

Dan asked, "How big are they?"

"Oh, they're about 1,500 pounds each, and I would say about eight or nine years old."

"How much do you want for 'em?" asked Dan.

"Oh, let's see, how about $40 each? And I'll throw in the harness."

Dan asked, "Where can I see them?"

Maggot said, "We're about ten miles south of here. We can meet you about halfway." Maggot asked, "Do you know where that small cemetery is? It's about five miles out. You have to keep a close watch out, it's kinda overgrown with weeds."

"Okay," said Dan. "How about tomorrow, early afternoon?"

"That sounds good, we'll be there." Dan drank up his drink and left. Joe was around the corner of the saloon while Billy stayed with the horses. When they got together, Dan explained to Billy and Joe what happened. Then they stopped at the sheriff's office and asked the sheriff if he knew anyone that had a barrel he could borrow.

"There's a whole bunch of barrels down by the train station."

"Who owns them?" asked Dan.

"Don't worry about it, they have been there for several years. Just help yourself."

"Thanks, John. We might have something comin' down. We'll let you know what happens."

They rode back to their camp.

Dan said, "Joe, if we fill four barrels with water and space them about two inches apart in a row in the wagon box, that would leave three spaces to aim the rifles through. I know Billy's goin' to throw a fit if we try to go without him. The barrels will protect Billy as well as us. We need to hitch the mules to the wagon and pick up one more barrel."

"I think it will work," Joe said. "You're right, Dan, that should work."

Dan continued giving Billy lessons. He knew that Billy would be a full-fledged bounty hunter in a few years, and he wanted Billy to be a marksman with any gun that he chooses to use.

After a shooting lesson, Dan said, "I'm going to church. Do you guys want to join me?"

Joe said, "We have to get ready for a showdown, and it might be good to have a little church in us."

Dan said, "Whenever I'm getting ready to make a capture, I like to go to church and have a few words with the Lord."

Billy said, "I'll go with you, Mr. Dan."

Joe asked, "Do you think Sammi can watch the camp? I'll go too."

Dan told Sammi to stay and watch the camp. Billy asked Dan if he could wear his knife to church.

"No, Billy, I don't think that would be a good idea." So Billy had to leave his knife at camp. They all went to church. After church, they rode back to camp. Dan and Joe remarked to Billy, telling how good he sounded singing the hymns.

Billy said, "Once I had to sing a song at our church's Christmas program. I was really scared standin' up there in front of all those people. I was so scared when I was singin' it sounded like I was yodelin'."

"You didn't seem scared when you were singin' those hymns at the church today."

"I wasn't standin' in front of about fifty people," said Billy.

Dan and Joe had a good laugh at that. They returned to camp and put their horses away.

Joe asked Dan, "Do you think we best wait to make a final plan until we see what happens at the saloon tomorrow?"

"Yep, Joe, we'll see if any of them show up. If they do show up."

Boom! Boom! It sounded like Billy was at it again. Many booms later, Billy's shoulder was getting a little sore.

"How far are you from bein' able to carry that .45 on your hip?" asked Dan.

"I've got about three-fourths of a box left. That mule still kicks perty hard," explained Billy.

"So how many cans did you hit with the .45?"

"I think I hit three cans, but I've been hittin' all around 'em," said Billy.

Dan asked, "Are you gettin' a better feel of it, Billy?"

"Yes, sir, Mr. Dan, but she still kicks perty hard. But it don't bother me, I'm a perty tough kid."

"Ya, I know, Billy."

"When we go to town tomorrow, can I wear my knife?" asked Billy.

"Ya, you can carry your knife."

"What do you think about me wearin' the gun and holster tomorrow, Mr. Dan?"

"No, Billy, you can wear your knife, but not the gun, as long as these killers are runnin' loose. After we get these guys taken care of, maybe we will let you carry it sometimes, depending how good you handle it. Tomorrow we will give you the test with the .45," said Dan.

The next morning was Monday; and after they took care of the camp chores and had their breakfast, Dan said, "Okay, Billy, it's time for the test."

"I'm ready," said Billy.

Dan went to the wagon and found the lid of a boot box. He took the lid and nailed it to a tree several yards from where Billy will shoot from. Billy got the .45 and loaded it.

Dan said, "Billy, I want you to stand right here. When you're ready, fire."

Billy raised the gun and *boom.* One after another, Billy fired all six rounds. They walked over to check the box lid. Dan was surprised at what he saw. Out of six rounds, Billy hit the lid four times.

"Did I do okay, Mr. Dan?"

"Ya, Billy, you did a remarkable job for only shootin' a few rounds with that gun. Now, Billy, take the big gun, load it with six of the .44 rounds. I will draw a circle about the size of a jar lid on the box lid. Then I want you to try to hit it as many times as you can."

"Okay, Mr. Dan." Billy loaded the big gun and knelt down on one knee and fired. *Boom.* Billy fired all six rounds. Dan went down to the lid and couldn't believe what he saw again. Billy had shot three rounds in the circle and three within an inch of the circle. Dan took the lid back to show Billy and Joe the target.

Billy said, "I missed with three of 'em."

Joe said to Billy, "That's remarkable. I had no idea you could shoot that good."

Dan said, "Billy, that's darn good shootin'."

Billy said, "Ya, but I missed with three of 'em."

"Billy, if that was a bad guy's head, you would have hit him with all six shots."

"Is that good, Mr. Dan?"

"Yep, Billy, that was remarkable." Dan looked at the sun and said it must be about noon and maybe they should go to town and have dinner at the café.

"Dan, you stay here and concentrate on our plan tomorrow. Billy and I will pick up another barrel and fill all four with water."

So Billy and Joe drove the mules to town to pick up one more barrel. Joe checked the barrels. They were dried out, and it would take too long to soak them to hold water. Billy was checking all the barrels and found some barrels that were full of water.

"Mr. Joe, come here and look at these."

Joe walked around where Billy was. Billy showed Joe the barrels that were full of water.

"Good deal, Billy. There were several sitting under the eaves from the train station. When it rains, the water keeps the barrels full. That's what we need."

Joe tipped a barrel over and dumped the water. They loaded the barrel in the wagon then drove the mules to the water trough where there was a water pump. They began pumping water in a bucket and pouring it in the barrels. Joe and Billy took turns pumping and filling the barrels. After an hour of pumping, they had filled all four barrels. They drove back to the camp.

Dan said, "Joe, see what you think of my plan. If we drive out to where we're supposed to meet 'em, then turn the wagon crossways on the trail, unhitch the mules, and hide them behind where we will be standing behind the barrels and shooting between them, they will also be protected from the wagon and barrels. Now if everything goes right, when the party's over and their guns are silenced, we will take the Mennonite team, and you will ride one of the team of horses and lead the other with the Mennonite blood-soaked wagon. Then bring it back here, and we can load Maggot and his other maggots in the back of the Mennonite wagon. We will take them back to Vega, then unload the maggots, and line them up side by side in front of the sheriff's office. We'll send Billy up to the photo shop and have them take the maggots' pictures. Then we better head out for the big hunt."

"That will work," said Joe.

"That will work," said Billy.

Dan and Joe had a swig of whiskey, and Billy had a sarsaparilla, a toast for tomorrow.

Billy asked, "Mr. Dan, do you think I could carry the .45 tomorrow?"

Dan said, "I'll let you under one condition, Billy—if you tell me that you will not pull it out of your holster unless something goes wrong and if one of us is in danger of gettin' killed."

"I promise, Mr. Dan." Billy turned and said, "I'm goin' to get some practice." Billy was shooting everything he could see. Bean cans, horse turds, sticks, little rocks, and whatever else he could find to shoot.

The next morning, all three of them were getting things ready to go. They unloaded everything out of the wagon except the barrels of water, a canteen, and their rifles plus three extra rifles.

Joe asked Dan, "What are you goin' to do with Sammi?"

"When it's time for the showdown, I'll put Sammi inside the wagon behind a barrel in front of me."

Dan said, "We need to get there about ten or eleven o'clock so we can get set up for the party. Billy, you better take a bucket in the wagon for you to stand on. Otherwise you won't be able to reach over the wagon box."

"Yes, sir, Mr. Dan." Billy had his gun and holster on one hip and his new knife on the other hip.

Dan asked Joe, "Which one comes the closest to his knees, the gun or the knife?"

They both had a good laugh. Dan asked Billy to get his telescope from his saddlebags.

"Yes, sir, Mr. Dan."

"We better head out and get set up."

All three of them and Sammi were on their way to a bounty hunters' party. The mules had a couple days' rest, so they were ready to go. They got to the meeting place a little sooner than they thought they would. They came to the small cemetery.

Joe said, "This is an appropriate place. When the fight is over, we can just throw them over the fence."

Dan took the reins from Billy and maneuvered the mules until he had the wagon sideways on the trail. They unhitched the mules and tied them to the side of the wagon and behind the barrels to protect them. They made sure they had ample room to maneuver their rifles.

"Now, when we need to take our places, it's Joe on the right, Billy in the center—to take the ones in the center—and I'll be on the left," explained Dan. "When they get within earshot, I will holler for them to get their hands in the air, and that they are under arrest. We all three will have our rifles ready. If any one of them reach for a gun, we all three open fire and take them as fast as we can. This should be over within seconds. One thing they will do after we take out the first few, the rest will try to cut and run, but we need to take 'em out as fast as possible, so we need to take aim." Dan was checking the trail with his telescope every minute or so. "Well, Billy, are you scared?"

"No, sir, Mr. Dan. I'm just waitin' for 'em." Billy waved his arm in the direction that they were coming from and said, "Come on, you chickenshits."

Dan shook his head and said, "Billy, I don't know about you. I guess you are a bounty hunter." Dan checked with his telescope and said, "I think they are on the way. There's a lot of dust. "So remember, when I say, put your hands up, you're under arrest, the first one that goes for his gun, we need to open fire—take them out as fast as we can."

Dan had Sammi get in the wagon and behind a barrel. They were coming down on them fast. Dan stepped out for a second, long enough to holler for them to get their hands up and that they were under arrest. Dan stepped behind the barrels. Joe and Billy were taking them out fast.

Boom! Boom! Boom! The noise from all the guns was deafening. They were falling fast. Dan was right, the last two tried to cut and run.

Dan yelled out, "Get 'em!"

Two more shots and they were all on the ground. After the gun battle was over, Joe's rifle was empty, so he grabbed one of the spare rifles and slowly walked around the wagon and saw one of them was still alive with his gun about a foot from his hand. Joe ran and kicked the gun away. Joe pulled his knife, grabbed him by the hair with one hand, and had his knife in the other. Joe asked, "Do you own that gray?"

"Yes, but I wasn't there."

Joe said, "I beg your pardon, sir." Joe took his knife and slit his throat and said, "That is for the Yoder family."

Dan said, "Looks like the rest are dead."

Billy said, "We have four leaks from bullet holes in the barrels."

Dan asked, "How you doin', Billy? Do you wish you had stayed back at camp?"

"No, sir, Mr. Dan, you needed help. Mr. Dan, we didn't kill men, we killed maggots. I just hope I got my share."

When Billy was out of earshot, Joe asked Dan, "Take notice, it's apparent that you and I make body shots, goin' for the heart. The three lying in the center have been shot in the head. Then notice one of the two that tried to run was shot right behind the ear."

"You're right, Joe, there's no doubt which ones Billy shot." They walked around, picking up the outlaws' guns, just in case some of them were playing possum.

Joe looked down and said, "That maggot son of a bitch got blood on my chaps."

Dan told Billy to start catching the maggots' horses. Joe caught the team that was stolen from the Mennonite family. He told Dan that he was heading out to get the Mennonite wagon.

"Okay, Billy and I will get things put together here." Billy picked up the maggots' guns and holsters and rifles. He had them loaded in the mule wagon. Billy had caught all the horses and had them tied. A couple hours later, Joe came rolling back with the Mennonite team and wagon. The wagon had three seats, so they had to stack them in the mule wagon. They could stack the dead maggots in the Mennonite wagon. They stacked the largest ones on the bottom. They had all nine of them, loaded with the smallest ones on top. They had everything loaded and were on their way back to Vega.

Dan looked up and said, "Thank you, God, for keepin' Billy, Joe, me, and Sammi from this load of maggots. Please, God, I know that the Yoder family is there with you. We ask them to not worry about the dangers of this outlaw gang in the future. Neither their relatives and their Mennonite friends have to worry either. Thanks, God. I'll be talkin' to you again soon."

The bounty hunters have made another successful takedown. With the wagon heavily loaded with bodies, after a couple hours, they finally pulled into town with the load of maggots and four leaking barrels. They pulled up in front of the sheriff's office.

The sheriff came out and asked, "What the hell happened?"

Dan said, "Sheriff, we had what we call a bounty hunter's tea party."

The sheriff laughed and asked, "How many are in there?"

"There's nine, and we have reason to believe that's all of 'em. Would you mind, Sheriff, if we lay the bodies in a row here in front of your office in a side-by-side position so the photo shop can take a picture of these maggots?"

"Sure," answered the sheriff.

Dan asked if there was anybody that could sell the nine horses and saddles.

"Ya, Dan, take them up to the livery barn and ask Matt if he can sell 'em for ya. He'll charge you for care and feed until they are sold."

"That's fine. I'll go talk with Matt. Billy, run up to the photo shop and ask them to come and take a picture of these maggots."

Joe said, "I'll go to the livery barn and talk to Matt about sellin' 'em."

The townspeople were coming from everywhere to see the dead maggots lying in a row. One woman got sick and ran around the back of the sheriff's office. She was white as a sheet. It seemed that all the people of Vega showed up. Most of the men were shaking hands with Dan and Joe.

Joe was telling the people that Billy played a big part in takin' the maggots down. Billy came back from the photo shop and was smiling. Everyone was shaking Billy's hand and telling him how brave he was and commented on the .45 on one hip and the big knife on the other. The sheriff asked Dan and Joe to step in his office.

The sheriff said, "I contacted the governor again. He said that he could approve $1,000 per head. Unless they have identification, he can't do any better."

Dan looked at Joe and asked if that would be okay with him.

Joe nodded his head and said, "That's plenty."

The people were still asking Billy questions. Billy said, "I was happy to bring these maggots in. This is for the Mennonite family."

Dan, Joe, and the sheriff had come back from their discussion. Dan asked the sheriff if he could send someone to the Mennonite's community and ask them to come and pick up the team and wagon and the family Bible and turn them over to the relatives.

The sheriff asked a man—his name was Robert—standing there with his horse if he would ride out and ask Gabriel Yoder, a brother of Jonathon Yoder, to send someone in and pick up these things.

"Sure, Sheriff, I'll go right now."

The man from the photo shop came and took some pictures. The sheriff asked Dan if he should get the funeral parlor to come and pick up the dead bodies and take them away.

About an hour later, Robert came back and said to the sheriff that Mr. Yoder said they didn't want the team nor wagon nor the Bible.

The sheriff said, "Well, Dan, I guess they're yours."

Dan looked at Joe and asked, "Do we have any use for another team and wagon?"

"Well, Dan, I don't know. But we can take 'em with us for now, and if we don't need 'em on down the trail, we can either sell 'em or give them to somebody."

"Billy, would you pull the wagon over to the pump and wash the blood off?"

"Yes, sir, Mr. Dan. Ol' Billy will get 'er clean."

"Billy, put the two seats on the wagon so you can wash them too."

Two young boys about Billy's age asked if they could help wash the wagon.

"Sure," Dan said, "if you want to."

One of the boys said they were in the same school that Wilma and Samantha Yoder were. The three boys cleaned the wagon the best way they could. They hopped in the wagon, and Billy drove back to the sheriff's office. Dan handed Billy some money and told him to take the boys and for all three of them to go and have a sarsaparilla. "God bless you, boys."

The sheriff asked, "How long, Dan, will you be in Vega?"

"We'll pull out in the morning as soon as we get loaded. Sheriff, I would like to get some more of the barrels, but I would like to pay someone for 'em."

"If you need more, help yourself, Dan."

"Now that we have this other team and wagon, we might as well carry more water. I'll take three more. If anyone claims 'em, I'll be happy to pay for 'em."

"Don't worry, Dan. There is nobody in this town that would take a cent after all you, Joe, and Billy did for us. You did this town a big favor, and you made the people feel safe again."

"Thank you, Sheriff."

"Oh, by the way, Dan, change the barrels with the bullet holes for good ones."

"Thanks again, Sheriff."

Joe, standing by, said, "I'll take the horse wagon, and Billy can bring the mule wagon and pick up the barrels."

Joe saw Billy and the two boys that he had made friends with. He asked Billy to get the mule wagon and drive them up to the barrels. The boys asked Billy if they could ride along.

"Sure, hop on."

They drove the mules up to the barrels. Billy's new friends helped him get the leaking barrels out and load the good ones in the wagon.

Dan asked, "Would you take the wagon, Billy, to the pump and start filling the barrels?"

"Sure, Mr. Dan."

"After you get the barrels filled, except the food barrel, then drive up to the livery barn and pick up four hundred pounds of oats. I'll be up to pay for 'em later."

Billy's friends asked if they could help.

"Sure, if you want."

Billy pulled the wagon around to the water pump. Joe pulled up behind with the horse wagon. The boys took turns pumping the water and filling the barrels. Two were still full. They didn't get hit with the bullets. The six barrels hold three hundred gallons of water. That would last about five days or so for the livestock and with about a dozen one-gallon canteens for the hunters. Dan and Joe were discussing what to do with the bounty money.

Joe suggested, "Why not have the sheriff send it to Maggie, and she can deposit it in the bank there in Lariat."

"That's a good idea, Joe."

So all business was taken care of. The hunters took the loaded wagons back to camp. The wagons were getting filled with nine more guns and holsters, nine more rifles and scabbards, and several more bowie knives— their bonus from the maggots.

The next morning, Billy had the stock fed and watered. He had his guns and his big knife loaded and was ready to get the mules headed out. Dan had the coffee, biscuits, and sorghum ready. They had breakfast. Sammi had all the biscuits that were left over. They harnessed the mules and the new black Mennonite mares.

Claude had the pack saddle and was loaded mostly with canteens of water. They were on the road again. Billy and Sammi and the mules led the train, with Claude and Cricket tied behind. Joe fell in line with the new black mares and wagon. He had Smoky tied behind.

Heading out, Billy said, "Follow me, men. Let's go to the big hunt and get some more maggots."

They were going down the road and making good time. They were out about four hours. Dan was riding beside Billy and the mule wagon.

Billy said, "You know somethin', Mr. Dan? I was thinkin' when we were on the road the other day, somethin' kinda popped in my head, and I kept thinkin' about it for a long time. And normally, I don't think about it that long of a time, but I have been thinkin' about it almost all day. Ya know, Mr. Dan, I think it's a really good idea."

"Billy, what are you sayin'?"

"Well, Mr. Dan, the question is a good one. Mr. Dan, if you promise me that you won't get mad at me, I'll tell you what I've been thinkin'."

"Well, spit it out, Billy. I can't get mad if I don' know what you are goin' to say."

"Well, like I was thinking."

"Come on, Billy, spit it out."

"Well, Mr. Dan, I'm thinking you should ask Ms. Maggie if she would marry you. I can tell by her eyes, when she's around you, that she loves you a lot. And when you're around her, I can see in your eyes that you love her a lot."

"Billy, I can't marry Maggie. Remember, I'm a bounty hunter, and as you know, bounty huntin' is a very dangerous occupation. She wouldn't know from day to day whether I may or may not come home."

"Well, Mr. Dan, I've been thinkin' about that too. When we get the big hunt over, you can retire. And you, Maggie, me, and Sammi can live on a little farm and raise a few cows and a few horses."

"Well, Billy, you make it sound good, but it's not that easy."

"Well, Mr. Dan, promise me that you will think about it."

"Okay, Billy, I'll think about it."

CHAPTER 9

After eight hours on the trail, they came to a log house that was vacated. There was a water pump in front of the house, so they decided to camp there overnight. They could fill their barrels even though they hadn't used much of the water. They set up camp.

Billy was checking out the old house. Billy let out a scream and came flying out of the house and grabbed his .22 rifle out of the wagon. Billy ran back to the house and *pop!*

Dan asked, "What the world is goin' on? Billy, what are you doin'?"

"Mr. Dan, there was a rat in there, and I shot it."

"What was the scream all about, Billy?"

"I'm scared of rats, and I'm scared of snakes too."

"I guess you took care of that rat."

"Mr. Dan, what happens if there are more rats?"

"You'll have to shoot them too, Billy."

"But what if they come after me when I'm asleep and get in my bunk roll."

Dan said, "You can have Sammi sleep with you, she won't let the rats get you." So Sammi slept next to Billy to keep the rats away.

The next morning, as soon as they fed and watered the stock and the hunters had their biscuits and coffee, Dan said, "Let's put a harness on Buck, and we'll hitch him with one of the mules."

So they harnessed the black team and one mule and Buck. Dan drove Buck a few rounds before hitching him and one mule to the wagon. They took it slow and easy so as not to scare him, but it was time to make the test. Joe held Buck's bridle and talked to him and patted him on his forehead to keep him calm. Joe walked beside Buck a few rounds. It was time to put them on the trail, to let Buck learn to pull. At first, he didn't know about having to push against the collar. A couple miles down the road, Buck looked like he had been pulling wagons forever. Dan had Billy drive the black team and the Mennonite wagon. They stopped a little more often because Buck wasn't used to pulling that weight. After they were out about four hours, they took Buck off and put the other mule back on.

"Do you want me to take the mules back, Mr. Dan?"

"I'll drive the mules awhile, and you stay with the black team, Billy."

That evening, they came to a small town with a few small farms on the outskirts and a few houses in town.

Dan said, "What do you think, Joe? Should we stop here tonight? I see they have a livery barn. We need to get some roughage, hay, in the horses and mules. They haven't been gettin' as much as they need. They can't live on oats alone."

"Let's stop," said Joe. They had plenty of room to camp beside the livery barn. They asked the man at the livery if he could feed and water the stock tonight and again in the morning.

The man said, "I'll take care of 'em."

Joe said, "It'll be good to have a good café meal tonight. Did you notice, Dan, they have a saloon?"

"Ya, Joe, I did. I guess we better stop in and have a sip." Dan walked in and asked if he could bring Billy and Sammi in the saloon.

A very little man tending bar said, "As long as you sit at a table and not at the bar."

Dan went out front and said, "It's okay." They came in and sat at a table. The small bartender came to the table and asked what they would like to drink. Dan and Joe said they would have whiskey.

Billy said, "Sir, what is your name?"

The little man said, "My name is Roy, what is your name?"

"My name is Billy. I would like a sarsparilla, Mr. Roy."

After Roy brought the drinks, he seemed kinda nervous but didn't say anything. He returned to the bar. There were two big slobs sitting at the bar.

They were talking loud, and they seemed to be picking on Roy. They kept getting louder and louder, and calling Roy names, and dipping their fingers in their beer, and flicking it in Roy's face. Dan asked Joe if he saw that.

Joe said, "I've been watchin' that."

They were filthy. You could smell them clear across the saloon. Their teeth were all rotten with some missing. Dan and Joe kept watching what was happening to Roy. One of them threw a mug of beer in Roy's face.

Dan picked up a quarter off the table and asked Joe to call it. Dan flipped the coin. Joe said, "Heads."

It was tails, so Dan said, "I'll take the one on the left."

Joe said, "I'll take the one on the right."

Dan and Joe stood up. Dan told Billy to stay at the table and keep Sammi with him. Dan walked up beside the one on the left and pulled his gun out his holster, and Joe did the same to the other guy. They handed the guns to Roy and told him to hang on to them until they said to let them have them again. The sleazy slobs become irate after Dan and Joe took their guns.

Dan said, "Sit tight, boys, you might get hurt."

Dan told Roy, "Give me a large mug of beer."

Roy was wiping the beer off himself with a towel. He turned around and poured the mug of beer and set it in front of Dan. Dan took the mug of beer and knocked the slob's hat off and poured the mug of beer all over the top of his head. The sleazy slob turned and made an attempt to swing at Dan, but it was too late. Dan got there first. The slob was lying on the floor, groaning.

Joe had hit the other slob and held him up long enough to hit him a second time. The second hit put him down-and-out. Dan dragged slob number one around by his hair and propped him up against the wall. He slept for some time. When he started to wake up and move, Dan said, "Stay where you are and don't move." Dan asked, "What's your name, slob?"

"Daryl is my name."

"Okay, Daryl, I want you to sit there until I tell you to move."

Dan told Roy to bring him a couple more large mugs of beer. Roy seemed to be enjoying the episode. Roy brought the two large beers to Dan.

"Let me ask you, Roy, how long has this been goin' on?"

Roy said, "Several years."

Dan said, "Things will get better. Daryl will be easier to get along with from now on." Dan took one of the beers and poured it all over Daryl's head.

Dan said, "I just wanted to buy you a couple beers before we hang ya."

Daryl had a scared look on his face and asked, "Why are you talkin' about hangin' us? All I did was pour some beer on Roy."

"Well, Daryl, where Joe and I came from, they hang people for throwin' beer on other people."

"No, sir, I promise I won't ever do it again."

"Daryl, Daryl, Daryl. I just can't take a chance like that. Roy is a good friend of ours, and when we leave, you would go right back to throwin' beer on him. So that's why we have to hang ya." Dan got up and took the other beer over and said, "I want to buy you another beer," pouring the beer on top of Daryl's head.

Joe's sleazebag had started coming around a little bit.

He asked, "What's goin' on?"

Daryl said, "They are talkin' about hangin' us."

Dan said, "You can get up now, Daryl. I want you to come with me." Dan took Daryl out front of the saloon. He asked, "Daryl, do you see that big cottonwood tree by the livery barn?"

"Ya, what about it?"

"Do you have anything against bein' hanged from that tree?"

"No, I don't want to be hanged on any tree."

Dan and Daryl went back in the saloon. Dan told Daryl to get a chair and sit there, where he could keep an eye on him. "What's your sleazy friend's name?"

"His name is Frank."

Dan told Frank to get a chair and sit by Daryl. "What do you think we should do with 'em, Joe?"

"Ya know, Dan, I was thinkin'. Let's say if we do let 'em live for now, when we come back through here next week or whenever we come back, we can ask Roy if they threw any more beer on him again. If so, we will hang 'em then."

Dan asked, "If we give you two one more chance, and you say you won't pour any more beer on Roy, I'm goin' to take your word for it. Do you take me and Joe's word for it that we will hang your ass to that cottonwood tree if your promise fails? You know the rest."

"No, sir, I promise," said Daryl.

"There are a couple other stipulations. One is you don't call Roy names. You don't torment him in any way, and most of all, don't be throwin' beer on Roy. You got that, Daryl?"

"Yes, sir, I promise."

"Okay, I'm goin' to trust ya."

Daryl asked if they could have another beer.

"Yes, you can. We need to see if you can drink a beer without throwin' part of it on Roy."

Frank asked if they could sit at the bar and have a beer.

"Sure," said Joe, "just be careful what you do."

Dan asked Daryl if he was trustworthy enough to carry his gun and not cause trouble. "Yes, sir, I promise. We won't cause any more trouble."

"Okay, Roy, you can give their guns back."

The hunters started out the door, heading to the café to have supper. Dan noticed a map hanging on the wall.

Dan asked Roy, "Does this map cover this area?"

"Yes, sir, it covers a lot of the states and territories. It has the miles between towns and water, and I've heard people say that it's really accurate. There's been lots of lives saved on account of that map."

"How much are they?"

"Twenty-five cents."

Dan handed Roy a quarter and took a map. They headed back to the café. After they left the saloon, Billy said, "That was fun watchin' you guys knock those ol' sleazers around."

Joe said, "Those slobs didn't seem to see the fun part of it."

Billy asked, "Do you think those sleazers will throw any more beer on ol' Roy?"

Joe said, "If they do, when we come back through, they'll think what happened today was a Sunday school picnic."

Billy said, "I can't wait to come back through to see if the sleazers poured any more beer on ol' Roy."

"When you guys were hittin' on those sleazers, Sammi dragged me halfway across the saloon. She's strong, and she wanted to get in the fight."

Joe said, "Ya know, Dan, I think you had ol' Daryl believin' we were goin' to lynch 'em. I think they became believers."

"But, Mr. Dan, if they threw just a little bit of beer on ol' Roy, you guys could whomp on those sleazers again," smiled Billy.

The next morning, they harnessed, saddled, and were ready to move on down the road. Joe was driving the horse wagon; Billy was driving the mule wagon. Dan was riding Buck. As they passed the saloon, Dan noticed that they were open.

Dan told Joe, "You guys head on out, and I'll catch up with you later." Dan tied Buck to the hitching post and went in the saloon.

Roy was washing glasses and getting the place open. Dan walked over to the bar.

"Well, Roy, how were the bad boys after we left?"

"What is your name, sir?" asked Roy.

"My name is Dan, and the other guy's name is Joe."

"After you guys left, Daryl and Frank shook my hand and said they would never throw beer on me again."

"So do you think they'll honor their promise, Roy?"

"I think so, Dan, as long as they know you and Joe are comin' back through. They both admitted that was the hardest they had ever been hit—by you and Joe." Roy said, "I certainly want to thank you and Joe for takin' my side. I'm a little man, and I just can't handle those big bullies. Please tell Joe thanks."

"I will," said Dan. "So, Roy, you take care. We will stop on our way back."

Dan and Buck headed out to catch up with Joe and Billy. After an hour or so, Dan hadn't caught up with them. Dan told Buck that they needed to speed up a little. Dan soon could see Joe and Billy at a distance.

Dan thought, *Billy must have those mules on fast-forward.*

When Dan finally caught up, Joe and Billy were curious as to what Dan had found out.

Billy asked, "Mr. Dan, did those sleazers throw any more beer on ol' Roy?"

"No." Dan told them what Roy said.

Billy said, "Well, maybe they will pour just a little bit on ol' Roy. Then when we come back, we can beat the hell out of those sleazers one more time."

Joe asked, "What do you mean 'we'? I didn't see you in there hittin' anybody, Billy." Joe looked at Dan and grinned.

"Well, Mr. Joe, I was busy holdin' Sammi off those sleazers."

Joe said, "I was just kiddin' you, Billy. I know you had your hands full holdin' Sammi back."

"Did you guys see that sign we just passed? It's so faded you can hardly read it. I think it says, 'You are now entering Oklahoma Territory.' We'll cross the Oklahoma Panhandle, which is about thirty miles wide. That means we'll be in Kansas by late tomorrow, if the good Lord's willing." Dan was checking the map. He said, "According to the map, there is a town called Eaglewood in Kansas, shortly after we get out of Oklahoma. That town has water. I'm goin' to guess they will have other supplies too, such as groceries. We can stock up then."

After they entered Oklahoma, it was quite desolate. There were very few trees, but there was wild grass for the stock to graze on. They had plenty of oats for their daily grain, but they needed the roughage. When they stopped for the night, they hobbled the ones they have hobbles for, which covered all of the animals except the Mennonite team. They hadn't bought hobbles for them yet. They had plenty of ropes to tie them to the wagons so they could reach all the dry grass they would need. Everything went well through the night, and the next day, they did reach Kansas late that afternoon.

The town was small, but they were sure it would have almost everything they needed. They pulled the mule wagon in front of the mercantile store.

Dan went in and ordered lots of canned groceries, cans of beans. They also bought dried beans, dried fruits, lots of beef jerky, etc. After they loaded everything in the mule wagon, they drove to the water pump by the water trough. Joe pulled the horse wagon up behind. All three of them took turns pumping and filling the barrels. They pulled the mule wagon to the livery barn and bought four hundred pounds of oats. Dan asked the livery man if they could buy some hay for the livestock.

"Sure, I have a large corral and plenty of hay troughs. So if you pull both wagons around the stable after you undress them, you can put 'em in the big corral. They will have all the water and hay they need."

"Okay, Billy, you can pull around the back. Joe can pull in beside the mule wagon. Billy, after you get the mules unharnessed, I'll give you some money, and you can run across the street to the leather man and buy two more pairs of hobbles for the black team."

"Okay, Mr. Dan."

After they put the horses and mules away for the night, Billy came back with the hobbles for the new team. The hunters were happy with the time and miles they made that day.

CHAPTER 10

The hunters were up early that morning. They harnessed, saddled up, and were ready to hit the trail again. A man walked up and asked Dan if he owned the big mules. Dan answered him with, "Yes, I do own them."

He said, "My name is Harold."

Dan introduced himself and asked, "What can I do for you, Harold?"

"I need a big pair of mules like yours. Would you be interested in selling them?"

"No, Harold, they are in use. We're goin' across country, and we need them. They're pullin' a heavy load."

"Well, Dan, I'm willing to pay a good sum of money for them."

"I'm sorry, Harold, but if we sold the mules, we wouldn't be able to get out of town."

Harold said, "I understand."

"What do you need them for?"

"Well, there is a county fair startin' next week, and they have a pullin' contest. People come from miles around to try to outpull Robert Noor's team. He has won it for the last six years. I was lookin' at your mules, and I think they might outpull Noor's team."

"Where is this fair?" asked Dan.

"It's up near Dodge City."

"That's the trail we're takin'."

"I can't sell you my mules, but if we happen to get there in time, you might be able to bet on 'em. We might give it a try."

"Is that lighter-built mare yours, Dan?"

"The black mare belongs to Billy here." He pointed at Billy.

Harold said, "You need to race her there. She's built like a racehorse. She has all the muscles in the right places."

Billy spoke up. "So they have horse racin' too?"

Harold told them all about the racing.

Billy got excited. "We can win, Mr. Dan."

Dan said, "It's not always that easy, Billy. There will be some fast horses entered."

"But, Mr. Dan, I know Cricket can win. When did you say the fair starts, Mr. Harold?"

"Friday, September the sixteenth. Maybe we'll see you up there."

"Maybe so, Harold, maybe so."

Dan unfolded the map and added up the miles between Englewood and Dodge City. It's about fifty miles according to the map.

"We can make it in two days." Dan looked at Joe and said, "We'll have plenty time, should we do it?"

Joe nodded his head and said, "Let's do it."

"Mr. Dan, I know that Cricket can win the horse race."

"We'll see, Billy. We'll see." They started making plans.

Dan said, "If we can make good time, we can maybe get there early. And that will give the mules and Cricket a two, maybe, three days' rest."

They pulled out. Billy was leading the way.

Dan told Buck, "We better hustle. Billy's got the mules on fast-forward, and we need to keep up."

Billy was anxious to get there. He was looking forward to winning that horse race. Dan kept telling Billy to not get too excited about winning, that there would be some fast horses entering the race.

"I know, Mr. Dan, but I'm perty sure that Cricket is faster."

They were on the road about four hours. Dan said, "Let's give the stock a few minutes' rest."

After a thirty-minute rest, they were moving out fast. Billy was pushing the mules. The three hunters were all excited to get to the fair.

Dan told Billy to pull up the mules. "I want you, Billy, to saddle Cricket. I'll drive the mules. When we pull out, I want you to take Cricket for about a half mile on a sharp gallop, and then turn her around and gallop her back. We need to let her out at a little faster pace."

"Okay, Mr. Dan." Billy nudged her a little, and Cricket reached a fast gallop. Billy had to keep a tight rein to keep her from a full-out run and took her what Billy thought was a half mile and turned her around and galloped her back. She did that without blowing. Tomorrow they'd do it again. They kept pushing the mules and horses to get there as soon as possible so they could have a longer rest before Friday. Billy is so sure that he and Cricket will win. Dan and Joe keep telling Billy not to be so sure about winning. Because if he loses, he'll be a very disappointed kid.

They told Billy, "If you loose, you have to be a good sport and shake the winner's hand and congratulate him or her."

Billy asked, "Will there be girls in the race?"

"I don't know, Billy, they have just as much right to ride in the race as the boys do."

Billy asked, "Mr. Dan, what if some girl gets in my way, and I can't get around her?"

"Well, Billy, you said Cricket always gets to the rail on the first turn, so you would be ahead of her."

"That's true, Mr. Dan."

The rest of the day went fast, and they had covered a lot of ground. That evening, they were making plans for the mule's pulling contest and Cricket's racing. All three of the hunters were getting more anxious to get there and sign up for the events.

Billy said, "I couldn't sleep last night thinkin' about the horse races."

Dan and Joe were having a couple sips, and Billy was slurping on a sarsaparilla while discussing the fair before getting some sleep.

The next morning, they got up and were on the trail again early. Billy and Sammi were in control of the mule wagon. Dan was riding beside the mule wagon. He asked Billy if he got some sleep last night.

"Ya, Mr. Dan, I did get some sleep. But I had a dream that me and Cricket won the race."

"Well, Billy, who knows, maybe so."

That afternoon, Dan took over the mule wagon. Dan had Billy saddle Cricket then told him to do the same as yesterday. "Don't blow her out, but put her at a good, strong and a little sharper gallop than yesterday. Make her work."

"Okay, Mr. Dan, we'll do it." Billy nudged Cricket and had her on a much faster pace. He took her down the trail, guessing where the half mile was, then turned her around and let her go the same speed back.

When he returned, Dan asked, "How did she feel, Billy?"

"Mr. Dan, she wanted to go. I could hardly hold her back. Yes, sir, Mr. Dan, she wanted to fly."

"Well, Billy, she doesn't seem to be winded much, and that's good. We know she's legged up as long as we've been on the trail. Her wind is the question. If it's a half mile, we stand a good chance. If it's a mile race, I don't think she's fit enough."

"How will we know, Mr. Dan?"

"As soon as we get there, we'll know. We should get there about tomorrow afternoon. You can have the mules back, Billy."

"Okay, Mr. Dan." Down the trail aways, Billy stopped the mules, pulled out his .22 rifle and aimed carefully and *pop!* He shot a rooster pheasant through the head. Then he saw two hen pheasants run in the weeds. He watched until they stopped. They thought they were hidden. Billy aimed carefully and *pop!* He shot one hen. The other hen flew away. Billy jumped down and said, "Ol' Billy got the supper for tonight."

"By golly, ol' Billy did get the supper," said Joe.

"We'll be eatin' high on the hog tonight," said Dan.

They covered a lot of ground again that day. They pulled over and set up camp. Wood was scarce, but Billy remembered seeing some rotted-off fence posts lying along the trail. Somebody replaced the rotted-off fence posts with new ones but neglected to take the old ones away.

So Billy saddled Cricket and rode back where the posts were. He piled five posts up and tied his lariat to them and pulled the posts back to camp. Joe was in charge of building a fire and cookin' the pheasants. Billy fed and watered the horses and the mules, and the chores were done for the night.

Dan, Joe, and Billy were showing symptoms of anxiousness, and the discussion was all about the fair. They were excited and couldn't quit talking about it.

Wednesday, September 13, they were up early and wanted to get on the trail. They rushed around. Billy had the stock fed and watered. They threw everything in the wagons and were on their way. Needless to say, Billy had the mules moving out as fast as they could go without them running. The mules didn't know what the hurry was, but they knew that Billy was in some kinda rush. Billy took the reins and smacked them on the rump and hollered, "Get up, you lop-eared shit for brains."

Dan said, "Billy, where are you comin' up with those dirty words?"

"Well, Mr. Dan, let me tell you something. These mules know that ol' Billy and Sammi are the bosses. You have to let them know in mule language. Notice how they settled down, and they are pullin' much better."

Dan said, "They look like they're pullin' about the same to me."

"Well, Mr. Dan, you're lookin' from a side view. Sammi and I are up here where we are lookin' down and can see the difference. Right, Sammi?"

Sammi let out her little bark.

Dan said, "I think you're brainwashin' my dog, Billy."

They all had a laugh. Later they rolled into the town called Cowtown where the county fair was held. Billy led the way on main street. Dan told Billy to pull up the mules.

"I'll check with the sheriff to see where we can set up camp out of the way." Dan went in the sheriff's office and introduced himself and asked the sheriff where they could set up camp. The sheriff had a map already printed out for the people who would be camping out. The sheriff explained what all they could expect over the three-day fair, starting Friday. The sheriff also gave the name of the fair organizer, Jane Crawford. So if there were any other questions, they could contact her.

Dan returned and told Billy to turn at the next cross street and then turn left. Then go to the next street and turn left again. Go out where the two big trees are, and that was it. They'd park there.

Billy said, "We're lucky to get here early so we get the shade trees."

After they unharnessed and unsaddled, they walked around town, checking things out. Dan was telling Joe and Billy some of the things that the sheriff told him. The races start in front of the saloon. It goes to the end of town and goes to the left around the street at the back of the business buildings and then goes to the other end of town. The track circles and then back down the main street and finishes in front of the saloon. It's just a little longer than a half a mile, although only about fifty feet longer.

"We can sign up tomorrow. It's $5 to start. The winners stay for the second day. That will be Sunday. Saturday is a rest day for the horses. Then they pay another $5 for the second-day race. They expect about twenty entries, and there would be four horses in each race. There would be five races. The five winners will draw numbers for the second day's race, and that would be the final race. The winner takes all the money."

Billy said, "Mr. Dan, I have enough bucks for both days."

"So is that what you want to do, Billy?"

"Yes, sir, Mr. Dan, I know we can win. Who do I give the money to, Mr. Dan?"

"Billy, tomorrow they will start takin' sign-ups, and you'll pay for the first day."

Dan, Joe, Billy, and Sammi walked the track where the races would be. Dan was explaining things to Billy, such as no bumping other horses. If he does bump, he will be disqualified.

Dan explained, "Try to get to the inside rail as soon as possible without bumping any of the other horses." Dan continued giving the do's and the don'ts of racing.

Billy said, "I remember when my dad was racin' at the fair, he would always get to the rail before the first turn, and he always won. Cricket loves to run."

"So, Billy, do you think that you can remember what I told you about racin'?"

"Yes, sir, Mr. Dan. I have it right here." He pointed to his head.

They spent the rest of the day checking out the rest of the town. They stopped at the livery barn and asked the man in charge if he could give the horses and mules plenty of hay now through Monday morning. The man said he would feed them twice a day at their campsite.

It was late afternoon, so they decided to stop at the saloon and have a drink. Dan went in first to check if it was okay for Billy and Sammi to come in. The barkeep said it was okay. So they had a few drinks, discussing the fair events again. Billy asked Dan if he could jump on Cricket and go outside of town and get some rabbits or pheasants for supper.

"Good idea, Billy. Don't get too far away."

"I won't," said Billy. Billy saddled Cricket and headed out.

Dan and Joe started to walk back to camp when they heard a *pop!*

Joe said, "I think Billy popped a rabbit."

About ten minutes later, there was another *pop!* Another rabbit. In less than a minute, another *pop!*

Joe turned and said, "Uh-oh, I think Billy had a miss."

Dan and Joe had a laugh about that and decided to tease Billy a little bit. They could see Billy coming back. So as soon as Billy came riding up, Joe said, "I guess you missed one shot. I thought you were Billy, the sharpshooter."

Billy said, "I am Billy, the sharpshooter."

Joe said, "Billy, we heard three shots."

"The reason you heard three shots was because I shot three rabbits."

Joe said, "I'll never doubt you again, Billy."

"That's good, Mr. Joe, because ol' Billy, the sharpshooter, doesn't waste ammunition."

CHAPTER 11

A tall, slender woman wearing a black Western hat with shoulder-length hair, tight pants, and black boots came riding up on a large chestnut mare. She was leading a big sorrel gelding packhorse. She had a black holster hanging over the saddle horn, with a .45 revolver with pearl handles sticking out of it. She had a saddle scabbard, which appeared to be a large caliber rifle. She was riding toward our campsite. The closer she got, the more it appeared that all her body parts were stacked in the right places. She rode up and stopped. She said, "Hi, my name is Abigail Lacey. My friends call me Abby."

"Hi, Abby, my name is Dan Colt." Pointing, he said, "This is Joe Cobb, Billy Priest, and my dog, Sammi." Joe and Billy said hi, and Sammi gave her little bark.

"I see you guys are bounty hunters."

"Yes, we are," said Dan.

She said, "I could tell by the big knives you're carrying. Only bounty hunters carry that size."

Joe said, "Why don't you step down and have a rest?"

"Thank you, Joe, I will." She stepped down from her horse. Billy took her horses and tied them. Abby said, "My husband was a bounty hunter."

Joe asked, "Did you say he was a hunter?"

"Yes, he got careless, and they got him."

"When did this happen?" asked Joe.

"About three years ago." She asked, "Are you hunting now?"

"No, but we are en route." Dan asked, "What brings you out here by yourself?"

"I'm headed for Broken Bow, Nebraska. My uncle died a couple months ago. I'm his only living relative. He never married, so he had no kids to leave his inheritance to, so he left his ranch and some money to me. I don't know how much, or how big the ranch is. The attorney that is handling the will sent a letter trying to explain what there was, but I don't think he knew anymore about it than I do, and I have no idea. I decided to go back and probably sell everything."

"Have you been traveling by yourself?" asked Dan.

"I have been so far. I've been hoping to find a wagon train going that way and join them, but it seems they are all moving west, and I need to go northeast."

"So are you here for the fair?" asked Dan.

"No, I'm just riding through."

Billy said, "Ms. Abby, I wish you would stay until tomorrow. I'm riding my horse, Cricket, in a horse race tomorrow, and I know she will win."

"That sounds like fun, maybe I'll stay and watch you win, Billy."

"We have to go sign Billy up for the race now."

"Why don't you walk with us?" said Joe.

"Okay, I will."

So they walked to the booth where they were to sign up for the events. Billy walked in and slapped his $5 on the counter and said, "I'm gettin' in the horse races."

The fair organizer, Jane, asked, "Who is signing for the boy?"

Dan said, "I'll sign."

"Okay, what is your name boy?"

"Billy Priest."

"What's the name of your horse, Billy?"

"Cricket," answered Billy.

"Okay, here is your stub. Keep it and come back at five o'clock for the drawing."

Dan asked Jane, "Could you sign us up for the pullin' contest as well?"

"Okay, who will be the team handler?"

"They are mules," said Dan.

"Who is going to be handling the mules?"

"Billy Priest," he said.

Billy looked up with his eyes ready to pop out of his head and said, "Mr. Dan, am I goin' to drive the mules?"

"Yep," said Dan. Billy was so excited.

Then Abby asked, "Billy, are you sure you're going to drive those big mules?"

"That's what Mr. Dan just said."

"Well, Billy, you're the only one that can make those mules pull. Don't you remember?" asked Dan.

"That's true, Mr. Dan, I remember now. I talk mule language." Everyone there had a good laugh.

Joe asked Abby, "If you're stayin' overnight, you are welcome to camp with us."

"Well, thank you, Joe. I would like that."

Later about five o'clock, they were ready to draw numbers to get their positions. Of course, Billy had been waiting by the booth for over an hour. Abby, Dan, Joe, and Sammi walked over to the booth to see where Billy would draw in. Dan asked Jane how many entries there was.

Jane said, "I assume they are all in. We have nineteen. Does everyone know how the drawing works?"

"This is our first time. If you don't mind, maybe you could run through it for us."

"Okay, we draw peas. The first round we draw for will be which race you are in. For instance, if you draw 2, you're in the second race. Second drawing will be position such as 4. You will be on the outside position. Does everybody understand? Okay, now there will be four peas with the number 1. There will be four peas with number 2, There will be four peas with number 3. There will be four peas with number 4, and there will be three peas with number 5, meaning there will be only three horses in the fifth race. Okay, we will start with our Billy boy. Now, Billy, you just take one pea only. Do you understand?"

Billy said, "Yes, Ms. Jane."

"Go ahead, Billy." Billy took one pea, and it was number 2.

"Okay, Billy, you're in the second race." They all drew their first numbers. "Okay, Billy, now draw one pea out of this cup. Billy drew number 3. Okay, Billy, you will be the third horse in the second race."

After the drawing was over, Dan asked Abby if she would like a glass of whiskey or if she drank alcohol.

"Well, thank you, Dan, I would like a glass of whiskey," said Abby. "I never drank whiskey before I started bounty hunting, but that drove me to drinking."

So they stopped at the saloon and sat at a table. The barkeep brought their drinks. Their conversation was mostly about Abby and the trip she was making alone.

Dan said, "We are going through that area. I know you can travel faster with you and your two horses, but I hate to see you out there alone on those trails. The drunken renegades and drunken outlaws are out there, and they would like to get hold of a beautiful woman like you. We would be happy to have you travel with us. Maybe you can think about it, and if you decide to, we will be pulling out Monday morning."

Billy piped up and said, "Ms. Abby, I'll help take care of your horses."

"Thank you, Billy, you're a very thoughtful boy, and I'll think about it. The only thing I don't want is to hold you guys back."

Joe said, "Don't worry about that, Abby, you won't hold us back. The bad guys will still be there."

"Maybe I should explain myself. As you can see, I carry a .45 revolver on my saddle horn and a .44 rifle in my scabbard. I used to back up my husband on most of his hunts. I wasn't with him when he got shot. I always wondered if he would still be alive if I had been backing him. We worked together—just the two of us. I've shot my share of the bad guys, and I might add that I'm pretty accurate with my guns. The reason I'm telling you this is so you know I can hold my own. I just want you to know if I do travel with you guys and trouble comes by, you can count on me as your fifth hunter. And if we get into it deeper than we plan, I won't cut and run. I know that even bounty hunters have a little fear, but if you have much fear, then you should change occupations. Plus, I'm a pretty good cook."

Billy asked, "Does this mean you'll travel with us?"

"Only if you three want me to."

Dan said, "You're forgetting there's four of us."

Abby said, "Oh yes, I forgot about Sammi. I'm sorry, Sammi. I mean if all four of you approve."

Dan said, "Whoever wants Abby to join us, raise your hand." Joe, Dan, and Billy raised their hands; and Sammi gave her little bark and raised her paw in the air. "I guess that was a unanimous vote," said Dan.

"Welcome aboard, Abby," said Joe.

"Welcome aboard, Ms. Abby," said Billy.

Sammi gave her famous little bark.

They finished their drinks and walked across the street and passed the icehouse where they freeze large blocks of ice. Noticing large boxes with a price tag on them, Dan was wandering about them. So they walked inside, and the man said, "My name is Bert, how can I help you?" Dan asked about the iceboxes. They all went back out front with Bert, and he explained how he makes them and all the different sizes. He explained how he insulates them. "The walls are three inches thick, and they hold ice for many days. Most of the people that live here buy one to hold their food. Once a week, they come in and buy a block of ice, and it will last another week. It tells you the size. This one says five feet by three feet by eighteen inches. This is the largest one, and that is inside measurements. So if you want the inside measurements, you add six inches to each of those figures."

Dan asked, "How sturdy are they?" Dan explained about the water barrels, each weighing about three hundred pounds. Two barrels would weigh about six hundred pounds. "Could that be too much weight?"

"That would be no problem," answered Bert.

"Okay, Bert, let us talk about it, and we'll let you know what we decide."

Back at camp, Dan said, "If we had this box lying down in the Mennonite wagon, then Billy could pick off an antelope once in a while, cut it up, and keep it on ice."

They discussed the icebox, and all five of the hunters agreed they needed the icebox. They decided to pick it up on their way out Monday morning. Most towns of any size would have icehouses.

Dan told Billy to saddle Cricket and gallop her around the track twice on a slow gallop to make sure there was nothing for her to shy at tomorrow. Billy did what he was told. When he returned to camp, Dan asked, "How did she go?"

Billy said, "She did great. She didn't shy at anything, but she sure did want to run, but I told her that she would have to wait until tomorrow."

People started coming from every direction. The people that were going to camp overnight. The saloon was going strong, and it was getting noisy, and the cowboys were starting to celebrate the fair. Billy came back from the mule wagon. Dan looked at Billy and asked, "Why are you wearing that .45 and your big knife?"

"Well, Mr. Dan, I was thinkin' the cowboys are gettin' noisy and probably will get cantankerous. I just want to be ready if there's a showdown between them and us."

"We don't need any trouble like that, Billy."

All went pretty well with the cowboys. Just a couple scuffles that didn't amount to much. Ol' Billy was ready, just in case he had to do a quick draw. He also had that big knife ready, in case he had to break someone's arm.

Abby had everything in her packsaddle. She got everything out that she would need for an overnight, including her bunk roll for sleeping in. They all retired for the day.

The next morning, Billy was up early and was ready for his race, which would take place at ten thirty. Abby was up and had her hair combed and tidied up and ready for the day. Dan and Joe were also up and ready for the day. Dan called for Billy to come over and take some last-minute instructions on the race.

"Okay, Billy, after the first race is over and all the horses are off the track, I want you to take Cricket from the starting line and take her on a slow gallop around the track and back to the start and finish line. When you get there and if they are not quite ready for the lineup, just keep Cricket walking around until they call for you to come to the starting line. When you hear the starter gun, you send her off at her best and hope you can have enough lead to take her to the rail. If not, try to get to the rail on the backstretch. Now when you're headed for home, don't use the whip unless you feel you have a horse coming on strong against you. Then reach back and give two quick whips and hope for the best. Okay, now tell me back what I just told you." So Billy told Dan, almost word for word, what Dan had told him. Billy was very nervous. He was walking in circles. Dan asked, "Is everything okay, Billy? Do you need to go to the toilet or anything else?"

"I'll go to the toilet right now," said Billy.

"Good idea, Billy, we don't want you to get excited and wet your pants."

When Billy came back, the man on the megaphone called the horses in the first race to come to the starting line. They had thirty minutes for the first race. That race would go off at exactly 10:00 a.m. Dan handed Billy a breast collar.

"Do I need that, Mr. Dan?"

"Yes, Billy. If she breaks real hard and the saddle slips, you're in big trouble."

"Oh ya, I didn't think about that, Mr. Dan."

Billy had Cricket saddled and had the breast collar on tight. Billy asked Dan if he would check his saddle and breast collar to make sure they were on properly. Dan checked and told Billy that it was all right. The first race went off, and Billy was watching close to see if there was anything helpful for him to watch out for. Dan was also watching to see if there was anything he could add to Billy's instructions. It was getting close to time for Billy's race. The announcer called for the horses for the second race. Billy hopped on Cricket. He asked Mr. Dan, Mr. Joe, Ms. Abby, and Sammi to cheer for him.

Abby said, "Don't worry, Billy, we'll be cheering for you."

Billy looked at Dan and said, "You know, Mr. Dan, I'm sure nervous."

"No, Billy, just think about Cricket being the leading horse at the finish line. Go, Billy, give'r hell."

Billy rode to the track and was hoping he could remember everything that Mr. Dan told him. He reached the starting line with the other three horses and riders. The starting judge told them to go ahead and warm up their horses for a few minutes. He would call for them when it was time to line up. Billy did what Dan had told him. He put Cricket on a slow gallop and had a tough time holding her back. Cricket wanted to run. Billy was talking to Cricket, saying, "Easy, girl. Easy, girl." Billy did manage to keep her on a slow gallop. The announcer called for the horses of the second race to come to the starting line. The judge announced the names of the horses and riders. There were four men heading, holding their bridles to give all of them a fair start. The judge had the starter gun. He raised the gun and *boom!* They were off. Cricket broke hard, just like Billy always said she does. He said she always gets to the inside rail before the first turn, and Billy did get to the rail before the first turn. The crowd was clapping and yelling, "Go, Billy, go!"

Billy came to the second and last turn. He turned to see if there were any horses trying to be competitive, but Billy could see there was no competition. Now all he could hope for was that she wouldn't tire out. He remembered that Mr. Dan said, "Don't whip her unless they were challenging her." They were coming down to the wire. Billy could hear Joe, Abby, and Sammi cheering, "Come on, Billy!" Sammi had her little cheering barks. Dan was yelling, "Don't whip, Billy, don't whip!" Billy started smiling as he shot across the finish line by more than a length. Billy was pulling up to slow her down.

He was on the backstretch, slowing as he should. The people that lined the backstretch were yelling, "You did it, Billy! We knew you could do it, Billy!" Billy had Cricket down to a walk. Billy waved to the spectators with a big smile. He turned Cricket around and made his way back to the finish line where Dan, Joe, Abby, and Sammi were waiting. There were hundreds of people lining the sidewalks. When he jumped down, he never had so many hugs and handshakes in his entire life. People swarmed around him. Billy had the biggest smile he ever had.

Abby hugged Billy and said, "Billy, you looked so professional riding that race, and Cricket looked like a professional racehorse."

"Thank you, Ms. Abby, I just knew Cricket could win. She loves to run. I just wish my mom and dad could of been here. They would be so proud of me and Cricket."

"You know, Billy, you can be assured that they were watching. And yes, they would be very proud of you and Cricket."

"Do you think so, Ms. Abby?"

"Absolutely, Billy. Trust my word, they're watching."

Dan pulled the saddle and breast collar off and put the halter on Cricket so Billy could walk her to cool her out. Dan was keeping track of the times of the winners.

		First Race	Final Race
1st race	56 seconds	(Dolly)	(Hog Wild)
2nd race	54 seconds	(Cricket)	(Carousel)
3rd race	57 seconds	(Carousel)	(Cricket)
4th race	56 seconds	(Patches)	(Dolly)
5th race	55 seconds	(Hog Wild)	(Patches)

Billy was walking Cricket, cooling her down. Sammi was walking with Billy and Cricket. Sammi even looked like she was smiling and happy for Billy. Dan could hear Billy telling Cricket, "I told everybody you would win. I told 'em, so now we have to show 'em that we can win one more race Sunday. I know we can do it. Thanks, Cricket, for winnin' today."

A well-dressed man in a suit approached Dan and congratulated him, saying, "That was a great race your boy won."

Dan said, "You need to congratulate Billy, the boy that's walking her."

"Oh, I will, but I just wanted to ask if you would be interested in selling that mare, at a very good price."

"You will have to ask Billy." The man asked Dan if he owned the mare. "No, she belongs to Billy."

"Isn't Billy your son?"

"No," said Dan.

"So I guess I need to talk to Billy."

"Yes, sir, but I don't think there is enough money in this world to buy that mare, but I guess it won't hurt for you to ask him." The man turned around and went to talk to Billy. Dan was watching and could see Billy shaking his head no. After a few minutes, the man went away, shaking his head. Billy had Cricket cooled down and came back to camp. Dan asked Billy, "Did that man offer to buy Cricket?"

"Yes, Mr. Dan, but I don't want to sell her."

"What did he offer to pay for her?"

"He said he would pay $200 for her. Do you think I should of sold her, Mr. Dan?"

"Well, let me ask you something, Billy. Would you rather have Cricket or $200?"

"I would rather have Cricket, Mr. Dan."

"Then you made the right decision, Billy."

"Mr. Dan, I don't want to ever sell her."

"I thought that, Billy. I don't blame you. I would do the same thing. Besides, you have a race coming Sunday." They were watching where the man went. It was obvious that he was the owner of the horse that Billy and Cricket just outran. A case of "if you can't outrun 'em, you buy 'em." Sorry, not this time.

Billy was so pumped up he couldn't sit still in one place. He wanted to talk about the race, and he had all the right. Billy had only been in this part of the country for two days. It seemed that at least 75 percent of the spectators were cheering for Billy and Cricket. Everybody that passed by their camp would stop and tell Billy what a good job he did and what a beautiful and fast horse he had. One man asked Billy if he was going to win the race Sunday morning.

Billy said, "I know Cricket can win."

The man said, "I'll be bettin' on you and Cricket." Billy was liking every bit of it. He felt so important.

Dan said, "Well, Billy, you need to think how you're going to get the mules to pull that big load tomorrow."

"I'll have a talk with 'em just before the contest tomorrow. Remember, Mr. Dan, I talk mule language."

"Well, that should help a whole bunch, Billy." Dan suggested they go to the saloon and have a victory drink for Billy and Cricket.

So they headed for the saloon. They were talking and laughing and bragging on Billy and Cricket. They made it to the saloon and sat at a table. The barkeep came and took their order. When he brought their drinks, he sat the drinks in front of them, including Billy's sarsaparilla. He asked Billy, "Aren't you the lad that just won the horse race?"

"Ya, me and Cricket."

"This first round is on me," said the barkeep. They all thanked him.

Billy asked, "What is your name, sir?"

"My name is Ted."

"Well, thank you very much for the drinks, Mr. Ted."

"Your name must be Billy?"

"Yes, it is, but how did you know?" asked Billy.

"Well, when your race started, I could hear the people yelling, 'Come on, Billy! Come on, Billy!'" Dan, Joc, Abby, and Sammi were just as proud of Billy as anyone could be.

CHAPTER 12

———

All the hunters were getting excited about tomorrow's pulling contest.

"Did Jane tell you, Billy, what time the drawing is for the pulling contest?"

"She didn't say. Maybe I should run over and ask her." Billy ran out the door and down the street to the contestant booth and asked Ms. Jane about the drawing.

"Hi, Billy, it's the same. At five o'clock. Oh, by the way, Billy, that was a beautiful race you and Cricket won."

"Thank you, Ms. Jane, ol' Cricket wanted to fly."

"Yes, she did, Billy."

Billy went back to the saloon and told the rest of the hunters about the nice thing that Ms. Jane said.

"That was nice of her," said Dan.

They had a couple more drinks, and they decided they better get going to the booth for the drawing. There were a lot of contenders there for the drawing. They all knew that Billy had won the second race. Some of the ladies gave Billy big hugs. The men were shaking Billy's hand and patting him on the back. Talk about feeling ten feet tall. Billy was loving every bit of it. Billy put his $5 up and got his stub.

Jane came out and said, "We are ready to start the drawing, but first I want to say the pulling contest will be the same as the past years. For those that are here for the first time, I will explain how the contest works. There

———

will be two contests. Number one is for teams with each horse or mule weighing 1,500 pounds each or less. Number two is for teams with each horse or mule weighing 1,501 pounds or over. The small teams will be pulling a sled weighted with 2,000 pounds. They will start at the starting line, and the team that pulls the sled the farthest will be the winner. If the team stops, they have ten seconds to get them moving again. If the team stops a second stop, that is your finish line. Are there any questions from the light team handlers?"

No questions.

"Okay, the heavy teams have the same rules except they will be pulling 3,000 pounds. Does the heavy team handlers have any questions?"

No questions.

"Okay, we will be starting with the light teams." They passed the cup around until they all drew their numbers. Jane asked who has number 1 as she wrote all the names from number 1 through number 12. "The light teams should be at the starting line a few minutes before 10:00 a.m. Now we will have the drawing for the heavy teams. We'll start with Billy boy." Billy drew his number, and it was number 7. After all were drawn, Jane said, "The heavy teams will do the same, starting with number 1 through number 9. Are there any questions?"

No questions.

"Then we will see you all tomorrow at ten o'clock sharp."

"So, Billy, you're number 7," said Dan. Dan stopped Jane and asked if there was a man there by the name of Robert Noor with a pulling team.

"Yes. See the man in the black hat? That's him walking away. And yes, he has a pulling team."

Dan said, "Billy, let's walk around and see if we can find Noor's team."

"Okay, Mr. Dan." They walked around the campground looking for the man with the black hat. They came across Harold, the man that wanted to buy the mules.

Dan stuck his hand out to shake hands with Harold and asked, "Do you remember us?"

Harold asked, "Aren't you the ones with the mules?"

"Yes, I'm Dan, and this is Billy."

"Billy, aren't you the one that won the second race?"

"Yes, sir, me and Cricket."

"Well, you sure looked good winnin' that race. I noticed you won by a length and never used the whip. You did great, Billy."

"Thanks, Mr. Harold. I'm goin' to be the mule handler tomorrow."

"Well, I sure hope you can beat ol' Noor and his team."

Dan asked Harold, "Do you know where Noor's team is?"

"You mean now?" asked Harold.

"Yes, Billy and I would like to take a look at them."

"If you walk straight down this row of campsites, about a quarter of a mile, you will see his wagon. It says Noor's Hardware on the side."

"Thank you, Harold. We'll walk down there and take a look." Dan and Billy walked down to see what his team looked like. They found his wagon with the team tied to it.

"Holy mackerel, those horses are huge. Our mules aren't near as big as his team."

"Well, Billy, if you notice, these horses are fat. And that means they haven't been working. They are in poor shape. Meaning, they will get winded real quick. Now the mules have been pulling the heavy wagon for several days and are fit and ready. I'm not saying they are going to win, but they will give it their best."

"Well, Mr. Dan, those ol' mules are perty strong, and if I have a good talk with 'em just before our turn to pull that sled, we might surprise them folks."

Back at the camp, the rest of the hunters were curious what Noor's team looked like. "Well, let me say, it's like this. His horses weigh about 2,200 pounds each, but they are fat, and they are out of shape."

Abby asked, "How much do the mules weigh?"

Dan said, "They weigh about 1,700 to 1,800 pounds each, so we are spotting them 1,000 pounds."

Joe mentioned something. "I've noticed with the mules. They work together. They lean into it at the same time, no seesawing, and that helps a lot."

"I guess we'll find out tomorrow," said Dan. The hunters were at their camp. Dan asked, "Does anybody want a drink?" Then he pulled out a bottle of whiskey. "Abby, you would probably rather drink from a glass instead of drinking out of the bottle like Joe and I do."

Abby said, "I'm a bounty hunter, right?"

Dan pulled the cork out of the bottle and handed it to Abby. Abby took a big drink and handed it to Joe. Joe took a big drink, then handed it to Dan. Of course, Dan had a big drink. They noticed some drunk cowboys that kept staring at Abby. It was evident there would be trouble before the night was over. They were camped about four campsites away. These guys kept getting drunker and talking louder. Dan told Joe, "We might have a little trouble in the making."

Joe said, "I've been watchin'."

It wasn't long before two of the drunks staggered over to their camp. They asked Abby if she would like to come to their camp for a drink. Abby answered with, "No, thank you."

"Come on, we'll have some fun." As he approached where Abby was sitting, Sammi walked between the drunk and Abby and was growling. The drunk said, "Whoever owns this dog better call her off, or I'll blow her head off." Dan jumped up in a fierce bolt and swung with his knife and cut into the drunk's muscles from his neck to his shoulder.

Leaving his right arm dangling, Dan said, "If you want to, you may try drawing your gun and shoot my dog." In the meantime, Joe smacked the other drunk, and he was out. The first trouble was calling Dan a son of a bitch because he had cut his neck. Dan said, "Get out of here before I cut the other side."

Dan and Joe were watching the other two that were still at their campsite. They seemed to be as drunk as the first two. Dan walked over to the one with the hanging arm and took his gun. Joe had his foot on his drunk's arm while he reached down and took his gun. Joe looked at Dan and said, "Maybe we better approach the other two before they come over here and somebody gets hurt."

"Let's go, Joe."

Joe and Dan walked over to their camp and asked if they wanted in on this little bit of bickering. They couldn't quite decide. Dan walked up within a foot of one, and Joe did the same with the other one. They just stood and stared straight into their eyes until they tried to go for their guns. Joe grabbed his knife and buried it in his belly. All fourteen inches worth. While Dan grabbed the drunk's handgun and aimed it toward the ground, *boom!* It shot into the ground. Dan had grabbed his knife and swung, cutting his head almost off. Joe said, "Took care of that job." They walked back to their camp, and there was Billy with his .45 aimed at the one that had just woke up. Joe dug up two pairs of handcuffs and cuffed the two that were still alive. Shortly after, the marshal rode up and asked about the gunshot. Joe said, "They had four drunkin' dummies that wanted to flex their muscles, so they accommodated them."

The marshal said, "That one"—pointing at the number one dummy—"is losing a lot of blood from his neck."

"That's true," said Dan. "He's lucky. I could have cut his head completely off. The two over there, we have reason to believe that they are deceased." The marshal handed them two pairs of handcuffs and said for them to exchange their handcuffs for his.

"I'll take these two in and book 'em. Then I'll bring a wagon back and pick up the other two. When I come back, can you guys help me load 'em in the wagon?"

"Certainly," answered Joe. After the marshal left, Dan suggested they have a drink on that.

Abby said, "I think I need a drink after that commotion. And Billy needs a sarsaparilla." And so they did. After Dan had a drink, he asked Billy what he would have done if the outlaw grabbed for his gun.

"I would have shot him in the head," said Billy.

Abby said, "Billy was taking care of things over here." They all had a couple more drinks. When the marshal returned, they helped him load the dead ones in the wagon. They decided to turn in for the night.

Today is Saturday, the morning of the pulling contest. All the hunters were up and getting ready for the contest. Billy was a little nervous, thinking, *What if the mules and I don't win?* Billy made sure the mules got their oats. That would give them a little extra energy.

Dan said, "Don't give them their hay until the contest is over." Abby was cooking ham, biscuits, and coffee. After everything else was taken care of, Dan told Billy, "You better have that talk with the mules about winning the pulling contest."

"Mr. Dan, I'm waitin' just before the pullin'. I'm goin' to have a talk with 'em. The reason for waitin' is because I don't know how long mules remember. So if I wait just before our turn, they will have it fresh in their minds."

"Well, okay, Billy, you're the one that talks mule language, so you will have to decide when it's time to talk with 'em. It's nine thirty, we better get the mules harnessed and be ready for our turn."

By the time they got the mules brushed and had them dressed and ready to go, the judge called for the light teams to line up according to the numbers that they drew, starting with number 1. "Does everyone understand the rules of the light horse teams?" Everyone agreed that they did know the rules. The judge said, "Where your team stops for the second time, that will be the marked distance of your pull. The first stop can't exceed ten seconds. There will be an iron stake driven into the ground to show your finish line. Okay, number 1 team, you are up."

"Mr. Dan, why are those four big horses hooked together?"

"They use them to pull the sled back to the starting line for the next team."

"Oh, I thought we were goin' to pull against them."

Billy was watching the teams pull, one after the other. The judge called for the heavy teams to start lining up, again starting with number 1.

"Okay, Billy, take the mules and drive them around until you have to get in line. They need to get their legs limbered up."

A man was hanging numbers on all the teams' harness. Billy was walking the mules like Dan had told him. They were lining up number 1 through number 9. Billy was number 7. The light teams were finished pulling, and now it was time for the heavy teams. Billy was standing behind the mules, holding the reins. Dan and Joe came over to talk with Billy. He was nervous, and they kept talking, trying to help him settle down. Before they knew it, it was Billy's turn. Billy went up to have his talk with the mules.

Billy said, "Okay, boys, I need to ask you to pull as hard as you can. We need to outpull ol' Noor's team. If we win, I'll promise you that I will never call you shit for brains ever again."

About that time, the flies were landing on the mule's noses. The mules were shaking their heads up and down, trying to shake the flies off. The spectators could hear what Billy was saying, but they were far enough away, so they couldn't see the flies. The crowd was roaring with laughter, so hard they were almost falling down. They were convinced that Billy was talking mule language, the way the mules were shaking their heads like they were approving of what Billy was saying to them. The judge was laughing so hard he couldn't get Billy and the mules started.

The judge, after he could get himself under control, motioned for Billy to pull up in front of the sled. Dan asked Billy if he could see the stake with the white flag tied to it.

"Yes, sir, Mr. Dan. Why?"

"Billy, that's Noor's position. To win, you have to get them mules to pull a little farther than that stake."

"I think these ol' mules can do it, Mr. Dan."

The judge said, "Go, Billy."

Billy slapped the mules on the rump with the reins and started yelling, "Haaaaa, haaaaa, get up you lop-eared canaries!"

The crowd was yelling, "Come on, Billy! Come on, Billy! Keep 'em going, Billy!" Then one of the mules fell forward; one of the tugs had snapped. Billy was out of the contest. The groans and aahs were coming from the crowd.

Dan and Joe went running to Billy and the mules. "What happened, Billy?"

"They were pulling really hard, and the tug snapped."

Dan took the broken tug of the sled and was looking at it. One-half of the tug had been sliced with a knife. At that time, the judge came to see what happened. Dan showed the broken tug to the judge. The judge asked Dan and Joe what they should do about it

Dan said, "I think I'm going to have a talk with Mr. Noor." Dan told Billy to go ahead and take the mules back to camp.

The judge said, "You know what, we had a tug snapped last year too. Now I wonder if that one had been cut also. The guy that's number 9 is the one that snapped last year." Dan and Joe went to find out about the tug that snapped last year. They walked back to number 9.

"Hi, my name is Dan Colt, and this is Joe Cobb."

"Howdy, my name is Carl Sands." They all shook hands.

Dan said, "I understand that you snapped a tug last year?"

"Yes, I did. Look at this."

He showed the tug to Carl.

Carl said, "That's been cut."

"Yep," said Joe, "We are wondering if your tug had been cut last year."

"Well, I don't know offhand. I didn't check it."

"Do you still have the broken parts?" asked Dan.

"Yes, I do."

"Maybe you should check the tugs here."

Carl walked around his team and, sure enough, one of his tugs was cut halfway through. Carl's face turned red. He was mad. "Why, that son of a bitch! Noor did this, I know he did it. That dirty son of a bitch!"

Dan said, "I'm going to get the judge and show him." So Dan brought the judge back.

The judge looked at it and said, "I think I know who did this, but I don't know how to prove it." The judge said, "Number 8 is up. Now let me have his pull, and then we will check this out a little closer." Dan asked Carl if he would like to borrow one of their tugs.

"Yes, Dan, I would like to see if I can outpull that son of a bitch."

Joe said, "I'll be right back with a tug."

Dan went to talk with the judge. Dan told the judge, "We are loaning Carl one of our tugs. Joe is after it now."

As soon as Joe returned, they buckled the tug on Carl's harness. After number 8 was finished, the judge said, "Carl, whenever you're ready, bring your team over, and we'll see if you can outpull Noor's team." So Carl brought his team, and they hitched them to the sled.

The judge told Carl, "I think you can outpull Noor's team. Go, Carl."

Carl's team was very powerful, and they laid into it. It was clear the crowd didn't like Robert Noor. Almost everyone was pulling for Carl. The crowd was getting louder and louder as Carl's team was trudging to pull the heavy load. The louder the crowd got, the more it seemed to inspire Carl and his team. The last few feet, the big horses were almost on their knees, but they held on long enough to pass the stake that Noor's team stopped at. Everyone was yelling yahoos and clapping. Carl, who just broke Noor's string of cheating, wins.

Dan and Joe figured that was the reason for Noor's six straight wins. He was picking out the ones that stood a chance of outpulling his team. Then he would slip in after everyone was asleep and cut one of the tugs deep enough, so when the team would get into some tough pulling, the tug would snap. After the confusion was over, Billy was off looking for Noor. Dan and Joe also went looking for Noor. They went to his campsite, but he wasn't there.

A fat woman said, "He probably stopped in the saloon to have a drink." Dan and Joe headed for the saloon. It was about an hour before they finally found Noor at the saloon.

Joe said, "I guess you know why we're here?"

Noor said, "No, I don't. Why are you here?"

"You cut the wrong man's tug," said Joe.

"I didn't cut any harness."

While Joe was talking to Noor, a young man stepped over and asked Dan, "Could you step over here for a minute?" Dan didn't know what he wanted but went with him anyway. The young man said, "I heard your conversation with that guy your friend is talking to. My friend and I are camped two campsites over from yours. We were sitting outside drinking beer, and we saw that guy in your camp last night. He was over by your mules and harness. I didn't think much about it, until I saw the tug snap when your boy was pullin' with the mules."

Dan asked, "Would you rather I not include you in this?"

"Well, let's see what he has to say," said the young man. They went back to where Joe and Noor were talking. The young man said to Noor, "You were in these guys' camp last night weren't you?"

Noor said, "So I would like to see you prove it."

Joe asked, "How long has it been since you've been unconscious, Noor?"

"I've never been unconscious."

Joe knocked Noor's hat off; and grabbed his hair, pulling his head down; and with a powerful driving fist, hit Noor on his jaw. Noor hit the floor and was out like a light. There was blood dripping from Noor's mouth.

Joe looked down and said, "You can't make that brag anymore, Mr. Noor."

Dan and Joe went back to the camp. Abby and Billy were sitting, talking about what happened with the contest. Dan and Joe could see that Billy was very upset. Dan asked, "Where were you, Billy?"

"I went lookin' for Noor."

Joe asked, "Did you find him?"

"Yep, I did."

"So what did you do?"

"I said, 'Noor, you son of a bitch.' Then I kicked him in the nuts."

Dan said, "Billy, don't forget there is a lady here."

"I'm sorry, Ms. Abby."

"That's okay, Billy." Abby was grinning and said, "I think Billy got even with Noor, don't you guys?"

"I guess he did," said Dan. "I guess ol' Noor has double trouble."

"Why's that?" asked Abby.

"Well," Dan said, "Joe just busted Noor's jaw. He's going to have a big headache when he wakes up. I'm sure he's still out on the saloon floor."

Abby said, "I think Joe and Billy both did a remarkable job."

The day wore on, and it was time for the hunters to go to the contestant booth. Billy was drawing for tomorrow's race. Dan asked, "Do you have $5, Billy?"

"Yes, sir, Mr. Dan, I still have eight and a half bucks."

"Well, Billy, you better give $5 to Jane so you can draw a number."

"Yes, sir, Mr. Dan." Billy stepped over to the booth and said, "Ms. Jane, I would like to pay my entry fee."

"Okay, Billy." Jane filled out his entry and said, "As soon as we get everybody's entries, we will draw for your position numbers." Finally the fifth entry was in. Jane called out to the ones that entered in tomorrow's horse race. All five entries were there for the position drawing. Jane asked, "Who wants to make the first draw?"

One of the guys said, "Let Billy draw first." So Billy put his hand in the jar and pulled out number 3.

Billy said, "That's my lucky number."

The other four drew their numbers. Jane said, "Remember, everybody, you must be here thirty minutes early, at 9:30 a.m. The race time is 10:00 a.m. sharp."

The hunters stopped by the saloon again. They found a table and ordered their drinks. They were discussing tomorrow's horse race. Dan asked Billy, "Did you see where the second fastest horse drew in?"

"I don't know, Mr. Dan."

"Well, Billy, the horse Hog Wild drew the rail. Remember he won his race in fifty-five seconds, where Cricket won hers in fifty-four seconds—one second faster."

"Is that good, Mr. Dan?"

"Yes, it's good that Cricket won in a faster time. That's good. Hog Wild already has the rail, so he will try to hang on to the rail to keep you from getting in. Do you understand, Billy, what I'm sayin'?"

"Yes, Mr. Dan."

"When we get back to camp, we'll make our plans for tomorrow."

Back at camp, Dan told Billy, "What you need to remember is that there are going to be two horses inside of you. When the judge fires the shot to start the race, let Cricket break as hard as she possible can, and hopefully, she can outbreak the other two—enough to get to the rail. If you don't get to the rail, just stay out until you get to the straightaway, and then try to get to the rail. If you still can't get to the rail, just hope that Cricket has enough stamina and speed to outrun them on the straightaway. Now, if you do get the rail, just let her set her own pace, unless one of them or both are a challenge to you. Then when you head for the finish, you might have to use the whip, but only if you have to. Okay, Billy?"

"Yes, sir, Mr. Dan. I think Cricket and ol' Billy will bring home the bucks."

Just then Carl Sands came to their camp and shook everybody's hand. Then he said, "I want to give you half of the money from the pulling contest."

Dan said, "No, Carl, you won the contest."

"I know, but I feel like your boy was doing a great job of handling those mules, and probably would have won, hadn't the tug broke."

"No, Mr. Carl," said Billy. "After I got even with Noor, that was pay enough for me."

"You did get even with Noor?"

"He did indeed," said Dan.

Abby walked away so Billy could tell the story. Carl asked, "Do you mind me asking how you got even with Noor?" Billy told Carl what he did. Abby could hear all of them laughing. She knew that it was time to come back to camp. Carl laughed so hard they thought he would wet his pants and couldn't quit laughing. "Well, God bless you, Billy. I'm glad you got him, Billy."

Billy said, "Mr. Joe hit and knocked ol' Noor out at the saloon."

"Oh, when did that happen?" asked Carl.

"About two hours ago, Mr. Carl. He's probably still layin' on the saloon floor, 'cause when Mr. Joe hits, he hits really hard."

Carl patted Joe on the back and said, "Good for you, Joe." He said, "I'll be right back." He went to his wagon. "I brought your tug back that you so generously loaned me, plus I brought you another tug for the one that broke."

"You don't need to do that, Carl."

"Well, Dan, I just wanted to give you something for loaning me a tug and allowing me to beat Noor, and thanks for noticing that the tug was cut."

CHAPTER 13

It was Sunday morning, and the hunters were up and getting the chores done. Billy was getting a little nervous, knowing in just a couple of hours it would be race time again. Billy was giving the mules their feed and water. He noticed that one mule was favoring one hind leg. Billy hollered for Dan to come over. Dan came to see what was wrong. "What is it, Billy?"

"It's James, he's limping."

"Uh-oh, he must of pulled a muscle on that pull yesterday. Billy, get the ointment out of the big wagon." Billy ran to the big wagon and found the ointment. Joe noticed that Billy was rushing around and asked him what was wrong.

"We have a lame mule."

Joe went to see how lame the mule was. "How bad is he, Dan?"

"I don't think it's too bad, but we're going to put ointment on him several times today and in the morning before we pull out. We'll have to harness Buck and let him and the other mule pull the big wagon, and we'll tie James behind the wagon." Dan showed Billy where to rub the ointment on. And they hoped that he wouldn't be too bad to travel by morning. "I wonder what time it is," said Dan. "Billy needs to saddle Cricket and get ready for his race in a little bit."

Billy finished putting the ointment on James. He caught Cricket and saddled her, and they were ready for the race. Dan had the last-minute instructions for Billy.

Dan said, "Billy, when you break at the start, you should have no problem getting in front of the number 2 horse. Make sure you're clear, and don't bump either horse. I'm sure you know to get to the rail if possible. If you can't get to the rail on the first turn, try the backstretch. If you can't get out far enough to get to the rail, then take her around on the outside. Then just hope she has enough stamina to outrun the inside horse. If it's close, you may have to go for the whip."

At that time, the judge called for the horses to come to the judge's stand. Billy hopped on Cricket and headed for the track. All five horses were at the judge's stand. The judge said, "You may warm up your horses. I'll call when it's time to line up."

Billy did the same thing that Mr. Dan had told him. A slow gallop all the way around the track. Billy was thinking, *Mr. Dan said "a slow gallop." That's easier said than done.* Cricket was about to pull Billy's arms out of the sockets. The judge called for the horses to come to the starting line. The five men that are the headers each took a hold on the bridles and had them ready. The judge aimed the starting gun in the air and *boom!* They were off.

Cricket broke extremely hard. Billy could see he had enough distance to get all the way to the rail. He took Cricket in with no problem. Billy let Cricket set her own pace, which was a fast pace. Halfway down the stretch, Billy turned to see if there was any horse challenging him. Hog Wild moved over trying to pass on the outside. The crowd was yelling and hollering, "Come on, Billy! Keep'er goin, Billy!" They got to the second turn, and Billy had a three quarters of a length lead. When they were out of the turn, Billy could see Hog Wild making a run at them. Billy waited. Hog Wild was slowly gaining on Cricket.

Billy could hear Mr. Dan above the noise from the crowd. "Spank her, Billy! Spank her, Billy!"

Billy reached and whipped Cricket twice, and she gave her last bit of energy. Billy could see that Hog Wild wasn't gaining, but he couldn't take a chance. Billy could feel Cricket starting to ease, so he reached back and gave her one more whip. When they shot across the finish line, Cricket had won by a head. The crowd's cheer was almost deafening. Billy was so proud of Cricket. As he slowed her on the backstretch, there were tears running down Billy's cheeks. Billy rode back to the finish line. Billy tried to wipe away the tears, but there were too many. The crowd was applauding, and again Billy had so many hugs and handshakes and pats on his back. "Good boy, Billy," "You did it, Billy," "Good riding, Billy," etc., etc., etc. Dan, Joe,

Abby, and Sammi were waiting for the rest of the people that wanted to tell Billy how good a job he had done.

It was at least fifteen minutes before Billy had a chance to thank Dan, Joe, Abby, and Sammi. They couldn't get a chance to tell Billy what a good job he did. Joe took Cricket and was walking her to cool her down. The man that was riding Hog Wild came over and shook Billy's hand and said, "Congratulations. You're a very good rider, Billy, and Cricket is one tough mare."

Jane came over and said, "Congratulations, Billy, you have won $120."

"Wow!" said Billy, "I'm rich." Jane handed Billy the envelope.

"Ms. Abby, would you take the money so I don't lose it?"

"Sure, Billy, I'll take care of it."

Billy said to Abby, "I feel like a nut with all these people seeing me with tears in my eyes."

"Billy, those were happy tears. That shows you have a big loving heart. I'm going to tell you what. When you crossed the finish line first, I had happy tears in my eyes too, and I'm glad I did, because I knew the young man that just won that race was definitely going to be one of my best friends for the rest of my life. That's why I had to cry happy tears."

"You know, Ms. Abby, I feel better now. You always make me feel better when I'm sad. Thank you, Ms. Abby."

"Billy, you're a special boy. Do you know how much you're loved by everyone that knows you and the people that don't know you personally? Did you hear all the people around the racetrack cheering for you? You know, Billy, Dan told me all about your past and about your parents. You are a very tough boy. Dan told me about the people in Lariat, and how much they love you, and Billy, I want you to be my special friend from now on."

"I promise, Ms. Abby, I will be your special friend for the rest of my life."

"Thank you so much, Billy."

Back at camp, the hunters were planning to pull out tomorrow morning. They were getting the big wagon loaded. Dan, Joe, and Billy were checking James, the mule, to see if he would be ready to travel tomorrow. Dan thought he would be ready, but they would still keep rubbing the ointment on his sore muscles.

Monday morning, Dan and Joe harnessed the black team and hitched them to the small wagon to pick up the new icebox and ice. When they got to the icehouse, Bert saw them pull up in front. Bert came out and said, "I have your icebox in the ice freezer room, so you can start with it being ice-cold. Then I will put four blocks of ice in it. That should last possibly two weeks."

They carried the box out and slid it in the wagon. After they put the ice in the box, Dan said, "How much do we owe you, Bert?"

"You owe $5."

"What about the ice?"

Bert said, "The ice goes with the box."

"Well, Bert, you're being overly fair with us." They paid Bert and headed back to camp.

"You know, Joe, let's remember to use the water out of the barrel that will sit on top of the icebox. That way we can get in the icebox when we stop at night, and in the morning before we refill them."

"Sounds good, Dan." So they harnessed John and Buck. Everything else was loaded and ready, except the food.

Dan asked Abby, "Would you want to go with me to the general store to load the icebox?"

"Sure, Dan, let's go."

They hopped on the wagon and headed to the store and loaded the icebox with a large smoked ham, twenty pounds of bacon, a crate of eggs, milk, dozens of jars of canned vegetables, pancake mix, biscuit mix, etc., etc., etc. All the perishables went in the new icebox. The rest was loaded in the wagon. They had everything ready, except filling the barrels that were going to sit on the icebox. Dan drove back to the camp to fill the barrels and meet up with Joe and Billy. Finally, they were on the trail. Dan was on the big wagon; Billy was on the small wagon. Behind the big wagon was James and Claude. Behind the small wagon was Cricket and Abby's packhorse, Ralph. The hunters were on their way with the string of horses, mules, and wagons getting longer.

Joe said, "This is the first time I've been on a hunt with our very own icebox, and lots of food on ice."

Dan said, "It's a first time for me too."

Abby said, "This is a first time for me too."

Billy said, "This is the first time for me too." They all had a big laugh at Billy.

Later Abby rode up beside the big wagon that Dan was driving and asked, "How am I to keep track of my share of food and other costs?"

"Well, Abby, we'll figure out something. Don't worry about it."

"Well, Dan, I want to cover my part."

Dan asked Abby, "Did you notice from the back there how mule James is doin'?"

"He's doing all right. You can hardly notice him favoring it now."

It was a hot day, but the horses and mules were making good time. Having plenty of water made them more eager to pull the heavy loads. It was midafternoon, and Dan suggested they pull over by some trees to give the horses and mules a little rest and a drink of water. They all pulled in the shade where it was a little cooler. Abby stepped down and reached in for a bucket. When she pulled the tarp back, she could see a bunch of saddle scabbards with rifle butts sticking out, plus a bunch of holsters with revolvers sticking out, not to mention the bowie knives. Abby stepped back and said, "Oh lord, where did all these weapons come from?"

Joe answered, "There were nine dummies that thought they were tough enough to take on Billy, Dan, and I. They were wrong. So we sent all nine to the fiery hubs of hell. We decided they wouldn't need guns anymore."

While sitting in the shade, Joe told Abby the story about the Mennonite family's murder and about the water barrels for protection and the fight that lasted less than one minute.

Abby said, "That's remarkable. What a good idea! Water will stop a bullet immediately." Billy was far enough away, so he couldn't hear.

The story went on. "You know, Abby, when we are in battle, Dan and I always shot for the heart or a body shot. Billy shoots for the head, and you know, Abby, out of nine, four of the shots were in the head, meaning Billy took out four of the nine."

Abby asked, "So I can assume Billy is a sharpshooter?"

"Yes, Abby, Billy is definitely a sharpshooter."

"Does Billy ever feel bad when he has to take a life at his age?"

"No, Billy's explanation was they're not humans, they're maggots."

"You know, Joe, I would bet that Billy's going to be one tough bounty hunter when he grows up. With you and Dan teaching him, that will make him better yet."

Dan came back and asked, "Is everybody ready to get on the trail again? We might get a few miles before we stop for the night."

They hit the trail and were moving right along. The stock had a good drink and a little rest. They were ready to go some more. After they went a few more miles, Joe said, "Dan, we have a string of cottonwood trees coming up ahead. That means there's water."

"I think you're right, Joe. We can stop there tonight."

When they approached the cottonwoods, they could see a small creek with cool, clear water and a lot of green grass. They had used enough water from the icebox barrels, so with them being half full, Dan and Joe could unload them so they could get into the icebox. Everybody had their chores done. Abby was cooking supper. They took the three seats off the small wagon to sit on. Dan dragged out a sarsaparilla for Billy and a jug of whiskey. He pulled the cork out and handed it to Abby. She took a drink and passed it around and around and around.

Next morning, the hunters had everything taken care of. The barrels were loaded, and they dipped the water from the creek to refill them. All the horses and mules drank out of the creek before they were hitched up. Joe said, "Let's hitch Smoky today with mule John. Maybe you can put a shank on Smoky for a ways until he gets the feel of pushing against the collar."

"Let's do it, Joe." They had the rest harnessed and hitched. Now it was Smoky's turn. Dan was on Buck and had the shank dallied up. Joe was in the driver's seat. They started out easy to let Smoky feel the collar. They pulled out on the trail. After a couple miles, Dan said, "I think Smoky has been broke to drive."

CHAPTER 14

They were about halfway across Kansas, still moving north. Midafternoon, Billy saw what looked like a man walking down the trail. Billy hollered at Dan and asked if he'd seen that. Dan took out his telescope and checked. Billy was right. There was a man, not only walking but staggering and could hardly stand up. Dan said, "I'll ride ahead and see what is wrong." When Dan reached the man, he asked, "What's wrong?"

The man said, "I need water, I'm too weak and can't go much farther."

Dan said, "You sit right here, and I'll be right back with water." Dan kicked Buck and had him running as fast as he could run. Dan reached the wagon and grabbed a canteen and kicked Buck and went back just as fast. Dan said, "I have water for you," and he jumped down and slowly gave him a little at a time for a short time until he was out of danger. Dan said, "I think you will be all right now."

The man said, "I'm with a wagon train. The others are dying from thirst and hunger. The livestock are also dying. They can't go any farther."

Dan asked, "Where are they?"

"See my tracks? They are about a mile or so."

The rest of the hunters were getting close. Dan hollered at Joe and said for him to come quick. They had to get to the wagon train fast. Joe and Abby were ready to pull out now. Abby grabbed the rope off her packhorse, Ralph. He had four full canteens on him. She then grabbed four more out of the wagon and also hung them on the packsaddle. Abby asked Dan, "Where is the wagon train?"

Dan said, "The man said they are about a mile away. Just follow his tracks, Abby." Abby gave Sally a kick and was on her way. Dan told Billy, "Help this man get in the wagon, then head out with the mules. You got that, Billy?"

"Yes, sir, Mr. Dan, we'll be there as soon as possible."

Then Dan grabbed Claude and loaded all the canteens he could hang on the packsaddle, then kicked Buck and said, "Let's go, Buck, let's go." Dan was on his way.

Joe jumped down from the small wagon and helped the man into the wagon with Billy. Joe climbed back on his wagon and headed out as fast as the black team could run. Shortly after, Abby reached the wagon train. Her heart broke when she saw the people that were already dead. There were dead people and dead livestock all over the place. Abby took the canteens from the packhorse. The people that were still alive came to her, begging for water. All Abby could say was, "Don't drink too fast, it will make you sick." There were people too weak to get to Abby. Just then Dan got there. Dan started giving water to the extremely weak ones, giving them just a little at a time. Joe rolled in and started dipping water from the barrels and giving water to the horses and mules. Abby saw to it the ones that came to her were out of danger. She started going from wagon to wagon. Some had dead people in their wagons. Abby came across a little girl that was lying on the seat of her parents' wagon. She was about three or four years old. She was almost dead. Abby said, "Honey, I'm not going to let you die." Abby put a few drops of water at a time in her mouth until Abby knew she was out of danger from thirst. Now she needed food, as do all the other people that were still alive. Abby continued taking a few of the canteens and looking for more people that were still alive. She found several as she checked every wagon. Dan was working on a different part of the wagon train, trying to save the people that were still alive—but that was just a start. They now had the ones that were dying of starvation. Billy rolled in with more water from the barrels. Billy was already distributing food and started opening the jars of vegetables and cans of beans, beef jerky, and any food that they had stocked up when they left Cowtown. They had enough food to possibly keep the rest of them alive temporarily.

After Joe had used up all the water they had in the barrels in the small wagon, Dan asked Joe if he wanted to go for food and water. Dan and Joe were looking at the map that Dan had bought. It showed a town about five miles from where they left the trail. It appeared by the map that it was one mile back to the main trail and five miles into town. A total of about six miles. "Joe, load the wagon with all the food you can, and fill all the water barrels with water." Billy had given almost all the food they had. Dan asked Billy, "Do you want to take Cricket and both your rifles? And your little gun and the big gun, just in the case you can find larger animals like deer, antelope, or elk? You could use the little rifle for small game."

Billy buckled another scabbard on his saddle for the big gun. He strapped on the holster with the .45 in it. Billy was after food to keep these people alive. Billy said a prayer to God, asking God to help him find some food. Billy headed for the clumps of trees where he was more than apt to find larger game. Within an hour, Billy was getting worried that he might not find meat for the starving people. Billy decided to ask God for help again. "God, please help me, I need to find some food for these starving people." Billy was riding out of the trees into an open field when he saw a small herd of antelope. Billy backed Cricket into the trees and stepped down, tying Cricket to a tree. Then he pulled the big gun out and moved slow and quiet and got behind a large tree and steadied the big gun on a branch, and *boom!* The antelope fell to the ground. The rest of the herd ran away. Then they all stopped with their heads high. They were looking for what made that sound. Billy stayed behind the tree and let them quiet down. Then Billy peeked through just enough to see which one he was going for next. One was facing straight at Billy. Billy raised his big gun and *boom!* Another one dropped. The rest ran away far enough that Billy's gun couldn't reach them. Billy got on Cricket and rode to the first antelope he shot and put his rope around the horns and slowly dragged it all the way back to the wagon train.

Dan said, "Billy, you're a good boy. Did I hear two shots from that big gun?"

"Yes, sir, Mr. Dan, I need to go back for the other one."

"God bless you, Billy."

Dan and Abby had a hot fire going so the meat would cook quicker. The hungry people were standing, patiently waiting for some food. Abby had given the little girl some of the canned vegetables, and she was doing better. She was so close to death. Billy came back with the other antelope. Immediately Dan hung the second one up and dressed it out and cut it up. This was slowly going to get these people out of danger. Joe came in with the wagon loaded with food and water. There were three other wagons following with two guys on each wagon. They had come along to help. The extra men asked Dan, "What can we do to help?"

Dan said, "We need to start burying the dead people. We need to get rid of the dead horses and mules too. What should we do with the dead animals?" Dan asked Billy to get the mules unhitched from the wagon, but to leave the doubles trees hooked to the team. "We're going to drag the dead livestock away from here. They are starting to smell bad from their decaying flesh." Dan asked Joe if he would unhook the black team and also leave the double trees hooked to them too. Dan asked if one of the men would take the team and help Billy drag the dead animals far enough away so they didn't have to smell them. One of the men from town volunteered to take the team and help Billy drag the dead animals. Everything was looking good as for keeping the rest of the people alive. It was getting dark, and the hunters had to get the people fed now. Billy and the guy from town, whose name was John, were still dragging dead animals away. They were down to the last few. The rest of the men from town were digging graves and burying the people as soon as they possibly could.

Abby had the little girl and didn't quite know what to do with her. Abby talked to some of the other people about the little girl. One lady said that Milly's parents and a brother were dead. Abby asked, "Do you know of anybody that would be willing to take her?"

"I don't know at this time," answered the lady.

Abby took the little girl by the hand and went to Dan and asked, "What should I do with this little girl?" Dan asked Milly if she had any relatives on the train. Milly said no, she has none. Dan suggested that Abby takes care of her just for tonight. Then tomorrow they'll see what would come out of it. Dan, Joe, and Billy and the six men from town were digging graves and burying the people by lantern light. By early morning, they had all the dead buried.

After sunup, the people were willing to help. Even those who were weak from the ordeal were willing to pitch in. Dan asked for the people on the wagon train to come as they needed to have a quick meeting and make some plans. The people that were already up went from wagon to wagon, rousing the others, telling them they were to come to the meeting. While waiting for all of them to get there, Dan asked Abby and Billy if they would start making plans for food distribution. This would be for all the rest of the food that was left on the small wagon. Dan asked the people to get their food. He asked that they all eat, but to only eat small portions so that there would be enough for all of them. Abby had Milly and made sure she got her share. The women went first, then the men went to eat theirs. Surprisingly, all were careful to not take too much.

After they ate, Dan said, "I want some of you to give your opinions on what we should do now?" Not one of them had any opinions. They were all so frightened about what just had happened. "Can I make a suggestion?" asked Dan. They all said yes and raised their hands. Dan said, "We need to move all of you to town and move all the wagons and the livestock too." Dan asked Joe if there was a place next to town that had enough room for all the wagons.

Joe said, "There is plenty of room."

Dan asked, "How many of you have a team that is alive? Raise your hand if any of you do." Eight of them raised their hands. "How many of you have only one horse still alive?" There were nine hands that went into the air. "How many of you lost all of your livestock?" There were fourteen hands this time. "Okay, how many wagons are there left?"

One man said, "There are thirty wagons in all."

"So the eight of you that have teams, harness your horses and hitch your wagon to them. If any of you are too weak to harness your animals, just ask me or Joe, and we will help you. Now those of you who have only one horse, you should pair up with the others that have only one horse. I will use Buck for the one with the odd number. So we will then have a total of fifteen teams. We need to get started now. Those of you who have no livestock left, we will come back after you after we take the first fifteen teams to town. Our men will use their teams to get your wagons to town."

The man they came across on the trail came over and said his name was Bill, and he asked Dan if he could use his horse Buck to team up with his wagon. He then said he would take as many people as would fit into the wagon with him. Dan said, "Yes, you can. We will hook up in just a minute. Joe and I need to harness for the ones that are too weak to do their own." Dan asked Billy to help back their teams up to the wagons and hitch them up. Dan started to harness their horses, and when he had a team harnessed, he would holler for Billy. Billy was running his legs off, trying to keep up. Soon they had the fifteen wagons hitched and ready to roll. Dan told the ones that were ready, "I'll lead, and all of you will follow in a line." Dan was driving Bill's wagon with Bill's horse and Buck.

After they had all fifteen in line and following, Dan asked Bill what happened to the wagon train and how they got into that deadly mess. Bill said, "We had a guide to get us to California. About a hundred miles back, we ran into a man that told us about a shortcut that would save us several hundred miles. So our guide went ahead and checked to see if everything was true. When he returned, he thought it was all true. Everyone in the wagon train agreed to take the shortcut. So we kept on traveling on that shortcut trail. The trail wasn't very well traveled, but we thought that it not being a well-known trail was why the man had told us to use it for the shortcut. So we kept moving. After several days and no guide, we were running low on supplies. We all started to get worried. We were pushing our horses, trying hard to get to find any kind of a town along the trail—but that didn't happen. When we stopped here, we were out of everything. We ran out of food first, and we were getting very low on water too. I guess you know the rest.

"Well, Dan, we never seen that man again. We don't know whether he was killed or couldn't find his way back. He was working on a 25 percent pay. We gave him 25 percent to start, then after we had traveled one-fourth of the way, we paid him his second 25 percent. If we would have known that there was a town this close, we would have been all right. We were so lost we had no idea where we were. I lost my wife a couple days ago. What a loss. I'm still having trouble believing that it happened. She was a great woman, Dan."

"Bill, I'm so sorry. That is a big loss. What do you think is in your future, Bill?"

"I don't know, Dan. Everything in my head is spinning. I can't even think. It still seems like a bad dream."

Dan asked, "Is there anything I can do to help?"

"Dan, you, Joe, Billy, and Abby have saved a lot of people's lives, not to mention all the animals you saved."

Dan said, "I wish we could of been here a few days earlier."

The wagons started pulling into town. Dan stopped and motioned for the rest of the wagons to stop, and he would check with the marshal. Dan walked to the marshal's office. The marshal was coming out to meet them. Dan introduced himself and asked where he wanted the wagons to set down. There would be thirty-one wagons total. "Well, Dan, there is plenty room on the south side. They will be parked next to the livery barn." Dan thanked the marshal and returned to the wagons.

They started making a circle with the wagons. Joe and Billy unhitched the mules and the black team and were ready to go back to help the ones that had lost both of their horses. Billy was riding one mule and leading the other, same with the black team. Joe was riding one black mare and leading the other. Dan said, "I'll stay here and see if I can help these people and make sure they are okay."

There were several of the men from the wagon train that rode their teams and followed Joe and Billy to help bring the rest of the wagons to town. The men were weak from lack of food and water for a long period of time, but they were willing to help their friends move their wagons to town. Joe and Billy were hitching the teams to the wagons. Abby asked Billy if he would hitch the mules to the wagon that belonged to the parents of little Milly. Billy said, "Yes, Ms. Abby, I sure will." Abby tied her horses to the back of the wagon. Abby, Billy, little Milly, and Sammi hitched a ride with them. After all the teams were hitched to the wagons, Billy walked around all the wagons, asking if everyone had their goods loaded in their wagons. Everyone was loaded and was ready to head out for town. Billy said for everyone to fall in line and follow behind him. The last of the wagon train was on their way to town. Billy helped little Milly in the wagon. Abby was also on the wagon and ready to go.

Abby hadn't had time to talk to little Milly. Abby was having trouble knowing what to say to her. She wasn't sure how to handle this situation. The little girl had lost her parents and her brother. Thank God Billy started talking to little Milly. Billy asked, "How old are you, little Milly?" She held up three fingers. Billy said, "Oh, you're a big girl!"

"Ya, I'm a big girl."

Billy asked if she knew Sammi. She said, "No."

Billy told Sammi to come up and meet little Milly. Billy said, "Sammi, meet little Milly, and little Milly, meet Sammi."

Sammi licked little Milly's hand. Little Milly patted Sammi on the head.

Little Milly said, "You're a good dog, Sammi."

Abby had to turn her head. Abby was thinking, *What is going to happen to little Milly?*

The wagons were rolling in, and Billy held his hand up and asked them to wait until he checked with Mr. Dan. Billy found Dan and asked him, "Where do you want these wagons, Mr. Dan?"

"Start with the wagon you're pulling. Park it where the half circle ends and have the rest to follow suit. Show 'em where you want them."

All the people were getting everything stable. Food was a question as they almost ran the town out of food yesterday. Dan and Billy walked to the general store. They met the owner, Robert. Dan asked, "How much food do you have to help us in this drastic time?"

Robert said, "Ya, I know, Dan, there's not much left. I wasn't geared up for fifty to sixty people that were staving. Right after, Joe came in and almost ran me out of food. I'm so sorry that these people went through this horrible situation. After Joe left, I went to the telegraph office and wired a very large order. It's on its way now."

"Robert, do you have anything that they can make large amounts of soup with, or do you have any suggestions?"

"Let me get my wife, and we can maybe come up with something."

"Thank you, Robert. I'm sure that you will come up with something."

Dan, Joe, and Billy decided to slow down enough to step in the saloon and have a couple drinks and start making plans. Dan said, "Billy told me on the way into town this morning that the guy that was the overseer was one that died. He also said they had a guide that left one morning to scout for water and food. He never came back. I certainly feel sorry for these people 'cause they are like a bunch of sheep. They have no idea what they're going to do next."

They drank up and went back to the wagons. Abby asked Billy if he would take little Milly and walk around the wagons for a few minutes. "Sure, Ms. Abby." Billy took little Milly's hand and started walking her around. Billy was talking to her and showing her different things.

Abby asked Dan, "What are we going to do with little Milly?" Dan asked if there was anybody with the wagons that might take her.

"I asked a woman if she knew anybody that might give her a good home, and she said, 'I don't think there's anybody that can afford to take on another mouth to feed.' These people are out of food and practically out of money, and they are going to hit a hard, cold winter.

"I'm simply afraid to turn this baby over to these people. These people are lost and afraid. They don't know where they are going or what they're going to do when they get there."

"What do you suggest, Abby?"

"I really don't know, Dan. This is late in August. If they stay here, they are going to freeze or starve to death. If they leave and get to the mountains in the next couple weeks, they are going to hit the beginning of cold weather."

"You know, Abby, you're right. These people need some guidance. I don't know what to do, Abby."

"Dan, you and Joe need to help me think of something to do with that baby."

Dan said, "I need to meet with some of the men." Joe suggested that Dan start on one side of the wagons, and he'd start on the other side to get them together to have a meeting. "Okay, Joe, let's do it."

So they went wagon to wagon, asking all men and women to come out for a meeting. Within a few minutes, they all came out. Dan started with asking how many were moving on to California. Several held their hands up. "Okay, how many are turning back?" Almost all the women that had lost their husbands held up their hands. "Okay, ladies, what means do you have to turn back to your home state?" Some said they would get to a train station and travel back. "How many are going to do the same?" Nine held up their hands. "Okay, what are you going to do with your horses and wagons?"

One woman said, "I don't know what to do with 'em."

"How many horses do you have between the nine of you? How many with no horses left?" One lady held up her hand. "Okay, how many have one horse?" Four held up their hands. "I take it the other four have a team left."

"Yes," said one lady.

"So you have a total of twelve horses. How many of you are willing to sell your horses?" All nine held up their hands. "Okay, what you need to do is make a deal with some of the people who are movin' ahead and need horses. Who is willing and qualified to take over as manager?"

One man said, "I think Roger Mann should take over as manager."

Dan asked, "Which one is Roger Mann?"

One man raised his hand and said, "I'm Roger."

"Are you willing to take over as manager?"

"Yes, I am. We need to get on our way. We are going to run out of summer weather."

"That's correct," said Joe. "You need to get going soon."

Dan said, "I will print out a map of the trails, and this will guide you all the way to California." Dan pulled out his map and asked Billy to take it down to the newspaper office and have it copied. "This should help you stay on the right trails. I might add, do not take any shortcuts." "Amen," came from several of the people. He then asked them to get together and work it out as soon as possible. "You need to get on your own. I think Roger Mann will be a good leader for you." So they started talking and making a deal between themselves.

Dan looked around and saw Milly's little hand clinched to Abby's finger. Dan thought, *Uh-oh, I think little Milly has just found herself a new home.*

Everywhere Abby goes, little Milly is by her side, holding Abby's finger. After the meeting was over, Dan went to where Abby and little Milly were sitting. Dan smiled and asked Abby, "Did you find someone to take the little one?"

"No, Dan, I can't let this baby go with these people."

"Well, I guess she will have to go with us."

"Do you mean that, Dan?"

"Well, we can't just leave her here in the middle of nowhere, can we?"

"Thank you, Dan. We will try not to hold you up after we get on the road again."

"Don't worry about it," Dan said. "I can see you and Billy have already adopted little Milly. I have a hunch she will get to all of our hearts before too long."

Billy came back with a copy of the trail map. Dan asked Billy to take the copy of the trails over to Roger Mann. "He was over there in that wagon." Dan pointed at a wagon.

"Okay, Mr. Dan."

Joe came by and asked Dan, "Are we going to be able to leave in the morning?"

"I hope so, Joe," Dan said. "I guess I should clue you in to what is happening."

Joe cut in and said, "Looks like we're gaining another little hunter. We can't leave her out here in the middle of nowhere, can we now?"

"You're a good guy with a big heart, Joe."

"Thank you, Dan, and the same with you."

"Well, Joe, I think we deserve a drink."

"Yes, sir, Daniel, I think you're right."

Joe walked over to where Abby and little Milly were sitting. Joe asked Abby if she wanted to have a drink with them. Abby said, "I didn't think you were ever going to ask. The answer is yes."

So all the hunters headed down to the saloon for a drink, including little Milly. When they got there, Dan stepped in and asked the barkeep if Billy, Milly, and Sammi could come in.

"Aren't you folks the ones who helped out the wagon train people?"

"I guess we are," answered Dan.

"You bet they can come in."

"Thank you," said Dan.

They all ordered their drinks, including Billy and Milly. The barkeep set the drinks on the table. Dan went to hand him some money. The barkeep said, "Your money is no good in here."

When the barkeep walked away, Billy asked. "What did he mean when he said your money was no good?"

"Well, Billy, it means he is not charging us for the drinks. It's his way of saying thanks for helping those thirsting, starving people."

"We did save a lot of them, didn't we, Mr. Dan?"

"We did our best, Billy."

Billy took little Milly by the hand and said, "Come with me, Milly." They walked over to the bar, and Billy said, "Could I ask you, sir, what is you're name?"

"My name is Markus."

"Well, we want to thank you for the sarsaparilla."

Little Milly said, "Thank you, Mr. Markus, for the sarsaparilla."

"You are very welcome, and what are your names?"

"My name is Billy, Mr. Markus."

"My name is Milly, Mr. Markus," she said with a cute little smile.

"Well, those are nice names, and I like them a lot."

He was looking at Billy, so he asked, "Is she your little sister?"

"Yes, Mr. Markus, she's going to be my little sister from now on."

After the hunters finished with their drinks, here comes the barkeep with another round of drinks. He set them on the table. Dan tried to pay him again. The barkeep said, "I told you your money is no good in here." Of course, they all once again thanked him very much. They started to debate about taking the wagon that now belongs to little Milly. She was the only one left from that family.

Joe asked, "Did she end up with any of the horses?"

Abby answered, "No, both horses were dead." Abby asked if she could make a suggestion.

Dan said, "Go ahead, Abby."

"Why don't we try my two horses and see if either or both of them are broke? Then Milly and I can follow with her wagon. That way, Milly and I can have a little privacy. Her wagon is small, but it has a canvas top and a fold-down front and rear. That would give us the privacy we girls need. It also has a pot that we girls need. That would beat us having to go in a clump of trees. What do you think of that, Dan?"

"We can do that. We do have Billy's harness that we can use. Okay, Billy?"

"Yes, sir, Mr. Dan, we can sure do that."

"Okay," said Dan, "let me suggest something too. We have Claude, Susy, Ralph, Buck, Smoky, and Cricket. Let's give the black team to Abby and Milly on little Milly's wagon. I'll take Buck and Claude on the Mennonite wagon. I have a feeling that Claude is already broke to drive. Does everyone agree?"

"Sounds good, Dan." They all stuck their hands in the air.

Billy said, "Milly, put your hand up." So little Milly put her little hand up.

"That's unanimous," said Abby.

The hunters were leaving the saloon when the barkeep motioned for Abby to come up to the bar. Abby went over to the bar and asked, "What is it?"

"Can I ask you what Billy meant when he said Milly was going to be his little sister from now on?"

Abby explained how Milly's parents and brother died on the wagon train. "Even their horses died. So we are taking her from now on. She is our little girl Milly and Billy's little sister."

Markus said, "I can see she is going to have a good home and a special home."

"Thanks, Markus," Abby said.

"I also can see that you have a big heart, and you are very generous, and you have a special love for children."

"Thank you again, Markus." Abby returned to the rest of the hunters and told the rest what Markus had said. "He seemed to have a big heart."

Joe said, "That is exactly what I told him."

They went back to the wagons. Dan, Billy, and Sammi went to Roger Mann's wagon and asked Roger if they were getting things worked out so they could get on their way.

"Yes, Dan, we have the horses taken care of. Food is the problem now. The general store has virtually no food. Robert, the owner, came by awhile ago and said he and his wife were making large pans of soup for today."

"What did he come up with?" asked Dan.

"Robert said he had two sacks of potatoes and a sack of onions in his cellar. Potato soup is on the way."

Dan suggested they wait two more days. Robert said that he has a large order of food on its way. Robert buys milk, eggs, and cured hams from the farmers. So Robert and his wife would still have to help them for a couple days since the hunters were leaving tomorrow.

Chapter 15

Dan asked Billy if he would run down to the general store and ask Robert if he had a couple of cured hams, some milk, and some eggs.

"Sure, Mr. Dan. Can I take little Milly and Sammi with me?"

"I think it would be all right, but stop at the wagon and ask Abby if it's okay to take little Milly with you."

"Okay, Mr. Dan."

So Billy went to the wagon to ask Abby. She said, "Sure, Billy, but watch out for her."

Billy took little Milly by the hand and said to Sammi, "Let's go, girl."

Dan went back to the wagon. He wanted to ask Abby about little Milly. "Has she asked about her parents yet?"

"No, Dan, that's what scares me. I know sooner or later she's going to ask, and I don't know what the hell to tell her."

"It's not going to be easy, Abby."

"What does Milly have in the wagon besides her clothes?"

"I haven't had a chance to look under the seat."

So Dan and Abby pulled out all the things that were under the seat. They found extra clothes, a teddy bear, a little necklace Milly's size. Just then a lady came and said, "My name is Mabel, and I came to thank you folks for saving so many lives. You people were sent by God to help all of us that couldn't help ourselves. You will be rewarded with a special place in heaven."

"Well, thank you, Mabel. We did our best. We did the same as any other folks would do," said Abby.

"Abby, do you realize how professional you people are? From the time you got to us, within a very short period of time, you had all the people who were alive out of danger. You even saved the livestock. Thank you again so much, Abby." Mabel turned to leave.

Abby asked Mabel if she would tell them as much as she knew about Milly.

"I sure will. Better yet, Abby, I will go back to our wagon and put it on paper." Then Mabel said, "I know the Montana's had a family Bible. There may be some information in there. I will give you all that I know."

Dan said, "Let's see if we can find that Bible."

They continued digging through all the things under the seat, and sure enough, they found it. Just then Billy, Milly, and Sammi returned from the store. Abby put the Bible back. She thought, *This is not the time, with little Milly being here.*

Billy handed a note from Robert Ness. Dan opened it and read what Robert had written. "Dan, I can get all the eggs, milk, cured hams, bacon, and bread that you need. Mrs. Olson is baking bread now. In the morning, you can pick up any amount you need."

So Dan said, "Our icebox is empty although we do have plenty of ice. So we'll stock up in the morning."

An hour or so later, Mabel returned with all the information on little Milly. Abby asked Mabel, "Do you think there is anybody with the wagon train that could use the clothes that Milly's parents and brother have in the wagon?"

"Oh, I'm sure they can be of use. If you want, I can take them and give them to whomever they fit."

"Okay, Mabel, I'll put them in a sack and send Billy over with them. I don't want little Milly to see them at this time."

So when Billy and little Milly were walking around the wagon circle, Abby dug out all the clothes of Milly's parents and brother. Abby had them packed in a burlap sack. She then hollered for Billy to come and take the sack to Mabel's wagon. Robert Ness and his wife came with two large pans of potato soup. Robert asked if somebody could put the tailgate down to set the soup on. Everyone brought their bowls and spoons and were just happy they had something to eat. The hunters also had some soup. Everybody thanked the Ness family for caring for the people that needed help at this time. The hunters returned to their wagons. They were making plans for leaving tomorrow. They had to replenish their icebox. Dan, Joe, and Billy took turns pumping and filling the water barrels and the oat barrel. Abby was preparing a place for little Milly and herself to sleep in little Milly's wagon. Billy was feeding and watering the livestock. Dan and Joe were making plans for traveling and came up with some ideas. They were making some way to be assured that everyone of the hunters would be safe.

Later the hunters all got together by their wagons and had to get everybody's opinion. Said Dan, "I think in a emergency situation—such as if we are attacked whether they are renegades, outlaws, or whatever—we need to be ready for them. Seeing how we made it work with the water barrels, we can make it work again. Abby, you and little Milly's team will travel behind Billy and the mules. Then the Mennonite wagon will follow behind Abby and little Milly. If anyone should try to ambush us, I want Billy to stop immediately, and Abby, pull little Milly's wagon close beside Billy's wagon, but save room so we can get between the two wagons. Then, Abby, you put Milly on the floor of the wagon and tell her to stay there. Okay, Abby?"

"Yes, I understand, Dan."

"Then, either Joe or I will be on the Mennonite wagon. We will pull up on the other side of the little Milly wagon. Again, leave enough room between the wagons. If we are being attacked from the right, Joe or I will jump down and pull the horses sideways as far as we can without moving the wagon. Then whether it be Joe or I, we will pull the team Abby's driving as far as possible. Billy, you will drag the mules around. If they are coming in from the left, then everything will be in reverse. Now there will be protection for little Milly from both sides, as well as protection for the rest of us. Does anyone have anything to add for protection?"

Joe said, "I can't think of anything better than that."

Abby said, "It's better than anything I can think of."

Billy said, "Ya know, Mr. Dan, I was just sittin' here thinkin'. That will work perty slick."

The next morning—with the horses and mules watered, fed, harnessed, saddled; water barrels filled; oat barrel filled; and food in the icebox—the hunters were pulling out. The train added one more wagon and one more little hunter. As they started to pull out, all the people from the wagon train were applauding and yelling nice things.

One woman said, "You wonderful people have a nice trip and a nice forever. We love you and thank you from the bottom of our hearts."

One said, "Thank you for taking little Milly. We know she will have a wonderful home."

As they pulled out of town, the applauding continued. The hunters finally were out of earshot, but it was the people's way of letting them know how much they loved them for saving so many lives. The hunters were happy to know they did save that many lives, but they wished they could have come a couple of days earlier and saved them all. The hunters were on their way, and the lineup was like Dan said. Billy and the mules were on the lead. Abby and little Milly were next, and Joe was on the Mennonite wagon. Joe was driving Smoky and Claude and found that Claude was previously broke to drive. Little Milly's covered little wagon was like Abby said. It gave the girls a little privacy.

They traveled several miles when they decided to stop and give the animals a rest and a drink of water. Billy took little Milly's hand as they and Sammi explored around the area. Abby pulled the Montana's Bible out to see if there was some information of any kind in it. Abby found exactly what she was looking for. All about the family and their birth dates, the city and state where they lived before joining the wagon train. Little Milly was born August 2, 1885. Abby asked Dan to come and see. Dan went to the Milly wagon to see what Abby found. Abby showed Dan the Bible. Abby said, "Milly has just barely turned three years old. Her full name is Mildred Beverly Montana. Her brother was born in 1882. Her mother was born 1866, and her father was born 1861.

After a few minutes' rest, they were on the trail again. They were pushing hard, trying to make up for some of their setbacks. Later on that afternoon, as they were moving on, all of a sudden the mules stopped and started backing up. Billy hollered, "It's a rattlesnake!"

Joe told Billy to back up a little more. Billy did as Joe told him. Joe had his saddle in the back of the wagon. He stepped down and reached into his saddlebags, pulled out a gun and walked around in front of the mules, and pulled both triggers. *Boom! Boom!* The snake was blown to pieces.

Billy asked Joe, "What kinda gun is that, Mr. Joe?"

Joe said, "Billy, it's a snake killer. I call it my equalizer."

It kinda surprised Dan also. Dan asked, "Is that a shotgun?"

"Yes, it is, Dan. I cut it down from a double-barreled shotgun to a ten-inch handgun. I cut both barrels down to five inch and cut the stock off and, with a little carving, made it like the handle of a handgun."

Dan said, "I haven't seen you use that one before."

"I use it when I'm hunting alone, and if I'm goin' after more than one, I carry it. And you can't imagine how those two shells scatter." Joe pulled his knife and cut the rattles off the snake and then returned to his saddle and pulled to load more shells in the equalizer. He put the gun and rattles in his saddlebags.

Billy asked, "Mr. Joe, what do you do with the rattles?"

"I save 'em. I have hundreds of 'em."

Joe was back on the wagon, and everybody was moving again. They did cover lots of miles that day. About dusk, they stopped for the day. After Abby sliced and cooked some ham, Billy brought a loaf of bread from the wagon. They all had ham sandwiches for supper, including Sammi. Billy told Abby, "That was a very good sandwich, Ms. Abby."

"Well, thank you, Billy."

Little Milly said, "This sandwich is good, Ms. Abby."

"Well, thank you, little Milly. I'm glad you liked it."

The hunters were sitting back away from the fire because the weather was still hot. Sammi was by Billy and had a low growl. They all knew there was something out there. Billy kept watching out into the dark night. Joe was watching Billy. Joe asked, "What do you see, Billy?"

"Well, Mr. Joe, there is something out there. Can you see their eyes shining?"

Joe said, "You're right, Billy, there is something out there. It's probably coyotes or wolves. We better keep an eye on Sammi. If they get her, they'll kill her."

"Should I shoot them, Mr. Joe?"

"Maybe, Billy."

Billy grabbed his big rifle, leaned over the wagon box, and *boom!* You could hear the predator yelp. Billy said, "I blew his lights out, huh, Mr. Joe?"

"Yes, you did, Billy."

The rest of the predators ran away. As the hunters were discussing the rest of the trip, Dan said, "We need to keep moving. We need to get there as soon as possible. If we don't, we could run into some cold weather. Of course, we don't know how long it will take to bring the gang down."

About that time, Billy noticed the shining eyes again. Billy grabbed the gun and leaned over the wagon box again and *boom!* Another yelp. The rest ran away but stopped and watched. They seemed to be getting braver. Billy aimed and *boom!* Another yelp.

"Dan, what do you make of this?" asked Joe.

"I'm not sure," answered Dan. "Normally, they don't get hungry this early in the year. After the snow gets deep and they start running in packs and sometimes they'll attack large animals. My thought is they may be in the early stages of rabies and could get dangerous enough to attack."

Joe said, "There is still several of them out there, and they are hungry or rabid. They would have left after the first shot." Joe told Billy, "Every time you see shining eyes, shoot 'em. I think they smelled that ham cooking,"

Ever so often, we could here *boom!* and then a yelp. Dan said, "They're committing suicide as long as Billy has the big gun."

The hunters were concerned because of their unusual habit and their behavior. Billy was thinning them out. As soon as Billy could see their shining eyes, *boom!*

Joe said, "There is more to this than meets the eye."

Dan told Abby, "You and Milly stay close to the wagon and, if they start coming in close, get in the wagon and pull the front and rear flaps and buckle them down."

Joe said, "We don't dare let the fire go out. The glow from the fire is what makes their eyes shine." Joe reached in his saddlebags and pulled out his equalizer and a handful of shells. He also pulled out his hunting knife.

Dan asked, "What are you going to do, Joe?"

"I'm going to find some firewood. I'll be right back."

Billy said, "Mr. Joe, there are some tree limbs on the other side of the Milly wagon."

"Thanks, Billy." After Joe got away from the fire, he could see plainer and could make out the silhouette of the predators. Joe wasn't sure how many there were as they mingled among each other. Joe put his knife back in the sheath and held the barrels with one hand and the butt and triggers with the other hand. He held it to his hip and *boom! Boom!* There were several yelps. Joe reloaded the equalizer and kept an eye on them. He could see there were some of them kicking their last. Joe continued watching for any movement other than those that were dying. After a few minutes, Joe returned to the camp, dragging some dead tree limbs.

Billy asked, "Mr. Joe, did you kill the rest of 'em?"

"I think we got most of 'em, Billy." Joe and the equalizer seemed to have taken care of the problem, but Billy wasn't quite convinced that Mr. Joe had killed them all. So Billy slept with his .45 on his one hip and his big knife on the other and the big gun by his one side. Sammi was on the other side.

The next morning, while they were hustling around to get on the trail as soon as possible, Billy said, "There's dead coyotes all over the place."

Joe walked through the coyotes and found one with foamy slobbers all around his mouth. That one had rabies, and it was covered with ticks. Joe said, "We are lucky that one of us or any of the livestock or Sammi didn't get attacked."

Dan said, "We need to watch out for more of the coyotes with rabies. There could be more infected. When they get to a certain stage, they are extremely dangerous. They could jump in our wagons and attack any one of us or one of the animals. So keep an eye out at all times."

Abby called Dan to one side and said, "It finally happened, Dan."

"Uh-oh," said Dan. "Little Milly must of asked about her mom and dad?"

"Yes, she did."

"What did you tell her?" asked Dan.

"The same old story. God needed them to do some special work for him."

"But did you tell her that they are not coming back?"

"I guess, in so many words, no. I'm a coward when it comes to seeing a baby like that cry. I'll go out there with the meanest, toughest outlaws, and I am not afraid for a second. But if that baby starts crying because she knows her parents and brother will not be coming back, my heart would be ripped from my chest. Dan, I don't know what to do. Please tell me, Dan."

"Well, Abby, let's leave it alone for now until we can come up with a better solution."

"Okay, Dan, but keep working on it."

"Will do, Abby."

The hunters pulled out and were on the trail again. Billy hollered at Mr. Joe and said, "We shot the hell out of those ol' coyotes last night, huh, Mr. Joe?"

"Yes, we did, Billy."

"That ol' equalizer of yours takes 'em out a half dozen at a time, huh, Mr. Joe?"

"It does that, Billy."

Dan was looking at the map and said, "We'll be coming to the Saline River some time today. We better hope the river's not too deep to cross."

Abby was busy trying to think what to say to little Milly about her parents and brother. Abby was thinking, *God, I need your help. Usually, God, I can take care of most of my troubles myself. But, God, this time I need your help.*

At that same time, Dan was thinking about little Milly and what they would have to tell her. *Abby loves that little girl, and I'm sure she will keep her and raise her, but this predicament is more than Abby can handle.* Dan then looked up in the sky and asked God to help them through this one. That afternoon, they did come to the river. They followed it around the edge until they came to a wider, shallower place to cross. Dan said, "The rest of you wait here, and Buck and I will test the depth." Dan told Buck, "Let's go." So they started across, and in the middle of the river, it was about to Buck's chest. Then it started getting shallower, so it was passable. Dan asked Joe to cross first with the Mennonite wagon.

"Sure, Dan, I'll go first." Dan snapped the lead shank to Claude's bridle, and he kept beside the team as they slowly crossed the river.

When they reached the riverbank, Dan and Buck went back across to get little Milly. He put little Milly behind him on Buck. In the middle of the river, little Milly laughed and said, "Look, Mr. Dan, Sammi is swimming along beside us."

Dan said, "Sammi is a pretty good swimmer."

"Ya," said little Milly.

They continued to cross, leaving little Milly with Joe. Dan went back after Billy and the mules. Dan snapped the shank on John the mule's bridle, and they slowly crossed. He then crossed back to get Abby and the Milly wagon. Dan asked Abby, "Do you swim?"

"Don't worry about me. Yes, I swim."

After they were all safe across the river, there was still a lot of daylight, so they decided to try and make it to a little town named Norton. The hunters were on the trail again. Late that day, they rolled into Norton, and everybody was tired and ready to stop for the night. "We covered more distance today than any other day on the trail," said Dan. On the very edge of town, they made camp, and Billy fed and watered the animals. Joe asked if they should just eat at the café across the street rather than lighting a fire and cooking. Dan said, "I was thinking the same thing."

After they had their supper and left the café, Joe said, "I'll stop at the saloon and buy a couple bottles of whiskey. We are running low."

So the rest went back to the camp, and Joe stepped in the saloon and asked the barkeep for two of the large bottles of whiskey and a dozen bottles of sarsaparilla. There were some drunks sitting at a table. One of them said to Joe, "You don't look like you can drink that much sarsparilla in one night."

"You're right, I'm not man enough to drink all those." Joe paid for the whiskey and the sarsaparilla.

As he was going out the door, the drunk said, "Who's the whiskey for? The dame that you had supper with?"

"Ya, it's for her," answered Joe. Joe just wanted to get out of there. One thing he didn't need was to fight a drunk tonight.

But the drunk said, "Is that how much she charges? Two bottles of whiskey?"

Joe sat the sack on the table and walked over to the table where the four drunks were sitting. He put his hands on the table and said, "You drunken bastards are sitting here, making fun of a lady that has more class than any one of you assholes has ever seen. Now which one wants to go first?"

One of the drunks stood up and said, "How about me?"

As usual, Joe knocked his hat off and grabbed his hair and—with one terrifying, powerful uppercut blow—blood flew everywhere. Only a few men have lived through Joe's powerful uppercut. Joe walked back to the drunks. He put his hand on the table and said, "Who wants to go next?"

All three drunks decided they would rather sit this one out.

One drunk said, "Big man, can I buy you a drink?"

"No, thanks," said Joe. "I have enough of my own. I do have a job for you though."

"What do you want us to do?"

Joe said, "I want you to drag the one on the floor out back in the alley. If he is still there in the morning, bury him."

"Yes, sir, will do."

Joe stayed long enough to make sure they did what they were told. Joe made it back to the camp.

Dan asked Joe, "Did you run into a problem?"

"Nothing I couldn't handle."

"The splatters of blood on your shirt, I hope it's not yours."

"No," said Joe.

Billy came up and asked, "Why do you think those three guys were draggin' another guy back in the alley?"

Joe looked at Dan and grinned.

The next morning, after breakfast, they had all the animals fed, dressed, and hitched to the wagons. They pulled out to the other side of town where the general store was to replenish the icebox. Dan and Abby went in to shop for groceries and bought enough to last a week or more. Who knows what they might run across next? Dan introduced himself to the proprietor then asked him what his name was.

"My name is William."

Dan asked William if he knew where they could buy ice.

He asked Dan, "Which direction are you headed?"

"We are headed north."

William said, "There is a town called Arapaho after you enter Nebraska. It's about twenty miles. When you get there, go through town, and it's the last building on the right. John is the owner. How much ice do you need?"

"About four blocks," said Dan.

"You are just traveling through?"

"Yes," answered Dan.

"Could I ask you why you need that much ice?"

"It's for our icebox."

"Where do you have an icebox?" Dan pointed out the window at the Mennonite wagon. "Would you mind if I take a look at it?"

Dan said, "Sure, come with me, and I'll show you." They walked out to the wagon. Dan took the two barrels out so he could open the box.

William asked, "Where did you get this icebox?"

Dan said, "We bought it from a icehouse just out of Dodge City, where they have a county fair and horse races. The owner's name is Bert. I don't think I heard his last name."

"How far is it to his place?"

"About one hundred and fifty miles. Give or take a little."

Abby came out and said she had the groceries bought. Dan hollered at Billy and Joe to carry the groceries out to the wagons. Next stop, Arapaho, Nebraska, at the icehouse. The hunters were rolling again.

Midafternoon, they rolled into town and were looking for the icehouse. It was easy to find, and they did get four blocks of ice.

Dan said, "I think we can make several miles more."

Abby and little Milly took on a hitchhiker named Sammi. Milly likes Sammi to ride with them. Milly and Sammi became good and close friends, and Sammi will certainly watch out for Milly. They traveled fast and hard for the next three days.

They finally rolled into Broken Bow, Nebraska. This was where Abby's uncle left her a farm and everything that goes with it, including a bank account.

Dan said, "We'll stop here overnight. The stock needs rest. We've been pushing them hard, and we don't want to break 'em down." Dan said, "I guess we leave you here, Abby."

"Dan, I've been thinking. Can you wait until I talk to the lawyer that's handling the will?"

Dan said, "Sure, we can wait."

So Abby pulled out the letter from the lawyer. They were thinking what to do next. A man was walking by. Abby asked if he knew a lawyer by the name of Albert Manson. She showed him the address on the envelope.

"Sure, he's straight down the way you're going. About six blocks. His office is on the right."

"Thank you very much."

Dan spoke up and asked the man if he could tell them where would be a good place to camp tonight.

"Sure, if you go past the lawyer's to the edge of town, there is the rodeo grounds. There are water pumps and plenty grass for your horses and mules."

Dan thanked him, and they pulled down to the lawyer's office. They pulled up and stopped so Abby could see Albert Manson.

Abby asked Dan if he would go in with her.

"Well, Abby, I can if you want me to."

"I would," said Abby. Abby asked Billy and Joe to watch little Milly.

They said they would watch her.

Abby and Dan went in to see the lawyer about the inheritance. They were greeted by a very overweight man.

Abby said, "My name is Abigail Lacy. Just call me Abby. This is a very good friend of mine, Dan Colt."

"I'm pleased to meet you. My name is Albert Manson. Just call me Albert. I assume, Ms. Lacy, that you are here about your uncle's inheritance?"

"Yes, sir, I am," said Abby.

"Okay, Ms. Lacy, you two have a chair, and I'll be right back." Albert went to a cabinet and pulled out a handful of papers and returned to his desk. "I need to ask you, Ms. Lacy, if you want me to give you figures in front of Mr. Colt?"

"Yes, I do."

"I thought that, but I have to ask. Your uncle has left you a large ranch with some livestock."

Abby asked, "Are you saying there is livestock on the ranch now?"

"Some. There are several hundred head of cattle, and probably thirty or more horses.

"Who is taking care of the stock?" asked Abby.

"The rancher next to your uncle's place. I guess I should say your place. He has been overseeing them for now. His name is Frank Adams. Can I ask you what your intentions are to do with the ranch?" asked Albert.

"I really don't know just yet."

Albert said, "Why I ask is, Mr. Adams would possibly like to purchase all the assets from you at a reasonable price. Now there is the ranch, cattle, horses, and the machinery."

Abby asked, "How honest of a man is Mr. Adams?"

"Very honest. He would never cheat you out of a penny."

"I need to think about it overnight. Tomorrow I will give you some kinda answer."

"Okay, Ms. Lacy, that will be fine."

"Albert, I thank you, and I will be in to see you tomorrow." Dan and Abby left.

"Abby, are you sure you want to give an answer this soon?"

"I need to ask you a question, Dan, but first let's go to the fairgrounds and set up camp and then get settled in."

After they got unhitched and all the chores taken care of, Joe and Billy took the seats off the Mennonite wagon for a place for them to sit. Abby had a question and couldn't wait to ask it. Abby asked Dan, Joe, and Billy to help her make a decision.

Dan asked, "What is your question, Abby?"

"I would like to continue to travel with you guys on the big hunt, and help take those rats in. I don't want any of the rewards. All I want is to go and help. You guys have been so special to me. Of course, I will have to take little Milly along."

Joe asked, "What about your inheritance?"

"Well, Joe, there is a neighbor rancher that is willing to buy everything, and I'm probably going to take the offer. I'm going to meet with the lawyer in the morning. I know you guys need to keep on moving on before the winter sets in, but I can catch up with you."

"So you would really like to go with us?" asked Dan.

"Yes, Dan, I really would."

Billy said, "Mr. Dan and Mr. Joe, I think we need her for two reasons. Number one, she's good with her guns, and number two, she's a good cook." They all had to laugh at Billy.

So Dan asked Abby, "Would you like to ride out to the ranch tomorrow and see what it's all about? We can saddle up in the morning and go there after you talk with the lawyer. We can shut down tomorrow and let the stock take it easy for the day."

"Are you sure about shutting down for a day?" asked Abby.

"Why not?" said Dan. "We'll get to the rats' nest when we get there."

"Thank you, guys, you are such special people."

Dan said, "You are a special lady, and little Milly is a special little girl. I know I wasn't looking forward to saying good-bye to you and little Milly, and I know Joe, Billy, and Sammi feel the same way."

Abby smiled and said, "Thanks."

Dan said, "I think this calls for a drink."

Billy jumped up and said, "I'll get 'em." Billy went to the Mennonite wagon and got two sarsaparillas from the icebox, one for him and one for little Milly. Then he brought the big jug for the rest of the hunters.

CHAPTER 16

The next morning after breakfast, Abby asked Dan if he would be ready to ride out to the ranch with her. But first they had to stop by the lawyer's office on their way.

Dan said, "I'm ready." Dan asked Joe and Billy if they would watch out for little Milly.

They both answered, "Sure, we'll take care of her."

Abby and Dan headed out, stopping by the lawyer's office. They stepped in, and Albert asked them to have a seat. "What can I do for you this morning?"

Abby asked about the bank account her uncle left.

"Yes, I have your last month's statement here." He pulled the statement out of his desk drawer and laid it in front of her.

Abby's eyes about popped out of her head. The statement read $86,000, plus some. "So Uncle John was quite wealthy?"

"Yes, he was wealthy. Now you are wealthy."

Abby looked at Dan and said, "This is quite a shock."

Dan said, "I'm happy for you, Abby, you're set for the rest of your life."

Albert asked Abby if she had a few minutes. He said, "I will walk across the street and have the bank make a bank draft from your account."

"No, Albert, I don't want it until we return back through here, and we have no idea when that will be."

"Well, okay, Abby, I will leave it in the bank until you come back."

Abby asked, "How far is it to the ranch from here?"

"It's about seven miles, and there is only one trail that will take you out there. Just take a right turn at the next street and that will take you out to the Frank Adams's farm. You will see a sign that says Adams Cattle Company. That will be his ranch. Frank will be able to tell you all about your uncle's place. Frank will tell you the truth about everything that is on the ranch and all your belongings."

"Thank you, Mr. Manson. We will ride out and talk with Mr. Adams, then we will get with you."

Abby and Dan headed out to the Adams's ranch. When they reached the ranch, they could see several hired hands. That told them that Mr. Adams had a large place, and they could see lots of cattle. One of the men asked if he could help them.

"Yes, I would like to speak to Mr. Adams."

"I will get him for you."

Frank came out of the house and asked, "What can I do for you?"

Abby said, "My name is Abigail Lacy. Just call me Abby, and this is my friend, Dan Colt. We are here to see if you can give us some idea what all goes with the ranch."

"Well, Abby, I can't tell you offhand, but the place has several hundred heads of cattle, several horses, and lots of ranch and farm equipment. I didn't do an inventory yet. I wanted to know if you were willing to sell all or part."

Abby asked Frank, "Are you sure you want to buy all of it?"

"Yes," said Frank, "if the price is right, but I don't know what it's worth."

"Mr. Manson said you are very honest, so if you want to take an inventory, we can work from that."

"Abby, how long will you be here?"

"We are pulling out tomorrow, and we don't know when we'll be back. Hopefully soon."

"If it's all right, Abby, I'll take an inventory on everything and the ranch. Then when you come back, we can have all the figures at Albert Manson's office."

"Thank you, Frank. We'll see you when we get back."

Abby and Dan headed back to camp. On the way, they stopped at Manson's office to let him know what the plans were. Then back at the camp, they started making plans on the route they would be taking tomorrow. Dan got out the map. He and Joe were discussing the trail heading northeast to a town called Burwell, Nebraska, then continuing northeast to a town called O'Neill, and then straight north to a town called Spencer. There they would be in the vicinity of the rat's nest. Dan and Joe agreed on that trail.

"Okay, we are headed out early in the morning."

"I'll have a drink on that," said Joe. They dug out two sarsaparillas, and the big jug was passed around a few times.

Abby asked little Milly if Joe and Billy took good care of her.

Little Milly said, "Ya, they were good to me. We walked all over town and saw lots of people and lots of stores, and Mr. Joe bought some candy for Billy and me."

Abby said, "Well, that was very nice of Mr. Joe. Did you say thanks to Mr. Joe?"

"Ya, me and Billy both said thank you to Mr. Joe."

The next morning, the hunters were moving around, trying to get on the trail and cover some ground. Dan hollered at Billy to get the mules moving.

Billy said, "Ol' Billy and these ol' mules are on our way, Mr. Dan."

Then Abby and little Milly fell in line. Little Milly said, "Ms. Abby and little ol' Milly are on our way too, Mr. Dan."

About noon, there was a little headwind that started coming up when they started dropping into a canyon. Joe was riding Smoky, ahead of the rest of the hunters. He saw a sign. He turned around and rode back to Dan's wagon and told Dan about the sign that said, "You are entering Windy Canyon. Be cautious for the next eight miles. Watch for severe dust storms." But they continued on. About an hour into the dust-blowing area, the winds continued getting stronger. They could see the dust storm coming. Dan hollered at Joe. Joe turned and rode back to Dan's wagon. Dan said, "Ride up and tell Billy what to do. We can't go any farther. We can't see." Joe rode up to Billy's wagon and told Billy to turn the wagon sideways and unhitch the mules and tie them with their butts to the wind. Joe told Abby to pull her wagon beside Billy's. Then Dan pulled his wagon directly behind the other two, and that created a pocket. Dan hollered at Abby to pull down both flaps and buckle them tight. "You and little Milly stay inside." Joe and Billy were unhitching the mules and horses with their butts to the wind. Dan told Joe, "It's going to be a nasty storm." By the time they had the stock taken care of, Dan pulled the tarp out of the big wagon, and the three of them fastened it to the wagon wheels and sat the three seats from the Mennonite wagon up against the tarp. They pulled the top of the tarp over their heads. That protected them from most of the dust. Dan hollered and asked Abby, "Are you girls okay in there?"

"Yes, we are fine. We're covered with blankets."

Little Milly said, "Ya, we've got blankets."

The storm blew all night. By early morning, the winds died down, so they could make the north rim before the winds came up again. The men hunters were harnessing, saddling, hitching and were on the trail. Dan told Billy to get the mules moving out. Billy had them moving as fast as they could go without breaking into a gallop. After the dust settled, they could see the north rim. Dan guessed it was about two hours away. After a couple hours of pushing hard to get out of the canyon, they were about there. The wind was coming up, but wasn't hard enough to raise the dust just yet. When they pulled out of the canyon on the north rim, they stopped to feed the animals. They hadn't had their oats yet. The hunters just wanted to get the hell out of that dusty canyon. So while the stock was eating and the men unhitched the stock and let them graze for an hour or so, Abby cooked the breakfast. They needed to get some roughage in them before moving on. All the men hunters agreed to get to the middle-loop river so they could clean up and get rid of some dust. After the animals grazed awhile, the men dressed and hitched up again. They were on their way. In less than an hour, they reached the river. Abby and little Milly continued on for about a quarter of a mile or so, while the men hunters stopped, shucked down, and dived in with a bar of lye soap and scrubbed up. They were on their last change of clothes, so that meant they needed to get to a laundry. When they caught up with the girls, Abby asked, "Did you guys get cleaned up?"

Little Milly said, "Ya, did you guys get cleaned up?"

"Yep," said Joe, "we feel better."

"Yep, me too," said Billy.

"Yep," said Dan.

They were going to try to get to Burwell before dark. They were moving out and making a good time. About an hour away from Burwell, according to the map, the three doe deer all of a sudden came running and jumping as fast as they could possible run. Dan said, "There's something in those trees that scared the hell out of those three does."

Joe was riding Smoky. He said, "I'll ride over there and see what's in those trees." Joe rode to where there was an opening. There were two mountain lions ripping a deer apart. Obviously, they got the fourth one. They were hungry. Even when they saw Joe, they continued viciously ripping, and tearing, at the deer. Joe stepped down, pulling his rifle from the scabbard, carefully aimed, and *boom!* One cat went rolling. The other cat jumped back in the trees. Joe decided to let the other one go, seeing as how he had the rest of the deer to eat. That should keep him from stocking them. An hour later, they rolled into Burwell's main street, looking for the rodeo grounds. Burwell has the largest rodeo in Nebraska. Abby noticed the sign on the front of the hotel, saying, Haircuts, Shaves, and Baths. Abby told the men hunters, as soon as they got the horses and mules put away, that she and little Milly were going back to the hotel to have a hot bath. They found the rodeo grounds, and they undressed the mules and horses and turned them loose so they could graze. Abby saddled Sally, and she and little Milly headed to the hotel to have a hot bath. Abby tied Sally to the hitching rail. They went in and asked the lady behind the desk about a bath. The lady pointed at a sign on the wall and said, "Cold bath, twenty-five cents; hot bath, thirty-five cents; haircuts, twenty-five cents; shaves, twenty-five cents."

"Well," Abby grinned and said, "I think we can get by with just the hot bath."

The lady hollered at her husband, who obviously was hard of hearing by the volume of her voice, to take two buckets of hot water from the stove to the bathtub. The girls had their hot baths and clean clothes. They rode back to camp.

Billy said, "You girls smell good."

Abby said, "Well, Billy, girls are supposed to smell good."

Little Milly said, "Ya, us girls are supposed to smell good because we put on some perfume."

Billy was wearing his .45 revolver on one hip and his big knife on the other. Some young man in his late teens or early twenties and about a hundred pounds overweight, who was obvious the town bully, was walking past the rodeo grounds and started making fun of Billy. He said to Billy, "Why are you wearing that big knife and gun? You're just a twerp. I bet you can't even shoot that gun."

Billy said, "Don't you ever call me a twerp."

The fat kid said, "You are a twerp."

Billy unbuckled his gun and knife and handed them to Joe. Billy took off running as fast as he could run.

Joe said, "We better step in, that other kid is twice the size of Billy."

Dan said, "No, Billy wants to be a bounty hunter. He needs to learn when trouble comes your way, you have to know how to get back out of it."

As soon as the fat kid saw Billy coming after him, he took off running to get away from Billy. At that time, Billy caught him and jumped up and grabbed his hair, pulled his head down and hit him as hard as he could with an uppercut that knocked the fat kid to the ground. He was bleeding from his nose. The bully was crying and was begging Billy not to hit him anymore. Billy asked, "Do you want to call me a twerp again, you fat bastard?"

Dan laughed and said, "I think Billy likes your style of fighting, Joe."

Joe said, "It's been successful for me, and it looks like it was successful for Billy."

When Abby came back, she noticed Billy had blood on his shirt. "Did you get hurt, Billy?"

"No, Ms. Abby."

Dan could see that Billy wasn't going to tell what happened. So Dan asked Billy if he would walk down the street to the blacksmith shop and ask the blacksmith if he could shoe nine head of horses and mules. Billy and Sammi headed down to the blacksmith. Dan was going to go to the blacksmith himself, but now he would tell Abby about Billy and the fat kid. When he told Abby the story, she laughed and said, "Good for Billy, he's learning. He's going to make a good hunter."

When Billy returned, he told Dan that, yes, the blacksmith could shoe four yet today, and the other five in the morning.

Dan said, "Billy, can you handle the mules and the black mares? Take them over so the blacksmith can get started."

"Yes, sir, Mr. Dan." Billy was on his way to the horseshoer.

Joe stood up and said, "I don't know about the rest of you, but I'm going to have a drink."

Abby said, "Well, don't leave me out."

"Don't leave me out, Mr. Joe," said little Milly.

"No, I won't leave you girls out."

"Can you get in the icebox, Milly?"

"Ya, Mr. Joe."

Joe asked Milly to get two sarsaparillas, one for her and one for Billy. While little Milly was getting the sarsaparillas, Joe asked Abby if she noticed little Milly had learned from Billy saying "Mr. Dan," "Mr. Joe," and "Ms. Abby."

"Yes, Joe, I noticed. Well, they are being polite. There's nothing wrong with that. But did you noticed Billy has us calling Milly, little Milly?"

"Yes, I did," said Joe. "Who says you can't learn from a kid?"

Just then, little Milly came back with the sarsaparillas. She said, "One for me and one for Billy."

Abby said, "You are a good girl, little Milly."

Then Joe dug out a jug that is a little stronger then the sarsaparillas, and everyone had some drinks. Later Robert, the horseshoer, brought the mules and the black team back and said to bring the others in the morning. Dan asked Robert if there was an icehouse in Burwell. "We need to buy some ice before leaving in the morning."

"Yes, Dave the slave driver has all kinds of ice. He has a big underground ice cellar."

"Could I ask you why they call him Dave the slave driver?"

"Well, Dan, it's kind of a joke around here. Dave cuts ice all winter long out at the reservoir. When it gets frozen a foot thick, he hires a couple of big kids to help him cut and haul blocks of ice to fill his ice cellar. Dave pays fifty cents a day. What Dave calls a day is from sun-up until dark, so he came by the name honest."

"Sounds like it," said Dan.

"Okay, Robert, we'll bring the rest of the horses in the morning."

"Thank you, Dan." Dan handed the lead ropes to Billy. Dan said, "Here, Billy, turn these four loose so they can get their bellies full."

The next morning, Dan and Billy led the other five horses to the blacksmith shop. Abby was fixing breakfast, and Joe was harnessing the black team. As soon as they had breakfast, he would hitch them to the Mennonite wagon with the icebox. They'd go pick up the ice while waiting for the rest of the horses to be shod. Abby and little Milly walked downtown and found a clothing store. Abby bought herself and little Milly some new clothes and little Milly some new shoes as hers were getting too small. Dan and Billy got back from the blacksmith shop and loaded the big wagon. It was about noon before Robert had the other five shod. Abby and little Milly were back and had the little Milly wagon ready to go. The hunters were on their way, heading for O'Neill. It looked like two days to O'Neill. All the hunters were getting tired of traveling. They were anxious to get there and find a place to live until they could round up the Robert Coulter gang. Even though they were getting tired, they still loved and respected each other as if they were one family. There were four sharpshooters on this small wagon train, which is unusual to see that many together at one time. Although Abby hadn't showed her skills with her weapons yet, her word was good enough for the others. The hunters were sure that once they got there, the Coulter gang would either be dead or in jail shortly after the hunters got on their trail. Outlaws don't stop and think that intelligent bounty hunters can perform many clever ways to catch them. These four are no exception. They could very well be the four best bounty hunters in the nation. Even though Billy has a lot to learn, he will be a top-notch hunter in time, Billy being the marksman that he is. The rest will come naturally to him. Bounty hunters that are not sharpshooters usually don't live long. Now that they were getting close to the Coulter rat's nest, the hunters became anxious. Just two days out of Burwell, they are entering the town of O'Neill. This is where the closest jail that can hold several outlaws at one time is. Dan hollered up to Billy, "When you see the sheriff's office, pull up the mules!"

Billy did see the sheriff standing in front of his office and stopped the mules. Dan and Joe stepped down and introduced themselves.

The sheriff said, "My name is William. Everyone just calls me Bill." Dan asked if they could meet with him tomorrow morning. "Sure enough," answered Bill. Dan asked if there was a good place to camp for the night. "You bet, Dan. The rodeo grounds, just out on the south edge of town. You can pull up by the barbershop and turn right, then go to the next street, turn right again. That will take you straight out to the rodeo grounds on the left. There is a water pump and lots of grass for your livestock. The Elkhorn River is just south of there."

They pulled in and set up camp and hoped they could meet with the sheriff and move out yet tomorrow. Dan, Joe, and Sammi went to town to meet with Sheriff Bill. Bill asked them to come in and have a seat. "What can I do for you, guys?"

Dan started with, "Bill, we are bounty hunters, and we need to ask you that this conversation goes no further than right here. We also ask that you keep from telling your wife also. We are going to get the Coulter gang. If they were to find out, it would be a death sentence for us. We have Joe, me, and Billy, a twelve-year-old orphan boy. Abby is a female bounty hunter, and little Milly is a three-year-old orphan girl. What do you think, Bill?"

"Dan and Joe, nobody will hear it from me, and that includes my wife."

"Okay, Bill, can you give us some information about the Coulter gang?"

"You guys need to talk to Rusty, the Boyd County sheriff. He's been dealing with those killers."

Joe asked, "Can we trust him?"

"Absolutely. Rusty would give his left leg if you can bring the Coulter gang in. He wants them bad, but there is too many of them. He has tried to get lawman throughout the state to help him, but nobody is interested."

Dan asked Bill, "If and when we bring 'em in a few at a time, can we use your holding cells until the state can pick 'em up?"

"Sure, you can," answered Bill.

Dan asked, "How many will your cells hold?"

"You guys take a look and see what you think." Bill opened the door leading to the cells.

"Well, Bill, I would say ten or more if we have to cram 'em in," said Dan. So they agreed to include Rusty in on the plan. "Does Spencer have a telegraph office?" asked Dan.

"Yes, they do, Dan."

"Would you mind if we telegraph you if we have a question?"

Bill said, "Absolutely, anytime."

So they went back to the camp and loaded up and pulled out for Spencer. Halfway between O'Neill and Spencer, there was a little store called Midway. They decided to stop there overnight because they had a late start. The next morning, Dan asked the older couple if they could use their water pump to fill the water barrels.

They said, "Help yourselves."

Joe and Billy filled the barrels, while Dan was getting everything else ready. Just as they were ready to pull out, Dan gave a warning to the rest of the hunters. "From now on, we need to keep a lookout. We could come across some of the Coulter rats. If we do see them, we need to do the same thing we did before, by having Billy turning the mules sideways, pulling the mules as far as he could without moving the wagon. Then Abby needs to pull in beside Billy's wagon, leaving enough room so we can get through between them. Me or Joe, whichever is on the Mennonite wagon, pulls in beside Abby's, with the barrels full and ready."

Before they pulled out, Dan asked the old fella at the store if there was anything to watch out for, such as outlaws or renegades or whatever.

The old fella said, "There is one of the largest outlaw gangs in the United States out there. When you get to Spencer, you might want to check with the sheriff. His name is Rusty. He will be able to tell you more about them. As far as the Indians, there are a lot of the Sioux Indians. Most of them are friendly, but every so often, some of them get a little too much to drink, and cause a little trouble, but not much. There are some renegades that split off the main tribe. They will steal. So watch out after dark."

The hunters were on their last leg of the trip. As they pulled out, they're looking forward to getting there. They rolled into Spencer early, making it a short day. Dan and Joe found Rusty, the sheriff, at his office. They introduced themselves. They asked Rusty if they could have a few minutes of his time.

"Sure," said Rusty.

They started out with the same as before, needing him to keep a lid on the hunters' identity. "We are bounty hunters, and we need to remain anonymous.

Rusty said, "Nothing will go any father than here. If you guys need some help, I know a couple of guys that would be willing to help you." Rusty asked, "Do you know how dangerous this gang is?"

"Yes, we do know, that's why we need to keep anonymous." Dan said, "We do not need help. We can work this out just between ourselves."

"Rusty, can you tell us where there might be a little farm that we might rent until this job is finished?"

"Yes, there are three in that area of the mouth of the canyon. There is one that's the most hidden, back up in the trees. It's a nice place. It has a log house, also a large barn and plenty corrals. It's not far from the Missouri River."

Dan asked, "Who can we contact to see if we can rent it?"

"Well, Dan, the couple that owned it was killed by the gang. They stole their cattle and horses. That was eight years ago. Nobody has ever claimed it yet, so I would just use it while you're here. There are two more farms that just packed up and moved away. They were afraid of the Coulter gang."

Dan said, "It sounds like the one somewhat hidden is the one we need to use. Can you tell us some of the places where the gang might be seen or hang out?" asked Dan.

"Yes," said Rusty, there are a few places where they've been seen. One is here, occasionally at the saloon, and sometimes they do shopping at the general store. Every Friday night, a little town called Bristow has a barn dance, and several of the gang members show up and get drunk and usually cause trouble, but haven't killed anyone as of yet. Also, every second Wednesday at Lynch, a town east of here. They have a horse and cattle auction. There are usually a few of them show up there."

Joe asked, "Why hasn't some of the people gotten together and brought 'em in?"

"Well, Joe, the people are scared to death of 'em. Some of the people steer away from the places that the gang members patronize. Some of the businesses are about to close their doors from lack of business."

"Okay, Rusty, can you draw us a map of how to get to the vacant farm?"

"Yes, I can."

"Rusty, could I ask you one more question?

"Sure, Joe."

"What do we look for to identify 'em?"

"The thing to look for is the brand on their horses' right hip. It's Rafter C. That brand is the one Coulter uses, but all their horses and cattle wear that brand."

"Thank you, Rusty. That will be a big help."

In the meantime, Rusty drew the map and handed it to Dan and said, "I wish you guys the best of luck, and if you decide you need help, just let me know." Joe asked Rusty if he had wanted posters with pictures. "Yes, I do, several, but I don't have all of 'em because we don't know how many there are. But they all are wanted. As soon as they join the gang, they are wanted. The state sent us pamphlets." Rusty handed them the package.

"Thank you, Sheriff."

The hunters were on their way to their new residence. They got lucky and made it to the little farm without being seen by any of the gang. When they pulled into the farm, Joe said, "I can see what Rusty meant when he said it was hidden."

When they arrived, they could see the house and the barn were built with eight-by-inch square lumber that was honed from logs that made them literally a fort and a good place to be in case of a shoot-out. They looked in the house first. There was dust a quarter of an inch thick on everything. There was a table and four chairs. There was one bed, a few pots and pans. There was a calendar hanging on the wall with the year of 1880.

It was obvious there hadn't been anybody in the house since the couple that owned it was murdered by the gang. Abby said, "In the morning, I'll start cleaning this place up."

Dan said, "We can all pitch in and get it livable." Dan asked Billy to check the barn and corrals to see where they could keep the horses and mules.

Billy was gone for a while, and all of a sudden, Billy let out a scream and came flying back to the house and said, "Holy shit, Mr. Dan, come here quick!"

"What is it, Billy?"

"Mr. Dan, come quick."

So Dan thought he better go see what scared the hell out of Billy. When Dan got to the barn and looked in, he could see a body hanging from a rope. It had been hanging there for quite some time. By then, Joe and Abby came to see what scared Billy so bad. Dan asked Abby not to let little Milly see in the barn. So Abby took little Milly by the hand and led her away from the barn. Abby knew she had seen all that she wanted to see. Then Dan turned to Billy and said, "Billy, untie that rope, and let the body down!"

Billy said in a very shaky voice, "Mr. Dan, if you ask me to ride the most meanest killer bronc in the world for an hour, I would do it, but I'm not going in there for one second." Dan looked at Joe and grinned. Abby and little Milly started walking back to the house. Billy said, "I'll go with you and help you, Ms. Abby."

Dan and Joe let the body down. There was no possible way of identifying the victim, so they agreed to bury the body in the morning. They were looking for a place to bury him. While looking, they came across the two graves of the couple that owned this place. They decided to bury this body in the same area. Sheriff Rusty had told them the couple were killed and buried here. But as to where this guy came from, chances are, nobody will ever know. Since Billy had vamoosed, Joe and Dan checked out the corrals, and there were all kinds of room, plus a windmill they turned on. There was a large pasture where the livestock could be turned out. They wouldn't be able to use the barn until the body was removed, so they would have to use the corrals for tonight.

First thing the next morning, Dan and Joe dug a grave for whoever that guy hanging was. Billy felt much better after the body was six foot under. Later, Dan had to tease Billy. He said, "Now, Billy, you told us you were scared of rats and snakes."

"Yes, sir, Mr. Dan."

"Now we have to add dead bodies hanging from ropes, huh, Billy?"

"Yes, sir, Mr. Dan. That gives me the heebie-jeebies." After that, they all had a good laugh.

Dan suggested they get started cleaning the house and getting it livable, before making plans to start capturing the gang. The hunters all pitched in. Even little Milly was helping clean the house. After it was all cleaned up, they moved in the things they needed to make it look like home. The bedcovers that were on the bed were covered with dust, but when they pulled them off, the rest of the bed was clean. So Abby and little Milly were to use the bed. The men hunters had their bunk rolls and could sleep in a room that was apparently built as a second bedroom, even though it was bare. Finally, they had the things that needed to be taken care first done. Finally, they had time to start making plans. It was difficult because there were so many of them. Dan said, "Let's take one place at a time. What if we take the Lynch auction first. Is that okay with the rest of you?" They all voted yes.

The Lynch auction was a few days away. They decided to check the mouth of the canyon first. There's only one way in and one way out. "We need to take Abby and little Milly with us," for fear of the gang finding them at the house. "We need to take the Mennonite wagon with the water barrels to be safe for the girls and Billy. Although Abby is capable of taking care of herself, we all have to take care of little Milly and Billy." Even though Billy didn't want anyone to think he needed protection, Joe and Dan knew they still had to watch out for him because he was a very brave boy and could very well get reckless and get hurt or killed If Dan and Joe were handling this hunt by themselves, they wouldn't need the wagon and barrels.

CHAPTER 17

Dan told Billy that he'd take the Mennonite wagon and the black team. "Do you think you can handle 'em?"

"Mr. Dan, ol' Billy can handle anything on four legs."

"I didn't know if you could remember how to drive horses after driving those mules so long."

"Mr. Dan, did you forget I've drove these ol' black girls before, and they know when ol' Billy's at the reins, they get kinda nervous. They know not to make any mistakes. They know the boss is handling the reins."

"Okay, I believe you, Billy. So round up those mares and we'll hitch 'em and we'll be on our way."

"Okay, Mr. Dan, I'm on my way." Billy took off running to get the mares.

Dan saddled Buck, Joe saddled Smoky, and Abby saddled Sally. They had the black team hitched, and they pulled out to take a look at the canyon. "When Rusty drew the map, he shows the mouth straight east from here," said Dan. Joe and Dan led the way, with Abby next and little Milly riding behind her. Last was Billy, Sammi, and the wagon. They were watching in every direction, in case some of the gang saw them and wanted to cause a little trouble. They have the wagon to give to Billy, Milly, and Abby, to keep them safe. Dan knew that Billy and Abby could handle about anything that comes their way, especially with Dan on one side and Joe on the other.

They came to the mouth of the canyon, and it was different than they expected. The canyon was a complete horseshoe. There were two openings about a quarter of a mile apart, with the center being a huge mound, about two hundred feet high. You couldn't see their hideout from the mouth. Joe said, "Let's go around all of this and see what is up there," pointing at a cluster of trees and thick brush.

"Let's go," said Dan. So they continued on. When they got to the top, the trees were getting more dense, and the wagon couldn't go any farther. Dan said, "Joe, why don't you stay here and help watch out for any trouble that might come our way? Very unlikely it will happen, but we need to make sure nothing happens to our little hunter family. I will ride back in as far as I can and see what's in there." So Dan rode in but couldn't see from there. He tied Buck to a tree and took his telescope and squeezed back in a little farther. He used his big knife to cut some of the brush so he could work himself a little closer. Finally, he came to the edge of the canyon. He sighted in his telescope. There it was. He could see the whole picture. It appeared there were lots of horses, some cattle, a pen with some large hogs. There were two houses and a very long building, which looked like a bunkhouse. Dan thought, *That's where the rest of 'em live.* He could also see why you couldn't ride in and arrest them. They had lots of firepower, and it appeared the buildings were built bulletproof. They were built somewhat like the house the hunters just moved into. Dan checked it out one more time with the telescope so he could remember as much as possible how the place was laid out. When Dan returned to the rest of the hunters, he had a lot to tell them about the layout.

Joe asked, "How many horses are there?"

"Somewhere between forty to fifty, but that doesn't mean there's that many outlaws. Some might have more than one horse. I'm guessing about twenty to twenty-five head of cattle. There is a small pen with about eight large hogs. There is a large garden area about two, maybe, three acres. My guess is they are trying to support themselves with meat and vegetables."

The hunters returned to the farm. They were trying to decide what to do with the gang after they capture them. They'd like to take ten or more before they take them to O'Neill. The men hunters were in the barn, looking for a safe place to keep the gang so they couldn't get away. While checking the barn, they found one door that was the old fella's workshop. Inside were his tools. Apparently, he would stock up on firewood for winter. He had a large bucksaw and three axes. There was a log chain about twenty feet long that he used to drag the logs home. They searched for a place where they could fasten the chain. He had lots of his tools hanging from nails on the wall.

Dan said, "Look here, Joe." Dan was pointing at a hand drill and several bits. They searched through gallon cans of rusty nails and bolts. Billy found a large bolt. Searching further, they found a nut that fit the bolt. They went to work and drilled a hole in an eight-by-eight-foot timber that was part of the structure of the barn. They bolted the chain to the timber. Dan stepped back and said, "When we handcuff 'em to that chain, they won't be goin' anywhere."

Late that afternoon, there was a man and a woman who came riding between the house and the barn. When they saw Billy, Joe, and Dan, they stopped and had a scared look on their faces. Joe said, "Howdy, folks."

They returned the howdy and then said, "We are sorry, we didn't mean to trespass."

Dan said, "You don't need to apologize. Can we help you with something?"

The man asked if they were going to live there and farm that place.

Joe answered, "We're thinking about it. By the way, my name is Joe Cobb." Joe pointed and said, "That is Dan Colt, and that is Billy Priest."

The man said, "My name is Frank Hartly, and this is my wife, Emma."

Dan asked, "Would you folks like to come in and have a cup of coffee?"

Frank said, "That sounds good." They stepped down from their horses and tied them to the hitching rail.

They all went to the house. Abby made a pot of coffee, and they had a long conversation about what all the Hartlys knew about the outlaw gang. Dan asked if they knew who owned the place.

"No," they answered. "As far as we know, the people that owned it were murdered. Nobody knows if they had relatives. That was about eight years ago." Frank asked if they knew about the outlaw gang that murdered them.

"We heard a little something about it," said Joe.

"Could you tell us what you know about the outlaws?

"Do you folks live around here?" asked Dan.

"Yes, we do."

Frank asked them if they were trustworthy people.

"Absolutely," said Dan.

Frank explained that the only reason they were still alive was because they don't know the trail to their place. "Please don't ever tell anybody else how to get to our place."

"It will absolutely not go any farther than here," promised Dan.

"We only live about a mile from here. If you pass on through this place and start up the trail, you will come to some trees that were toppled by a big storm. It looks as if it's a dead end. When you ride around the toppled trees, you will go through tree limbs and branches for a ways, and then you will come to an opening. Then you'll be on our property. I ask you again to never tell anybody else."

"A double promise," said Joe.

Dan asked Frank if they knew somebody they could trust and if they knew of a safe place to leave little Milly. "The rest of us have a job to do, and it could end up with us being in a dangerous place."

"Yes, Dan, my wife and I would be happy to watch her and Billy anytime."

"Thank you, Frank, but we don't have enough ropes to hold Billy back. He thinks he is needed as much as the rest of us. We are here to do a job, and it could be good for you and the other people of this area." Joe and Dan shook hands with Frank, and the Hartlys left.

They were on their way home. Frank asked Emma, "What do you think their jobs are?"

Emma said, "I don't know, but it seems it's a secret of some kind. Did you see the big knifes they carry? Even Billy was wearing one."

"Ya, Emma, the part where it will benefit us and other people in this area. I don't understand." They rode up through the trees to their home. Frank shook his head and said, "The only thing I can think of is to stop the gang of outlaws. You know, Emma, I wonder if they are bounty hunters. The big knifes and all."

Emma said, "You know, Frank, I bet you're right. Oh Lord, wouldn't that be wonderful?"

Frank said, "The only thing is, I've never heard of a woman or a kid bounty hunter."

"No, I haven't either, but maybe there could be."

The next morning was Wednesday and the day of the Lynch auction. Abby saddled Sally and took little Milly behind her and rode up through the trees to the Hartlys' house. When Abby knocked on the door, Emma opened the door and was very friendly. She asked Abby if she would like a cup of coffee.

"Thank you, Emma, but I have to get back. We have a job to do. Could I leave little Milly until later this evening? I'll be back then to pick her up."

Emma said, "You can leave her as long as you want."

Abby was on her way back to get everything ready for the first leg of the big hunt. Dan had a plan for the auction capture. They didn't need the water barrels on this one. Dan explained to the other three how they could make it work. "Let's head that way now." They all mounted and were on their way. "We want to get there early so we can be there when they come riding in and check the brands on their horses and look for the Rafter C. Then we can get a close look at their faces so we are sure we recognize them when they come out of the barn. We don't want to hurt any innocent people. Abby, if there is a window where you can see them when they go in and sit down, you signal Billy. Now, Billy, once they're in the barn and set down, you take their horses somewhere where they can't be seen and tie them to something. Joe and I will stand on each side of the door. Abby, you will go to the auctioneer, and as soon as he sells a horse or a cow, when he says sold, you walk up to the auctioneer and stand and motion for him to lean over to see what you want to say to him. Then you tell him there's a loose horse, and it has a brand on its hip, it's Rafter C. We will assume there will be two or more that will come out to catch the horse. Joe, you stand on the door side so we can close the door before we take 'em down, fast and hard. Now, Abby, after you tell the auctioneer and he announces it, you start back toward the door and let Joe and I know how many got up to come out."

The hunters were on their way. An hour later, they reached the sale barn. They finished making their plan. They found where Billy would take and tie their horses. The window was in the wrong place for Abby to see in, so they had to make a new plan.

"Okay, I will signal Billy when to take the horses." Joe said, "I sure hope Rusty knows what he's talking about."

The auction started, and the gang members hadn't showed up yet, but a few minutes later, Billy said, "Look," pointing at several riders coming up the trail.

Dan said, "Let's spread out so if that is them, they won't suspect anything."

There were six of them that rode up and tied their horses to the hitching rail. They walked into the sale barn. Everything was looking good. After a couple minutes, Dan made a motion for Billy to take the horses. Billy did his job well. Now it was Abby's turn. Abby went in the sale barn, and the auctioneer was selling a horse. When he said sold, Abby did her job, telling the auctioneer about the loose horse and the brand. Abby started making her way to the door. She saw three of them stand up and were coming to catch the horse. Abby stepped out the door and said, "Three." Then she stepped sideways behind Dan with her gun in her hand. When the door opened, all three stepped out, and the door shut. Joe, with his famous attack, knocked the first guy's hat off, grabbed his hair, and drove a powerful, wild uppercut to the guy's face. The guy went down. Dan took him by the collar, swung him around, and slammed his head into the barn. He went down. Joe and Dan went for the third one. Abby had her .45 in his ear. He had no intentions of causing any trouble. She had taken his gun. Joe was dragging his victim around the corner toward their horses. Dan helped his victim on his feet. He had blood everywhere. Dan was leading him toward their horses. Abby had her gun to number 3's head. She said, "Don't try anything, or I'll blow your goddamn brains all over that barn."

The hunters put all three on their horses and handcuffed them to their saddles. Dan said, "Billy here is going to be watching you guys. Billy, if any one of them tries anything or makes a noise, kill 'em." They went back to the door and were waiting for the other three to come out. Dan said, "The other three will come out when these three don't come back."

After about an hour, they did come out the door. Dan did about the same thing—grabbed one, slamming him against the barn. Joe must have felt sorry for his. He just grabbed his gun from his holster and said, "I'm letting you off easy. Just don't try anything stupid, or you will be coyote bait." Abby had also taken his gun away and pretty much warned him the same way. When they had all six chained to their saddles, the hunters were on the way back to the barn with the first catch. Six down. They didn't know how many to go. They took one at a time in and handcuffed them to the log chain. They weren't going anywhere. Dan had Billy take their bunk rolls behind their saddles and throw them in the stalls that the prisoners were chained in. Dan explained to Billy not to get close to them.

Abby rode to get little Milly. When she got to the Hartlys', they were very, very nice. They fell in love with little Milly and asked if they would be able to watch her again.

"Maybe, Friday night. Would you like keeping her overnight?"

"That would be just great," said Emma.

The next morning, Dan hitched the black mares to the Mennonite wagon. He needed a couple barrels of oats for the horses and mules, and now they had six more horses to feed. He needed one hundred pounds of beans for the prisoners. He asked Joe and Billy to stay and watch out for somebody looking for the six outlaws. Dan made the trip to Spencer. He stopped by the sheriff's office, and he and the sheriff had a good talk. He told Rusty about their successful catch. Rusty was about to do a little dance. He was so excited. "Well, Rusty, I have to go now. I thought you might like to hear the latest."

Rusty said, "That's the best news I've heard in a long, long time. God bless you, bounty hunters." Rusty shook Dan's hand.

Dan walked to the telegraph office and asked the operator to send a message to Maggie in Lariat, Texas, to tell her they were there and that yesterday they brought in six coyotes. And they were going hunting again on Friday. He told the operator to sign it "Love, Dan."

"How much do I owe you?"

"How about twenty-five cents?"

Dan paid, then said, "Maggie will probably send back a telegraph. Just make a note, and I'll be here in Monday."

He drove the wagon to the feed store and bought two barrels of oats. Dan stopped by the market and asked the grocer if he had some beans.

"What kind of beans do you want?"

"It doesn't matter," said Dan.

The grocer asked, "How many? Well, I have what you see in those barrels, plus I have a hundred-pound sack in the back room."

"I'll take the hundred-pound sack."

The grocer said, "Could I ask what are you going to do with that many beans?"

"We are raising some pigs, and we are raising them on a special diet."

"Well, okay, I'll bring them out to your wagon." They loaded the beans. Dan asked if he had ice. "Yes, I have ice in the back room."

"Could I buy four blocks?"

"Yes, indeed, you can. Drive your wagon around the back, and we can load 'em in your icebox."

After Dan loaded the ice, he asked the grocer for a large slab of bacon, a large ham, and a crate of eggs. When Dan got back to the farm, Dan asked Abby if she would start cooking beans for the prisoners. Joe had put a bucket of water and a dipper in their stall. Abby was cooking beans in a large pot. Dan went to the barn and told the prisoners that they would have beans in a little while. "I want to tell you guys something. If any one of you tries to escape or cause any kind of a problem, I will light the barn on fire and listen to you scream and yell as you're cookin'. Do you guys know what I mean?"

They answered one at a time. They all answered the same answer. That was yes. "We won't cause any trouble."

Abby finished cooking beans. Dan and Joe took the pot of beans, some bowls, and spoons so the prisoners could eat.

That evening, they were discussing the barn dance at Bristow. "I don't think we need the wagon and water barrels on this one either," Dan said. "Again, we need to get there early so we can get everything worked out. We need to take them quietly so nobody sees us take them out. We don't need the story getting around and back to the rats' nest. Coulter is probably wondering why these six didn't come back. At this time, Coulter could think those six might have decided to split off and leave the rats' nest. Very likely, after a few catches, they will get suspicious. That's why we need to take 'em without the public knowing what's up."

Abby was busy cooking beans for the prisoners. Six mouths to feed twice a day takes a lot of beans. The next morning when they got their beans for breakfast, one of the prisoners complained to Dan. "There are rats in this barn."

Dan said, "Yes, there are, and six of them are handcuffed to that big chain." Later, Dan told the rest of the hunters, "In a while, we need to head for the barn dance."

Abby said she was taking little Milly to the Hartlys' and that she would be right back. The rest of the hunters were saddled and ready to go when Abby returned. There was hope among the hunters that this might be another good catch. When they rode into Bristow, there was not much town, but there was a big barn with a sign on the door that said, "Barn dance every Friday at eight o' clock." They rode through town to get a picture of the layout. Billy asked if he should look for a place to hide their horses.

"Yes, Billy, let's get down and look behind the barn for a good place to tie 'em."

Around the back, there were hitching posts. Dan pointed at them and told Billy, "Right there."

They walked around town, and it didn't take very long. There was a saloon, a small market, a barbershop, a stable, and the marshal's office. The whole town's population was less than a hundred people. They had the plans for two different situations. One was if there were two or three of the bad guys. A different plan was if there were five or more. Later, the people started coming and tying their horses, wagons, and buggies to a long hitching rail that ran all the way across the front and all the way down one side of the dance hall building. They were surprised to see how many people were coming to the dance. The hunters didn't hang out together so that nobody would wonder what was going on. The band was getting tuned up. The band consisted of a fiddle player and a piano player About the time the band started to play, three riders came in and tied their horses to the rail. They appeared to be drunk. They were talking loud and pushing each other and acting like little kids. The hunters all looked them over so they could identify them. Dan told Billy to walk down where they tied their horses and see if they had brands on their hips. When Billy came back, he nodded his head yes. Dan told Billy, "Get their horses." Billy no more than took the horses around behind and tied them. When two more riders came and there was no doubt they had been drinking with the other three because they were also drunk, Billy came back and asked Dan if he should take their horses too. "Ya, Billy, take 'em." The hunters assumed that most of the people who were there were coming to the dance. The more people the better. It makes snagging the gang much easier.

Abby went in the barn and saw a long bench to sit on. Abby sat down and waited for one of the bunch to come and ask her for a dance, and that was exactly what happened. Abby accepted his offer to dance. They danced, if you could call it a dance. He fell all over Abby. After a few minutes, Abby said, "It's too hot in here. I think I'll go outside and get some fresh air."

The scum said, "I'll go with you."

"Sure," answered Abby. When they stepped outside, Abby walked toward the back of the barn. The scum followed her.

Joe stepped out from behind a tree and said, "I'll take him from here." Abby quickly grabbed his gun. Joe pulled him over to the horses and asked, "Which horse is yours?"

"What's goin' on?" asked the scum.

"Well, it's like this. You are under arrest."

"What for?" asked the scum.

Joe said, "For dancing with my wife." Joe handcuffed him to his saddle. "Billy, keep an eye on him. If he doesn't do what you say, kill him."

After Joe walked away, Billy looked up and said, "Hey, weasel, did you hear what Mr. Joe said?"

"Ya, I did, kid."

Abby told Dan and Joe, "I'll be back with another one, so wait here."

"Go get 'em," said Joe.

Abby went in and saw the other four talking. She sat down on the bench. Being as attractive as Abby was, it didn't take long for her second catch. Another outlaw came and asked Abby for a dance. The same thing happened. Abby was trying to hold the drunken outlaw up. Abby, after getting her toes stepped on a few times, decided enough is enough. Abby asked the outlaw if he would like a drink of whiskey.

"Sure, ma'am."

At that time, another one of the gang came over to try to get a dance with Abby. When he asked her, she said, "Sure, when we get back. But first, your buddy and I are going out to have a drink of whiskey. Would you like to come along?"

"Sure, I could stand a good drink," said the drunken outlaw.

So Abby had two this time. They stepped outside. Dan was leaning against the barn, and Joe was leaning against a tree. When they got next to Dan, Abby said, "We have two more." Dan reached out and grabbed one, and at the same time, Joe grabbed the other one. Abby grabbed their guns.

Joe said, "Three down, and two to go."

Dan said, "We can't use Abby anymore. They may get suspicious. We can't take the chance."

Billy said, "Mr. Dan, let me pull the loose-horse trick."

"What do you have in mind, Billy?"

"Mr. Dan, it will work like this. Ol' Billy will go in and tell the last two that there's some horses loose, and they need them to come and help him catch 'em. Then you, Mr. Dan and Mr. Joe, be on each side of the door. And that will take care of that."

Dan looked at Joe and said, "I guess that would be safe for Billy, don't you?"

"I can't see any danger for Billy," said Joe.

Abby said, "That shouldn't be dangerous for Billy."

Dan told Billy to do this exactly like he said he would. "Okay, Billy?"

"Yes, sir, Mr. Dan."

"Take that big .45 and that knife off your hip so they won't be suspicious."

Billy left the gun and the knife with Abby. Billy went in and said everything exactly like he said outside. Within a couple of minutes, the door opened. As soon as they got out the door, Dan closed the door and shoved one against the wall. Joe grabbed the other one. Abby was there almost instantly to grab their guns. Joe and Dan took the outlaws and chained them to their saddles. The hunters were on their way back to the farm, with five more outlaws. Billy asked, "Did this catch work perty slick or not?"

All the hunters agreed that it did work slick. Dan said, "Everybody did a perfect job. We got them, and nobody got hurt."

They reached the farm and added five more to the catch chain. After they handcuffed them to the chain and all the horses were put away, the hunters went to the house. Joe lit the lamp, and they all sat around the table and passed the bottle around a few times. Billy had a sarsaparilla. Needless to say, they were very happy this catch went off so easy. None of the people at the dance ever even knew the outlaws were taken out. Nobody knew the difference. Dan said, "Tomorrow night, I will take them to O'Neill and turn these eleven over to Sheriff Bill."

CHAPTER 18

Dan was about to head out for O'Neill with the first eleven outlaws. Dan said, "Joe, you and Billy stay here and watch out for Abby and little Milly. If I leave here after dark, I should get to O'Neill fairly early the next morning. I should make the trip in twenty-four to thirty hours. Then we can start planning how to get the rest of the rat's nest."

Billy asked, "Mr. Dan, why are you leaving after dark? Couldn't you see better in the daylight?"

"Well, Billy, if I leave here in the daytime and the gang catches up with me, I'm going to have big trouble. After dark, all the bad guys should be in their rat's nests."

"Oh, I didn't think about that, Mr. Dan."

The next morning, Abby fixed breakfast for the hunters and had a pot of beans cooking for the prisoners. Now she has eleven mouths to cook beans for. After breakfast was over, Abby asked Billy, "Will you stir the beans while I'm gone after little Milly?"

"Sure, Ms. Abby. Ol' Billy can handle that job."

Abby saddled Sally and rode up through the trees to the Hartlys' to pick up little Milly. When she arrived, little Milly came running out to meet her. By this time, little Milly had definitely considered Abby her guardian. She very seldom asked about her mom, dad, or brother. Little Milly loves Abby with all of her little heart. Abby loves little Milly with all her heart too and will do so for the rest of her life.

Later that day, Dan asked Billy to take all the rifles and scabbards off the outlaws' saddles and put them under the tarp with the rest of the rifles. "Ya know, Mr. Dan, I was thinking, by the time we catch the rest of the rats, we'll have a wagon full of guns."

"That's right, Billy. That's how we keep track of how many outlaws we put away."

A few hours later, Dan, Billy, and Joe were busy saddling the outlaws' horses and Buck. They used ropes to tie the outlaws' horses together. They tied them three abreast except the last two, and they were tied together. Dan was ready to go. The sun was down, and it was getting dark. There was enough moonlight, so Dan could see the trail. Dan said, "Let's load 'em one at a time." Joe went in and unlocked one and brought him out and put him on his horse and chained him to his saddle. They continued until all eleven were locked to their saddles. Dan said, "I'm going to leave Sammi here. If anybody comes around, Sammi will let you know." Then he said to the other hunters, "See you when I get back." Dan and all eleven prisoners were on their way to O'Neill. They rode all night and had no rest stops. Dan wasn't about to unchain the outlaws, so there were no problems.

It was daylight when Dan rode up to the jail. When Sheriff Bill saw Dan ride up, he came out and said, "Dan, you guys were serious. Eleven of 'em. I can't believe you brought them in this soon. Dan, you are a hell of a bounty hunter."

"No," Dan said, "I'm one of four hell of a bounty hunters."

They took in one outlaw at a time and checked the wanted posters and identified which ones had posters and which ones didn't. There were seven with posters, totaling twenty-three thousand dollars bounty. Sheriff Bill had all eleven of them locked up. "Well, Dan, I'll send a telegraph and have these all picked up. The state will send a money draft here to the jail."

"That's fine," said Dan. "If you would, have the bank hold the money drafts in the vault until we catch all of 'em, and we are on our way back to Texas." Dan took his lariat and tied knots ever so far apart and tied six horses down one side of his horse and five down the other. Dan told Bill, "I'll be back with some more soon."

Bill said, "I'm lookin' forward to that."

Dan was on his way back to the farm. He was tired from traveling all night, but couldn't stop and rest. He was leading eleven horses and had a long ride ahead. Dan had ridden about three hours when he noticed some renegades at a distance. They were rooted to the spot, watching Dan and the eleven horses and saddles. Dan took a deep breath and a sigh. He knew this could turn into a bloody battle. He was looking for any kind of shelter, but so far he'd seen nothing. He was keeping a close eye on them. It appeared there were four of them. Dan stopped and took out his telescope and sighted in on them. Dan looked through the telescope ahead for shelter, but still nothing. He was thinking, *I might just have to shoot it out with 'em.*

Dan was pushing Buck and got him and the rest of the horses on a fast trot, pushing to get to a shelter to shoot it out. Dan could see them coming his way, but only at a slow pace for now. Dan kept pushing. Now he could see their horses at a full run toward him. Dan quickly found the shortest horse of the eleven. He grabbed his rifle and leaned over its saddle. As they came closer, Dan could see that only two had rifles, which helped a whole bunch. When they got close enough, Dan aimed carefully and *boom!* That took care of one of the rifles. The other three started to turn, so he aimed and *boom!* The second one with a rifle went down. Dan went for more. He aimed carefully and *boom!* The third one went down. Dan didn't try for the fourth one. He had ridden out of range. Dan checked the horses and found out that one of the outlaw's horses took a bullet in the gut. "Well, buddy, we have to get you back to the farm and doctor you up." Dan walked out and caught the three Indian ponies. They weren't much, but he didn't want anybody else to get them. He added those three to the string. He picked up the two rifles and strapped them to one of the saddles. Dan was on the trail again with the string getting longer.

It was about dark when Dan pulled into the farm and was greeted by the other hunters. Joe said, "That is one hell of a string of horses following you."

"That's true," said Dan. Dan asked Billy to bring the iodine and some gauze. "One of the outlaw's horse is packin' a bullet."

Joe asked, "Did you have a run in with somebody?"

"Yep," said Dan, there were four Indians that liked the looks of all the horses and saddles."

"Did you get 'em?" asked Joe.

"Ya, three of 'em. The fourth one got out of range. But don't tell Billy one got away. I'd never hear the end of it."

Joe had a big laugh and said, "On my honor, Dan. My lips are sealed."

Billy returned with the iodine and gauze. Dan cleaned up the horse and sterilized the wound in hopes that it would live. They unsaddled all the horses and turned them out in the big pasture. Dan asked, "Is there any whiskey left? I need a drink."

"You bet," said Joe.

They went to the house. Dan told them what all happened on the trip and about the twenty-three-thousand-dollar bounty. Everybody was happy about the first two catches. Dan was tired from being up for twenty-four hours, so they called it a day. The next morning, while eating breakfast, they discussed what to do with the outlaw's horses and saddles. Dan said, "I was thinking, while on the trip, after we bring in the rest of the nest of rats, that maybe we should have an auction and sell all the livestock and whatever else that we find in their hideout, then give the proceeds to the families that were robbed and had their property stolen by the rats. What do the rest of you think?"

They all put their hands up and said it sounded like a good idea.

Billy said, "Hold your hand up, little Milly." So little Milly held her little hand up.

Dan said, "It looks like that was a unanimous vote."

Abby asked, "What about the brands on all the livestock?"

"The sheriff will sign to approve it," said Dan. "What we should do is go back up where I cut the brush away to get to the rim and check and see how many horses are still there."

The hunters all saddled up and rode to the spot. Abby, Billy, and little Milly stayed out front, while Dan and Joe rode back in as far as they could. They squeezed their way to the edge of the canyon. Dan had his telescope. He looked down on the rat's nest. He could see about thirty horses. "Here, Joe, see what you can see."

Joe took the telescope and searched the entire place. Joe said, "I can't see any easy way to go in and get 'em."

Joe and Dan and the rest of the hunters headed back to the farm. They were thinking how they could get them all at once and finish the job before cold weather hit. When they reached the farm, Abby asked if they should go into town and get some groceries.

Dan saddled Abby's horse, while Joe harnessed the team and hitched them to the Mennonite wagon. They backed the wagon up to the house and unloaded the icebox on the porch in the shade. Dan asked Billy, "Do you want to drive the team and wagon?"

"You betcha, Mr. Dan."

So Billy and Sammi crawled up on the wagon and were ready to go. Abby and little Milly were on Sally. The hunters were off to town.

When they reached town, Billy pulled the team and the wagon up in front of the market and tied them to the rail. Abby and little Milly went in to shop for groceries. Billy could see two horses tied in front of the saloon. He couldn't quite make out the brand on the closest one's hip. Billy reached in the wagon and pulled out his little .22 rifle and carried it down by his side, then walked up to the saloon, and sure enough, the horses were wearing the Rafter C brand. Billy looked in, and he could see two outlaws sitting at the bar. Billy pointed his rifle at the back of their heads. He then told them to keep their elbows on the bar because if they moved, he would kill them. The outlaws were watching in the mirror behind the bar.

The one asked Billy, "Is this a joke, you little bastard?"

Billy's way of showing that it was not a joke was by shooting one of their beer mugs. He blew it all over the place. Billy asked, "Does that look like a joke? Barkeep, come around here," said Billy.

"What do you want?" He was coming around the bar.

"Take their guns and get rid of 'em." The barkeep did exactly that. Billy told the outlaws to get on the floor facedown. Billy said, "I hope you try something because I would like to blow your brains all over the walls."

They hesitated for a short time. Billy blew the other beer mug all over the place. The outlaws slowly stepped down and laid on the floor facedown. One of the outlaws told Billy, "You are going to get killed for this."

Billy said, "You let me worry about that. Barkeep, I want you to go to the market and ask for Dan or Joe, and tell them Billy needs two pairs of handcuffs."

Dan and Joe were talking when they heard the *pops*. Joe said, "That was a gunshot, from a small caliber gun. It sounded kinda like Billy's little gun." Just then the barkeep came up and asked for Dan or Joe. Joe said, "That's us."

"Billy needs two pairs of handcuffs."

"Are you serious?" asked Dan.

"Where is Billy?" asked Joe.

"He's in the saloon with two guys pinned down on the floor."

Dan reached in the wagon and pulled out two pairs of handcuffs. Dan and Joe started running toward the saloon. When they ran through the door, sure enough, there were two guys lying on the floor facedown. Dan asked, "What the hell are you doing, Billy?"

"I've got two rats pinned down."

"I can see that, Billy, but how do you know that they are part of the rat's nest?"

"Well, Mr. Dan, take a look at the two horses out front."

Joe stepped outside and looked at the brands. Joe said, "He's right, Dan."

Dan put the handcuffs on them. "Well, Joe, why don't you take their horses around the back so we won't be seen as we take them out of town." They took the two out back and chained them to their saddles. Dan stepped back in the saloon and asked the barkeep if he knew who those two guys were.

"Yes, I think they are part of the outlaw gang."

"What did Billy shoot at?"

"He shot two beer mugs off the bar. He did that to prove he was serious."

"Here." Dan tossed a silver dollar on the bar and said, "That should cover the mugs. Can I ask you to keep this quiet, barkeep?"

"Sure, I didn't see a thing. By the way, Dan, here are those guy's guns."

"Thanks, barkeep." Dan told Billy to run down and bring Smoky around the back for Joe. From then on, everything went good.

Joe took the outlaws in the back way out of town so people wouldn't see what was going on. Dan and Billy went back to the market. Abby and little Milly were finished grocery shopping. Dan loaded the groceries in the wagon. Billy and Sammi were on the wagon again. Dan, Abby, and little Milly were on their way to the farm. Outside of town, they met with Joe and the outlaws.

On the way back to the farm, one of the outlaws said, "You do know that you all will die for this?"

Dan said, "Shut up, or I'll tie you to a tree, and let Billy do some target practice."

The hunters and Billy's captors rode to the farm and the latter were locked to the chain. One of the outlaws was calling Billy names. Billy said, "You weasels better shut your mouths, or I'll get my gun and finish the job."

Joe was standing close by. He turned and grinned at the outlaws and said, "He'll do it too."

When all were taken care of, Dan asked Billy, "Why didn't you come and get me and Joe to help you take these guys?"

"Well, Mr. Dan, there was only two of 'em. When I popped that mug of beer, they knew ol' Billy wasn't kiddin'. When I popped the second one, they decided to believe what ol' Billy said, and they laid on the floor like I told them."

The next morning, Sheriff Rusty came riding into the farm. Dan and Joe stopped what they were doing and greeted the sheriff.

Rusty said, "I don't know if it means anything, but there is a money shipment coming in tomorrow. Two years ago, the Coulter gang robbed the delivery, right in front of the bank. They killed two of the men that were delivering the money. They got by with it. The company that shipped the money was the loser. Nobody had guts enough to go in and get 'em. Nobody knows how they knew when the money was going to be dropped off at the bank, but they did. But anyway, I thought I would let you know. Who knows? They might not show at all, and then again, they might."

"Well, thank you, Rusty. We'll work on that," said Dan.

After Rusty left, Dan and Joe started working on something that might get most of the rest of them. Joe said, "I wonder if we use both wagons with the barrels in them. We could park one sideways, on the south side of the mouth of the canyon, then put the other wagon backed up to make it L shaped. According to the trail's wear, it's obvious that they are using the south side. The only thing is that we don't know how many will come out—if any, if they should show up. They'll know how fast we took out the other nine maggots. It was less than one minute, I would guess. With an extra rifle, we should take out twenty or more without any of us being in danger."

"So," Dan said, "that might get us out of here and on our way back to Texas." They went back to the house and discussed it with Abby and Billy. They were all for it. "What time do you think we should get set up and be ready for 'em?" asked Dan.

"Well, Dan, let's get around somewhat early and get set up and use the tarp to drape over the wheels to cover the wagons so we can't be seen under the wagons." Dan started to explain all their positions. He said for Abby and Billy to stay behind the two center barrels. "Joe, you take the right, and I'll take the left. Joe can take out the guys on the right. Abby and Billy can take out the center ones, and I'll take out the ones on the left. When they get about hundred yards, I'll holler for them to put their hands up and that they are under arrest. We can be assured that they will go for their guns. We need to make sure that every shot counts. All four of us are crack shots, so we should have no misses. This, of course, is if there are several of them."

The hunters had been there for several hours. They became doubtful that any of the rats would show up. Dan and Sammi were keeping a close eye on the trail. Dan handed the telescope to Billy and told him to watch out for them for a while. A short time later, Billy said, "There are two riders coming up out of the canyon."

Joe said, "Dan, let's take these two alive. We'll see if we can get one of them to snitch on the rest of them."

When the rats got close, Dan and Joe stepped out from the wagon with both rifles pointed at their heads and told them to put their hands up and keep them that way. "If either of you reach for anything, you'll be dead before you hit the ground." They never moved. Dan asked Joe to keep his rifle aimed at their heads. Dan leaned his rifle against the wagon wheel and pulled out his revolver and said, "Stay where you are until I get your guns." Dan reached up and pulled one gun out, then walked to the other rat and pulled his gun out of his holster. Dan pointed to one and said for him to step down very slowly. They were both in handcuffs and locked to a wagon wheel.

About ten minutes later, Billy said, "Here comes a whole bunch of 'em."

Dan took the telescope and said, "Billy's right, there must be twenty or more.

CHAPTER 19

The big fight is about to start. Dan asked, "Is everybody ready?"

Billy said, "Yes, sir, Mr. Dan, I'm ready." Then Billy said, "Come on you chickenshits. Ol' Billy has a surprise for ya."

About that time, Dan stepped out and said, "Put your hands up, you are under arrest." Nearly everyone of the rats went for their guns. Dan hollered, "Get 'em!" *Boom! Boom! Boom!* The sound of all the guns was deafening. The hunters were taking them out so fast. The last five rats threw their guns on the ground.

Joe said, "Let's get the five in cuffs and drag the dead ones around the back where they can't be seen from the canyon." The sound of the gun battle might pry some more rats loose from the canyon to see what the gunshots were all about. Obviously, it worked.

Abby said, "Here comes four more." These four were a little skeptical. They could see some of the horses even though the hunters brought all the horses behind the wagons. There were too many to hide. The four riders stopped their horses and stayed there for some time. They started coming toward the wagons very slowly. Dan and Joe were waiting for them to get a little closer.

Dan had told Abby and Billy to be ready in case the rats decided to shoot it out. Dan and Joe stepped out and said, "Don't try for your guns because you are heavily covered, and you don't stand a chance." The rats were convinced. They never moved.

Joe said for them to ride toward them with their hands up. The rats did what they were told. When they were in cuffs, Joe went over to one of those chained to the wagon wheel and pulled his revolver out and stuck the barrel in his ear. Then he knelt down and whispered, "I have a question for you, sir. Have you ever had a bullet go in one of your ears and out the other?"

The rat said, "No, I haven't."

"Well, would you like to have that happen, sir?"

The rat said, "No, sir, I wouldn't like that."

Joe said, "Then, I have something to tell you. If you don't cooperate, you are going to have it happen for the first time. How many more rats are in the canyon now?"

"I think only Coulter and his woman."

"Are you sure of that?" asked Joe.

"That is all I know of," answered the outlaw rat.

Dan asked Joe, "Are we ready to go get Coulter and his honey? Maybe we can finish this sweep and have all of them in jail or six feet under."

Joe said, "Let's make sure all of these are safely chained and tied securely. Abby and Billy, you keep them still, and if any one of them moves, shoot 'em."

Dan said, "I'll leave Sammi here also."

Joe asked Abby if he could borrow her horse.

"Sure, Joe, anytime," answered Abby.

Dan and Joe headed out. They decided to split up. Joe was on one side of the entrance, and Dan was to take the other. The rat snitch told Joe that they would be in the house on the right. They split and were taking each side to make sure that Coulter and his woman didn't get away. They both got within vision of the house that Coulter was supposed to be in. Dan hollered for Coulter to come out with his hands up. Dan could see a rifle barrel stuck out of a window. Coulter wasn't going to get caught without a fight. Coulter sent several bullets at Dan. Dan tied Buck where he couldn't be hit. Joe did the same thing with Abby's mare. They both started closing in on the house. They were staying behind anything they could for shelter. Dan was running between shelters when Coulter had changed windows and shot. Dan was shot in the leg. He dropped to the ground. Dan said, "Coulter, you son of a bitch, you just signed away your right to life." Dan took out his kerchief and tied it as tight as he could on his leg.

Joe hollered, "Are you okay?"

"Ya, for now." Dan hollered at Coulter and said, "If you don't come out now, I'll burn your house down with you in it."

Coulter said, "I have a bunch of men that will be coming back at any time. They'll kill you in one minute."

Dan said, "Are you talking about the nest of rats that are up on top? There are about a dozen of them dead, and the rest are in shackles. Your outlaw days are over. If you want to live, you must come out. Now."

Coulter asked, "If I come out, are you goin' to shoot me?"

"No, we will not shoot you as long as you and your woman come out with no guns, and with your hands up."

"Okay, we'll come out now." Coulter stepped out with his woman in front of him and had his revolver pointed at the woman's head. He hollered, "If you don't let me have a horse and leave here, I'll kill her!"

Joe hollered back and told Coulter to go ahead and kill her because he didn't give a shit. The woman pulled away and started to run. Coulter raised his gun, and *boom!* He shot her in the back of the head. At that time, Joe and Dan both opened fire. *Boom! Boom!* They shot at Coulter until they both ran out of ammunition. Joe hollered at Dan and asked if he was all right.

"Ya, I'm okay."

Joe said, "I guess that took care of Coulter." Joe and Dan went to the house to make sure there wasn't any more hiding in the house. "I think the snitch was telling the truth," said Joe. "I guess we better get the Mennonite wagon and come back for these two." Joe asked Dan to ride back to the wagons and get the iodine to fill his wound with it. He said, "I'll stay here and make sure nothing happens to Coulter. After all, he was the main one we came for."

Dan went limping back to Buck. He headed back to get the wagon. When he got there, Abby said, "Dan, you're hurt. What happened?"

"Oh, I got a little careless, and I took a bullet in my leg. But that's a long ways from my heart. I'll be okay."

Billy said, "I'll get the iodine."

Abby asked, "Is Joe okay?"

"Ya, Joe's okay."

Abby asked, "Did you get Coulter?"

"Coulter is full of bullet holes." Abby took the iodine and poured some in the wound. Dan said, "Damn it! That iodine burns worse than the bullet."

"Billy, can you dump those barrels in the Mennonite wagon and set them on the ground? We have two bodies to go get."

Dan asked Abby, "Is everything okay here?"

"Oh ya, one of the rats moved his leg, and Sammi was on top of him. Billy had to talk to Sammi and get her cooled down. He pulled her away, or she would have torn him to pieces. From that time until now, none of them moved—not even a finger."

Dan took a look at the rats and asked, "Does anybody want to challenge my dog?"

They all answered the same. "No."

Dan left with the Mennonite wagon and went down to pick up Coulter and his woman. Dan and Joe loaded them in the wagon and headed out of the canyon. When they reached the other dead and chained rats, they filled a wagon with dead outlaws. Dan asked Abby if she had a count on the dead.

She said, "There's ten dead and eleven alive."

Dan asked Joe if he and Abby, Billy, and Sammi would take the big wagon and the live rats and get them chained in the barn. He'd take the dead ones to town and dump them off at Sheriff Rusty's.

Dan was pushing the black mares pretty hard, trying to get to town before dark. Dan was noticing the weather had cooled down. A norther wind was blowing. Dan pulled into town and made it to Rusty's office. Rusty saw Dan pull up and met him at the door. Rusty said, "What the hell have you got there?"

"I've got a load of dead rats. Where do you want these bodies?"

Rusty said, "Let me see if I can get permission to put them in that building across the street." Rusty jumped on his horse and said, "I'll be back in a few minutes."

Rusty did get permission to use the building. Dan pulled the wagon around in front of a large door. Rusty opened the door. Rusty and Dan were pulling the dead out of the wagon and laying them in a row. Dan said, "What is this cool weather all about?"

"I don't know, Dan, but it is getting cold out here."

"Rusty, I need to ask you if you can have an auction in a few days. It seems to me that cold weather might hit soon."

"What for, Dan?"

"We, the hunters, decided to sell everything that comes out of the canyon. Horses, cattle, pigs, harness, and much more. That's why we need wagons and cowboys. We'll drive the cattle across. But we'll need a place to hold the cattle, horses, and pigs. And a room for everything else. After the auction, we'll give the people that were robbed and had all their things stolen from them part of the money. These people moved to get away from the Coulter gang. Then we can divide the rest of the money accordingly. I ask you to help us get this auction going."

"Dan, I will get started right away. I think I know enough people around these parts, and they will be willing to help. When you come in tomorrow morning, I should have a bunch of volunteers."

"Thanks, Rusty, I'll see you in the morning."

Dan headed back to the farm to see if everything was okay there. When Dan got there, all the rats were chained to the big chain. Abby was cooking beans for the rats. It smelled so good. Dan asked Abby if she would cook some beans for them.

"Absolutely," answered Abby. She said, "I'll cut up some ham for our beans. The rats get beans, but no ham."

Little Milly said, "Mr. Dan, we're going to have some good ol' beans for supper."

"Well, I'm glad. Thank you, little Milly." After supper, Dan said to Abby, "Those were the best beans I've ever eaten."

Billy said, "Those were really good beans, Ms. Abby."

Little Milly said, "I really liked the beans too, Ms. Abby."

"Well, thank you, I'm glad that you all enjoyed the beans. That was nice of you to say that."

The next morning, Dan was up and ready to ride to town to see what all Rusty had planned for the auction and where it would take place. Joe and Billy stayed at the farm to get all the outlaw's horses in line. Then Billy was going to drive the black mares to the Mennonite wagon to haul the thirty-four saddles. Joe had the thirty-four horses. He tied them three abreast and had the other half tied behind Billy's wagon. The rest were tied behind Smoky. Abby and little Milly were riding Sally. Dan had already ridden to town. There were teams and wagons lined up and ready to haul everything Coulter owned for the auction. Rusty came out to tell what all he had accomplished. There were cowboys going to go get the cattle. Rusty had pens for the livestock and a vacant building to store everything else in. Rusty said, "Dan, I picked out seven of the ten outlaws. There are two men and a woman. I don't have posters on those three. I marked on the posters which ones they were. But you will get bounty on them also."

"Rusty, we are wanting to head south real soon. Do you think you and the town's people can go ahead with the auction and get everything taken care of?"

Rusty rounded up the people that were ready to take their wagons out to pick up Coulter's stuff. Also, there were cowboys that would be driving the cattle back to town. While Dan and Rusty were making plans, Rusty had asked the auctioneer to help. He said he would do the auction at no charge. Joe, Billy, Abby, and little Milly were coming into town with thirty-four horses. Rusty said, "I have never seen that many horses in line, in all my life." Rusty pointed and said, "Just outside of town, there are large corrals to put horses and cattle in."

So Joe and Billy put the horses in a pen, and Joe turned the windmill on. Billy drove the wagon to the building where he could unload the saddles. Everyone was ready to start the hauling. The seven wagons were strung out. Six cowboys and two cowgirls were following. It was something how these people were willing to help, not to mention how much they were appreciating the hunters' bringing in the infested nest of rats. Most of the people made it plain that they preferred the ones they brought in horizontal. The train of wagons pulled down in the canyon. They were loading the wagons with everything imaginable. The seven wagons were stacked clear full. They loaded the hogs in one wagon. The cowboys and girls headed out with the cattle.

Later that day when the wagon crew had hauled everything there was at the Coulter hangout, the hunters were back at the farm, getting ready to head south. Now that their job was finished successfully, Abby rode up to the Hartleys to let them know that the Coulter gang was out of business and won't be back. The Hartleys were so happy and excited. They just couldn't get over what a wonderful job the hunters had done. Emma said, "Frank thought you were bounty hunters, and he was right."

Abby grinned and said, "I thank you for keeping little Milly for us."

"Oh, Abby, we enjoyed keeping little Milly so much."

Abby got back to the farm and started getting things packed in the little Milly wagon. Dan, Joe, and Billy were getting things loaded into the other two wagons. They had to load the two seats from the Mennonite wagon to the little Milly wagon so they had room for the thirteen outlaws chained together. They had to drop them off in O'Neill on the way through. Dan said, "When we get to O'Neill, I'll get a doctor to dig out the slug in my leg."

Dan asked Abby, "Are you and little Milly about ready to head south?"

"Yes, Dan, we are ready."

Joe, Dan, and Billy had everything ready, with all the outlaws chained in the wagons. They had to leave the icebox because there was not enough room. The wagons were totally filled. The weather was getting much cooler, so they wouldn't need the icebox. The hunters were on their way heading south.

By the time they reached O'Neill, the north wind was getting colder and colder. Abby and little Milly had blankets wrapped around them. They pulled up in front of the sheriff's office, and Bill, the sheriff, stepped out and shook Dan's hand and said, "Dan, you and your hunters have to be the best bounty hunters in the world."

"Well, Bill, we got 'em, but I'm not that sure that I did so good as I got careless. Now, I'm carrying a bullet in my leg. Maybe you can guide me to the town doctor. I need to get it dug out."

"Sure, Dan. Old doc Jones is up the street. He's somewhat crude, but he'll dig 'er out. You might want to take a few drinks of whiskey before lettin' ol' doc start diggin' on it."

"Sounds like I should take your advice."

Bill, Dan, Joe, Billy, Sammi, and Rusty took the outlaws in one at a time and locked them up. Sammi walked beside each outlaw with her hair standing up and constantly growling. Each of the outlaws was a little nervous as they walked beside Sammi. Bill asked Dan, "Where do you want me to send the bounty money?"

"Bill, can you send this money and the other bounty money that you put in the bank here? Just send all of it to the bank in Lariat, Texas."

"I'll do it, Dan."

The next morning, all went to the general store to get heavy clothes. Dan, Joe, and Abby were seeing to it that Billy and little Milly had plenty of warm clothes and warm coats for them too. The north winds were cold, but it hadn't started snowing yet. It could hit at any time. They went back to the saloon hotel where they had their wagons, horses, and mules. The next morning, the men hunters were getting the horses and mules harnessed and saddled. They had them ready to go. Abby and little Milly went across the street to the market and loaded up with food because they didn't know what the weather would bring or how soon. At this time, it didn't look good. Billy and Joe went to the market to carry the food that the girls had bought. They stashed away the groceries under the seat of the wagon and covered it with blankets. They headed out of O'Neill and were headed for Burwell. The wind was cold, but it was at their backs, so that helped some. Everybody was enjoying their new winter clothes. Little Milly looked like a little Eskimo down in her warm clothes.

So the hunters drove to the doctor's office. Before Dan went in, he dug out the bottle of whiskey and took a big, big pull off it before going in to see Dr. Jones. Ten minutes later, Dan came out with his leg wrapped and saying, "That damn doc Jones should be hanged." Dan said, "We better get a hotel for the night and buy some more winter clothes in the morning. The horses and mules have taken on a heavy coat of hair. That tells me that the cold and nasty weather is going to hit soon."

CHAPTER 20

A big storm was coming. The horses and mules were willing to move out a little faster. The more they put to it, the warmer they stayed. All the animals had heavy coats of hair and that included Sammi. The wind seemed to be getting stronger. The hunters were hoping that it would not snow. Dan said, "We need to get as many miles behind us as we can so we can continue trying to outrun this storm."

The days were getting shorter and that meant less miles each day. When the sun was dropping fast, Dan motioned for the rest of the hunters to pull over for the night. They unharnessed and unsaddled the horses and mules. They tied them to the wagons with their butts to the wind. The hunters had to settle for a can of beans and some jerky. There was no such thing as starting a fire in the high winds. They got the tarp tied down for the men to have a place to sleep out of the wind. They had their bunk rolls and some blankets. Billy had his new winter cap with earflaps pulled down and tied under his chin. Abby and little Milly had the Milly wagon covered to sleep in with heavy clothes and plenty of blankets. Sammi decided to sleep with the girls. She was already in the Milly wagon. The wind blew hard all night. No letup at all.

The next morning, the wind was still blowing, but there still was no snow yet. They were all anxious to get on the road heading south. They reached Burwell late that afternoon. They pulled into the rodeo grounds to spend the night. The city of Burwell's rodeo grounds had a row of stalls, so they had a place for the animals out of the wind. They pulled the wagons on the south side of the barns, getting out of the winds as much as possible. It would be much more comfortable spending the night.

Bad news when they arose the next morning. There was light snow mixed in with the blowing wind. Dan, Joe, and Abby had to make a decision. Do they take a gamble and pull out, or do they stay where they are until the storm is over? Dan said, "We have to remember, we have little Milly and Billy with us."

"Mr. Dan, don't worry about ol' Billy. Ol' Billy is a perty tough kid."

"Ya, I know, Billy, but we have to be concerned about all five of us."

Abby said, "We have food that will last us for a week or so. We have warm clothes and lots of blankets. Now I'm going to let you and Joe make that decision."

Joe said, "I think we better shut down here and see what happens. We can see what tomorrow brings. The storm could quit, or we might see three or four feet of snow. We are better off here in town than to be out ten miles from nowhere, being stranded and having a chance of running out of food."

They voted to stay. It snowed through the night, and by morning, there was a foot of snow on the ground. The wind had let up some but was still blowing, although it had stopped snowing—at least for then. Dan said, "It's obvious the storm is not over." They decided to wait awhile to see if they were going to get more snow. Dan told Billy, "Saddle Cricket and ride downtown to the general store and pick up some extra food to take along. In case we decide to pull out and something goes wrong."

"Yes, sir, Mr. Dan. Ol' Billy is on his way."

Dan handed Billy a $20 gold piece and said, "Get two burlap bags full of groceries."

Joe said, "I'll ride with Billy. If we decide to pull out, we better have more whiskey."

When Joe and Billy returned, the weather was looking more promising.

"What do you think, Joe? Should we pull out and hope for the best?"

"Let's harness up and go, Dan."

The guys were hurrying around to get on the road. Billy had the lead with the mules and the big wagon. The foot of snow did slow them down some, but the powerful mules had very little problem with the snow. They broke the trail for the other teams. After they pulled out of Burwell and got to the trail, somebody else had already made a trail with a team and wagon. That helped and made their traveling much easier. The next destination was Broken Bow. Dan told Billy to make the mules move out, that they'd keep up. The hunters were running for it. When they stopped for the night, it was so dark. Joe had to light the lantern so they could see to undress the horses and mules and so Joe could find one of the bottles he bought.

The weather was cold but not snowing. The wind had almost stopped. The hunters were praying for no snow. Broken Bow was probably no more than fifteen miles away. They could get there early tomorrow. They might get Abby's business taken care of, and they could be on their way again.

When they did roll in to Broken Bow, it was before noon. Dan and Abby pulled in front of the lawyer's office. Joe and Billy went straight to the fairgrounds. Dan and Abby went in to meet with Albert Manson to see what he and Frank Adams had come up with about the farm. Albert had all the figures in front of him. The ranch, 4,000 acres, at $6 per acre would be $24,000. The cattle, numbered 409 head, at $6 per head would be $2,454. The thirty-eight head of horses at $30 per head would be $1,140. All the machinery would be $3,000. That made a total of $30,594.

"Ms. Lacy, this is what he is willing to pay you for everything."

"I assume this is a fair price?" asked Abby.

"Yes, Ms. Lacy, it is. I had an appraiser go out and do an appraisal. Here is what the appraiser wrote: 'The price that Mr. Frank Adams has offered Ms. Abigail Lacy is a fair price for buyer and seller.'"

"Mr. Manson, I will except Mr. Adam's offer," Abby said. "I also ask if you can send a bank draft and the bank account that Uncle John left me to the bank in Lariat, Texas, under my name."

"I will take care of everything, Ms. Lacy. Your balance should be $116,594."

Abby signed the agreement and shook Albert's hand. Dan and Abby were heading back to the fairgrounds. When they returned to the fairgrounds, Joe and Billy hadn't unharnessed. They didn't know how long it would take to get Abby's business taken care of. Dan said, "We might as well head out. It's barely noon."

They did pull out, and the farther they went, the less snow there was on the ground. That made it easy traveling. They made several more miles before it was time to stop. In the middle of the night, the wind came up again. The hunters were nervous, and Dan peeked out under the tarp. He could see snow in the wind. It was too dark to hitch up and try to get on the trail. So they would have to wait until daylight, then pull out. And that is what they did.

They pulled out early the next morning. It appeared the snow was getting thicker. Visibly, they couldn't see very far, so they traveled as close to each other as they could, in case the snow got worse. Dan could see a farmhouse and a field with several stacks of hay. Dan waved for the rest of them to pull into the field and pull the wagons close to each other. Dan explained, "The reason why we pulled in this field *is* the stacks of hay will keep our stock alive if we get buried with snow." It wasn't looking good. The wind was howling, and the snow was getting thicker. After about thirty minutes, they couldn't see ten feet in any direction. Dan told Billy, "Don't attempt to go anywhere. If you were to attempt to get to the horses and lose your direction and get lost, you will freeze to death out there, as cold as it is." Dan hollered and asked Abby, "Is everything okay in there with you and little Milly?"

"Yes, Dan, we are doing okay."

"Abby, you girls don't leave the wagon under any circumstances."

"Okay, Dan, we won't."

Dan told Billy to hop in the big wagon and get the hammer and break the ice on the top of the barrels and to throw the broken pieces of ice out. "In the morning, we'll do it again." Dan and Joe were wrestling with the tarp, trying to get it tied down. The wind was whipping it so bad they could hardly hold on to it. They finally managed to get it tied and that helped block the wind. The wind and snow hadn't let up. It was a full-blown, ugly blizzard. In the morning, they could see at least three foot of snow, and it was still snowing pretty hard. They had plenty of food, although some of it were frozen. They made do with what they had. Jerky was always good in a bad situation. The hunters were tired of snow and cold. They were blocked in. They didn't know at this time how bad or how long they'd be blocked in. The blizzard was not giving up. It blew all through the day and went into the night and hadn't let up yet. About midnight, Dan noticed the tarp wasn't whipping nearly as bad. Dan stuck his head out of his bunk roll and said, "Thank you, God. Let's make plans to get back on the road."

In the morning, there was no wind. No snow. Just blocked in. Dan said, "Joe, you and Billy lead the horses and mules and take 'em to the closest stack of hay and turn them loose so they can fill up." Dan was waddling through the snow on his way to the farmhouse. Talking about snow up to your butt. Dan got to the house and was greeted by the farmer's wife. Dan asked, "Who do I talk with about buying a stack of hay?"

"Just a minute and I'll get my husband."

The husband came out of the back room and asked," What can I do for ya?"

Dan said, "My name is Dan Colt."

"Hi, Dan. Percy Hall is my name."

Dan said, "I would like to buy a stack of hay."

"Come on in. I seen you pull in last night, but thirty minutes later, I couldn't see past my porch. Is your group okay?"

"Ya, we're okay. It wasn't the most comfortable two nights I've ever spent, but everybody is fine."

"You say you want to buy a stack of hay?"

"Yes, I need to pay you for the hay my animals eat."

"How about one dollar?"

Dan said, "You are being overly fair. Are you sure that is enough?"

"Ya, I'm sure."

Dan paid and waddled through the snow, getting back to the camp. Billy said, "Mr. Dan, guess how I got through the deep snow."

"I don't know, Billy. How did you get through the deep snow?"

"I hopped on mule John and rode him to the haystack."

Joe and Dan were discussing how they could get out of there. They knew that the horses and mules would play out real fast. Dan looked and noticed Percy coming through the tracks Dan left. "Hi, Percy." Percy said hi back." Dan introduced Joe. "Joe, this is Percy Hall." They shook hands.

Percy said, "I didn't think to tell you, if you are wanting to pull out, there is a log wagon that comes through every day, except Sunday. One day it's the father. The next day will be the son, with a load of logs. They usually come through about nine o'clock, but he will be a little later today because of the deep snow. He will have a six up hitch of big horses. He usually has a four up, but when it snows this deep, he uses the lead team to break the way through the deep snow. His other four are pullin' the load. After they go through, you'll be able to follow him."

"How far does he go?" asked Dan.

"I don't know how far he goes, but he comes back late."

They thanked Percy and started thinking this could be their way out. They caught the stock and harnessed them and were ready to roll. They had waited for quite some time. They were getting disappointed. Billy hollered,

"Here he comes, here he comes!" They hitched to the wagons and were ready to pull out. Within ten minutes, the hunters were moving again. The horses and mules were full of hay, and Billy had broken the ice out of the barrels, and the stock all had a drink. Traveling was a little slower, but every step was one step farther from the storm. They were getting out of the storm area. The hunters followed the log wagon for miles. They could see ahead of the log wagon. There were tracks from the other wagons that had gone through. Dan hollered at Billy to go around the log wagon and get the mules moving. After all of them passed the log wagon, they could move a lot faster. They could see the snow was getting less as they traveled south.

The day was coming to an end. They were looking for a nice place to camp. They found an old, vacant farm. They could tie the horses and mules in the old barn, and it would be shelter for the wagons. Sammi was growling and staring toward the back of the barn.

Dan asked, "What is it, Sammi?" Dan walked around the barn and found an old man sitting on an old broken chair. He had a white horse tied to the fence. Dan asked, "How you doing, old-timer?"

He answered, "Fine, just fine."

"What brings you here?"

The old man said, "Just passin' through."

"Where you headed?" asked Dan.

"Don't know."

"Where do you live?"

"I don't have a home."

Dan said, "You look a little gant. Haven't you been eatin'?"

"No, not much."

"Are you spending the night here?"

"I was thinking about it. Do you think it would hurt anything?"

"No, I don't think so," said Dan. "We are staying here too. My name is Dan Colt. What's your name?"

"My name is Arnold Hicks."

"Well, Arnold, you can eat with us tonight."

"You sure you don't mind?" asked Arnold.

"No, we don't mind."

So Abby cooked a meal, and there was plenty for everybody. Arnold was their guest. Arnold was hungry and took on a big fill. They talked for a couple hours. Dan asked Arnold a lot of questions. Arnold didn't have a home. He had no relatives—nothing, other than what he had on and what he had in his saddlebags. He had a soiled blanket tied behind his saddle and his horse, Bud. The hunters all were feeling sorry for Arnold.

The next morning, they were getting ready to move on. Abby had baked some biscuits and made gravy and coffee. Abby asked Billy to go wake Arnold up for breakfast.

"Okay, Ms. Abby."

Billy shook Arnold's arm and said, "Mr. Arnold, it's time for breakfast."

Arnold said, "No, young man, I don't want to impose. I ate with you last night."

"Come on, Mr. Arnold, you're going to eat breakfast with us."

Dan heard Billy and Arnold talking. So he came over and told Arnold, "You are invited to eat with us, and if you don't eat with us, Abby is going to feel real bad."

"Well, okay, if you're sure you don't mind."

After breakfast, they had the horses and mules harnessed and ready to go. Abby called Dan to one side and asked, "What are we going to with Arnold?"

"What do you mean, Abby?"

"Dan, I can't drive away and leave Arnold out here by himself. He has no money and no place to go. He would go right back to starvation."

"What do you have in mind, Abby?"

"Why can't he travel with us until we can find some place where somebody can help him?"

"Well, Abby, I guess we can ask him to go with us."

So Abby went and had a talk with Arnold. At first, Arnold kept shaking his head no. Little Milly had a hold on Abby's finger and said, "Mr. Arnold, we want you to go with us."

Dan came over and said to Arnold, "We want you to go with us."

Billy heard them talking. He came over and said, "We really do want you to go with us, Mr. Arnold."

Arnold said, "I have no money. I wouldn't be able to pay my way."

Joe said, "Don't worry about the money. We want you to go with us."

Dan said, "How about helping Billy take care of the horses and mules? Then you will be paying your way."

"Well, okay, if you're sure."

Abby smiled and said, "We're sure."

Billy spoke up and said, "Mr. Arnold, if you want, you can tie your horse, Bud, behind the wagon, and you can ride with me and Sammi on the mule wagon."

—

They did just that. The string has just gotten a little longer. Arnold was smiling, sitting beside Billy and Sammi. The weather was still cold, but not as bad, after getting away from that snowstorm. Arnold didn't have much for warm clothes either. His blanket was about worn out. His jacket was thin and had several holes in it. That afternoon, they pulled into Dodge City. When they saw a general store, Abby hollered for Billy to pull up the mules. Abby stepped down from her wagon and walked up to the mule wagon and said, "Come with me, Arnold." She got him down from the mule wagon and insisted he come with her. So in the store, she told the clerk, "We want new boots, a heavy coat, a warm new blanket, and a warm winter cap."

"But, missy, I can't accept all these things."

"Let me ask you. If you and I were good friends and you saw me cold and hungry, would you help me?"

"Well, sure. I would, missy, but—"

"Well, but what?" asked Abby. When they came out of the store, Arnold looked like a new man.

They were rolling again, heading for Texas. The next two days, they drove hard. They pulled out of Kansas into Oklahoma where they spent the night. One more full day and they would be in Texas. Dan asked Joe if he remembered the name of the town in Texas.

"No, I don't think, I do."

Billy put his hand in the air and said, "I do. That's where you guys whomped on the sleazers that were throwin' beer on ol' Roy."

Joe said, "That will work out just right. That's a full day's drive from here. We can stay there overnight and check with Roy to see if Daryl and Frank are bein' good boys."

Arnold fit right in with the hunters. He and Billy took care of the mules and horses. Arnold felt like he was doing something to help pay his way. All of the hunters liked Arnold, and Arnold thought the hunters were very special. When Arnold got up in the morning, he would say a little prayer, and when he would go to bed at night, he would also say his little prayer. The hunters were moving through the Oklahoma Panhandle. They're getting anxious to get back to Lariat and settle down for a while and be with their friends. Dan wouldn't admit it, but he was anxious to get back with Maggie. Billy was anxious to get back and see Maggie too. He missed all the rest of his town friends. As the day wore on, the hunters finally entered the little town where the home of Roy's Saloon was. Billy was excited to see if the sleazers had been throwing beer on ol' Roy. They stopped at the edge of town and set up camp. Billy and Arnold unharnessed the mules and horses. They put hobbles on all of them so they could graze. First, they gave all of them a drink of water. Billy was wanting to hurry up the rest of the hunters so they could go to the saloon and check with Roy. Finally, they headed for the saloon to have a drink before they went to the café for supper. They walked in and sat at a table. Roy came over to their table to take their order. Roy remembered Dan, Joe, and Billy. He shook all their hands and took their order. Dan asked, "Arnold, do you drink whiskey?"

Arnold said, "Sometimes, a little, but not much."

Dan told Roy to bring a bottle of whiskey and four glasses and two sarsaparillas for the kiddies.

Billy spoke up and asked, "Mr. Roy, have those sleazers thrown beer on you anymore?"

"No, they have been real good. You guys put the fear of God in those boys."

Billy asked, "Did they ever act like they might throw beer on you?"

"Nope, they never did. When they come in, they always come up and shake my hand."

Billy asked, "Did you ever think that they might have been thinking about throwin' beer on you."

"No, you guys have done a miracle for me, and I will owe you for the rest of my life." The hunters enjoyed a couple of glasses of whiskey. Dan went to the bar to pay. Roy shook his head no. "You don't owe me anything. I owe you guys." Roy totally refused any money.

They were ready to push on the next morning. Billy and Arnold had the teams harnessed and hitched to the wagons. Everybody was aboard, and they were off again. After two hard days of travel, they pulled into Vega—the town where they took out the maggots. They pulled up to the livery barn and asked Matt if he sold the nine horses.

Matt said, "I sold eight of them. I still have one horse and one saddle."

Dan asked Matt, "How much do we owe you?"

"Twelve dollars," answered Matt. Dan paid Matt. "Dan, I'll write a note so you can take it to the bank and pick up the $320."

"Oh, the sheriff said, when you stop by, to let you know that he sent the bounty money to your bank in Lariat." Matt said, "I'll be right back." A couple minutes after, Matt came out leading the horse with the saddle. "Billy, jump down and take the horse and tie him to the back of your wagon."

Dan shook Matt's hand and thanked him for everything. The hunters pulled out to the same place they had camped before. Dan rode to the bank and picked up the money from the sale of the horses. The bank gave Dan the money in a small canvas bag. When he got to the camp, he asked Abby if she would put the bag of money in a safe place.

"Sure, Dan, I'll put it with Billy's racing money."

The hunters were dragging in their tracks. It had been a long, hard venture. The hunters, the mules, the horses, and Sammi were all very tired. Two more hard days had passed. They pulled into a little town called Hub, Texas. Dan saw a telegraph office. He stopped in and told the operator to send a telegraph to Maggie at the Wagon Wheel Saloon. "I want you to say, 'Maggie, have a bottle of whiskey, four glasses, and two sarsparillas ready. We'll be in tomorrow afternoon.'" When Maggie received the telegraph, she couldn't understand why four glasses instead of two, why two sarsaparillas instead of one.

The hunters came rolling into Lariat right on time. People came running out to the street, yelling, "Welcome back!"

CHAPTER 21

A welcome home party was about to start. The people of Lariat were so glad to see that everybody came back alive. They were all hugging Billy. Needless to say, Billy was wearing his .45 on one hip and his hunter knife on the other. The crowd were shaking hands with Dan and Joe. Sammi was getting many pats on her head. Sammi let out her little, friendly barks. Little Milly was getting a lot of attention too. Abby was learning how friendly the people of Lariat were. Arnold asked Dan, "Can I take the wagons one at a time so we can put the horses and mules away?"

"If you want, Arnold. Pull up by the livery, and ask Frank where to put everything. He'll show you."

Dan asked Billy to find out from Abby where he could find the two sacks of money. He wanted to bring them in and have Maggie put them away.

"Okay, Mr. Dan."

The news of the hunters' return spread fast. It wasn't long before the saloon was packed with people. It was a big celebration. Everybody was wanting to know what all took place on their trip. Maggie cleaned a table and sat Dan, Joe, Abby, Billy, and little Milly. She even saved a chair for Arnold. Maggie said, "Dan, I'm so happy that you're back." The party went on for several hours. Dan, Joe, Abby, and little Milly rented rooms in the hotel. Arnold insisted he wanted to sleep in the wagon. Of course, Billy had his bedroom in the back of the saloon. They were all so tired. They just wanted to get some rest.

The next morning, the hunters gathered at a table in the saloon. Dan asked Abby, "What are your intentions, now that the big hunt is over?"

"I don't know, Dan. For some reason, I really don't want to go back to my place fifty miles south of here. Every time I ride into my town, Littlefield, it brings back old memories. I was thinking after the celebration last night and seeing how nice and friendly the people are in this town, I might stick around here for a few days and just look around. Who knows, I might decide to buy or build a house here in Lariat. I did a lot of thinking when we were traveling. I remembered that Lariat didn't have a school. When I was a little girl, I always wanted to be a schoolteacher. Now that I have little Milly, she's going to need schooling. Billy and all the kids in this town need schooling."

Maggie said, "Abby, that would be wonderful. You're right about this town needing a school." Dan said he would be willing to help with the expenses. Maggie said, "I can guarantee you, the people of Lariat will volunteer their labor, with no charge."

Abby asked them not to say anything just yet. She wanted to look around and make sure that's what she wanted to do. Abby was going to saddle Sally and ride out and see if there was anything of interest to her. Billy offered to ride with her and show her around. So they left. Abby and Billy rode all around Lariat. While riding on the outskirts of town, Abby saw a level piece of land with an old fallen down house. She asked, "Do you know, Billy, who owns this vacant property?"

"Yes, Ms. Abby. The old guy died, and it never resold. Carl Jones was his name. I think it could be for sale. I think Ms. Maggie will know."

After riding all of the close, outlying properties, Abby and Billy returned to the saloon. Abby asked Maggie if she knew who to contact about the old Carl Jones place. She wanted to see if it was for sale.

"Yes, Robert Stoner, the owner of the bank."

"Thank you, Maggie. I'm going to walk down and see what Robert knows about the place."

Abby and Billy went to talk to Robert. He invited them in and asked them to have a chair. Then Robert asked how he could help them. Billy introduced Robert to Abby. Robert asked, "Are you Ms. Lacy?"

"Yes, I am."

"Ms. Lacy, I received a bank draft in your name. It was a rather large sum of money."

"Yes, I would like you to hold it in your vault for now. What I'm here for, Robert, is to ask you about the Carl Jones place."

"What did you want to know, Ms. Lacy?"

"I was wondering if it is for sale."

"Yes, Ms. Lacy, the land is for sale. The old house is absolutely beyond repair. So the ten acres at $20 per acre would total $200. I realize that sounds kinda high, but it is close to town. In fact, the road in front of the property is in the town limits. So that's a real fair price."

"Okay, Robert, I want to buy it."

Billy jumped up and said, "Yahoo!"

"Ms. Lacy, if I would be guessing, I would guess that Billy wants you to live in Lariat." Abby and Robert had a good laugh.

When Billy returned to the saloon, Dan asked Billy to start unloading the 48 rifles, 48 handguns, and all the knives, then stash them in the back room of the saloon. Billy had a full day's work. Billy started carrying guns and stashing the guns as Dan had said. When Billy went back to the livery stable, Frank told Billy, "Tell Dan I sold three horses with saddles, but I still have one horse left, and I don't know what happened to the fourth saddle."

"Mr. Frank, I know where it is. Mr. Dan gave it to me before we left for the big hunt."

"Oh, okay, Billy. Now I know. Tell Dan he can pick up the money from the others that I sold for him."

"Okay, Mr. Frank, I'll tell him."

Dan and Joe checked with Robert at the bank to see if the bounty monies had arrived yet. If it had, they'd now have to decide how to divide the money. Dan and Joe had the figures from the bank. They went to the saloon. They sat at a table and tried to figure how to make it fair. Joe said, "If it is okay with you, Dan, let's split it four ways."

"You mean you, me, Billy, and Abby?"

"Well, Dan, I feel they played a big part in the captures too." Abby and little Milly came in and sat down at the table.

Dan asked, "Abby, would you be satisfied with the money split four ways?"

"No, I wouldn't. I told you when I joined in with you guys that I did not want any of the bounty money, and I refuse any part of it."

Joe said, "Abby, you put yourself in harm's way. You played a big part in the capture of the rats."

Abby said, "I was a voluntary hunter, and I enjoyed every part of it. It was fun to bring that many bad people down."

"Okay, how about if we build the new schoolhouse?"

"If you guys want to donate to the new school, that would be up to you. And if you do, that would be very nice."

So that's what they did. They also put $10,000 in Billy's bank account. Tears welled up in Billy's eyes when he found out about the deposit. Billy doesn't even know how much $10,000 is. Abby had a meeting for the town's people at the saloon. She wanted it there because it was the largest building in town. Saturday evening, the town's people filled the saloon. Abby started the meeting by asking if they would approve of her building a new schoolhouse on the ten acres she had recently purchased. Maggie stood up and said, "Let me make this more clear. Abby is willing to furnish some of her property to build the schoolhouse on. She is going to teach the school with no pay. Now I'm going to ask for volunteers to help build the schoolhouse. Okay, if you are in favor of Abby building the schoolhouse on her property, raise your hand." Every hand in the place went up. "Okay, how many are willing to pitch in and help with the labor?" Every hand in the room went up.

Dan stood up and said, "Joe Cobb and I are willing to pay for all the materials." The people all stood up and started applauding. It was so loud it hurt their ears. Dan said, "Now that you are all here, I need to have you witness something for me."

All the people said, "Sure," and nodded their heads.

One man said, "Sure, Dan, what is it?"

Dan went to Maggie. He took her to the center of the floor. Every eye was on the two of them. Maggie and Dan were facing each other. Dan held her hands in his and asked Maggie, "Do you love me enough to marry me?"

Yes, yes, yes, I do, and yes, I will marry you," answered Maggie.

The people were so excited. They clapped louder than before. Dan said, "Maggie, could I ask you for a very special request?"

"Sure, Dan, what is it?"

Dan asked, "Maggie, will you wear that beautiful green gown that you were wearing the first time I seen you at the wedding?"

"Sure, Dan, if you want me to."

Dan said, "Now I want to buy everybody a drink."

Everybody was having so much fun. They were hugging Maggie and shaking Dan's hand. Some of them were buying Dan and Maggie drinks. This went on for a couple hours.

The next morning, Dan, Maggie, Abby, Billy, and Sammi started planning the wedding. They finally decided that it would be on Saturday, at the church in one week. Maggie asked Abby, "Would you be my maid of honor?"

"Absolutely, Maggie, I am honored to be asked."

Dan looked at Billy and asked, "Are you going to be the best man?"

"Sure, Mr. Dan, I'll be the best man."

All through the week, Maggie and Abby made all the plans. They made a big sign that read "Maggie and Dan are getting married, Saturday, Feb. 25th at the church. The whole town is invited."

Dan was at the bank, asking Robert if he had a nice house for sale.

Robert said, "I have several. Tell me what you're looking for."

"I would like something with a little acreage, something with two bedrooms because Billy is probably going to be living with us."

"Let me see what I can come up with, Dan, and I'll see you around the saloon a little later."

"Thank you, Robert." Dan went to the clothing store. He asked Richard, the owner, if he had two suits—one his size and one Billy's size.

"I think I can fix you up. I have to take some measurements." He measured Dan and asked him to send Billy down so he could measure him. Abby also bought a new gown. She doesn't pack one when she's traveling.

Friday, Dan picked up the suits for him and Billy. He also bought a diamond ring for Maggie. Dan told Billy that he would carry the ring, and when the preacher asked for it, he would hand it to him, then Dan would put it on Maggie's finger.

"Okay, Mr. Dan, I can do that."

Everything went well right up to and through the wedding. Maggie was wearing the beautiful emerald green gown that Dan had requested she wore. She was so beautiful. Dan could not keep his eyes off her. Abby was dressed in her beautiful pastel, green gown. Little Milly was dressed in a little pink dress, with the little pink necklace that Abby had found under the seat of the wagon.

It was time for the wedding, and they were all a little nervous. First, Billy walked down the aisle and stood exactly where he was told to stand. Dan walked down the aisle and stood where he was told to stand. Then it was Abby's turn. She walked down the aisle and stood where she was told to. Now it was Maggie's turn. The church was full. There were a lot of people standing outside. When Maggie started down the aisle, Dan, Abby, and Billy turned to face Maggie as she walked toward them. All the people in the church stood up. Maggie had a very big smile on her face as she walked and stood beside Dan. The preacher was just about to start with the wedding when Sammi came down the aisle and sat down by Billy. Billy looked down and saw her. Billy whispered to her, "Sammi, you're not supposed to be in here."

The preacher looked down and smiled and said, "She's all right. She's part of the wedding party."

Sammi just couldn't hold it back. She had to give her little bark. All the people couldn't hold it back either. They all busted out laughing. That was part of the humor of the wedding. The wedding was short and sweet. After they said their vows and kissed, all the guests headed for the saloon for the reception party. Needless to say, the party started immediately after the wedding at the saloon.

Maggie hired Bart, a piano player, to play for the dance. Bart was pounding out the songs. Sisters Emma and Caroline began to sing with the music. People were dancing in the saloon and outside on the walkway and even some in the street. One woman said it was the largest turnout for a wedding party that she'd ever seen. Bart kept hammering out the tunes. Emma and Caroline were singing every song that Bart played. The dancing went on until the wee hours of the morning. The town's people were so happy that Maggie, being one person the town loves, and Dan, being another person that the whole town had taken in as a very special person, were finally married.

Several days after the wedding, Dan did buy a house with twelve acres so he could keep the mules, Buck, Claude, the black team, Maggie's mare, Nancy, and, of course, Cricket. Within a month of Abby's purchase of the ten acres, she hired two strong young men to dismantle the old house. Abby hired two carpenters to start building her new house and the new schoolhouse. In the spring of 1889, Abby and little Milly moved into their new house. The schoolhouse was built and ready for school. Dan, Billy, Arnold, and Sammi pulled out for Amarillo to pick up all the supplies to run a school. They had to take the mule wagon and the Mennonite wagon to pick up a desk for the teacher and twenty desks for the pupils. Billy was on the mule wagon, and Arnold was riding with Billy and Sammi. Dan was on the Mennonite wagon.

Abby and Maggie were becoming very good friends. Abby spent a lot of time at the saloon visiting with Maggie. They both enjoyed little Milly. The whole town loves little Milly and Billy. Abby and Maggie were making plans for a birthday party for Billy when they get back. They should get back on March 3. Billy's birthday is March 5. Abby was having Billy's party at her new house. The word got around town about Billy's birthday. Maggie had everybody in town trying to find somebody that raises German shepherd pups like Sammi. Robert from the bank had a relative that raised shepherds, but they were thirty miles away. Robert sent a telegraph asking if they had any that would be ready to wean. Buddy from the telegraph office brought a note saying they had four puppies that were ready to be weaned. Maggie said, "I don't know how I can get there having to run the saloon." Abby volunteered to go and pick up a puppy for Billy. Maggie said, "I can't ask you to go."

"No, Maggie, I want to go. I want to see the look on Billy's face when he sees the puppy."

"Are you sure, Abby?"

"Yes, I'm sure, Maggie. Maggie, are there any ladies here that would watch little Milly for two days? I'll be one day going and one day coming back. I'll leave early tomorrow morning."

Maggie found a place for little Milly. Abby was on her way to pick up the puppy. Her horse, Sally, was strong and could make thirty miles in one day. The weather was still cool. That made it much easier on Sally. Sally did make thirty miles as she pulled into a small town. That was where the people lived that raised shepherds. It was late, so Abby decided to get a room at the hotel. The hotel was like Maggie's, a saloon with the hotel above. Abby put Sally away but decided to buckle on her gun and holster. She was in a strange place. She went back to the saloon and rented a room. Before going to her room, she sat down at the bar and asked the barkeep for a glass of whiskey. After he sat the glass in front of her, the barkeep asked, "Are you travelin' through?"

Abby said, "I'm here to pick up a shepard puppy."

The barkeep said, "By the way, my name is John."

"Hi, John. My name is Abby."

John asked, "Are you looking for the Adams' place?"

"I guess," she said. "All I know is there's people here that sell shepherd puppies."

"Ya, you're lookin' for Dick and Ina Adams. They're the people that raise the puppies."

"Where is their place?" asked Abby.

"Well, Abby, there is an alley next to the saloon."

"Yes, I seen that."

"Okay, if you go out the front door, go around the corner and down the alley, about—maybe—four blocks, you'll see the dogs. They have lots of dogs."

"Thank you, John. Save my drink. I'm going down and take a look, so if I can buy one tonight, that will let me get an early start back in the morning." Abby went out and down the alley to the Adamses' house. When she got there, she thought, *Boy, John was right, there are lots of dogs.* Abby knocked on the door. When the door opened, a lady stood there. Abby asked, "Are you Ina?"

"Yes, I'm Ina." After Abby told her what she needed. Ina took her out back and showed her the puppies.

Abby said, "There is nothing cuter than puppies." After ten minutes of playing with the puppies, Abby picked a little male puppy that was marked exactly like Sammi. Abby asked, "How much is this one?"

Ina said, "They are $2 each."

Abby said, "I want this one."

"Can I pick him up tomorrow morning, about six o'clock?"

Ina said, "I'll have him cleaned up and ready to go."

Abby went back to the saloon. There were two guys that had come in and sat at the bar, the next seat from Abby's. They seemed to be somewhat intoxicated. Abby was a little nervous, but was watching from the corner of her eye. The one that was closest to Abby was staring at her. He reached over and touched her arm. Abby flinched and said, "Get your slimy hands off me, you son of a bitch." The drunk reached over and took hold of her arm a second time. Abby jumped up and grabbed her gun, swung it as hard as she could, hitting him across the nose and eye. When he hit the floor, Abby grabbed his gun and jumped over him and surprised the other drunk. Then she grabbed his gun out of his holster and handed the guns to the barkeep and said, "Keep these guns until these two bastards sober up."

John said, "You guys get the hell out of here before she kills both of you." He pulled their drinks away and said, "Now get out!" The one that was still sitting at the bar slid off his stool and was trying to help the one on the floor get up. John went around the bar and grabbed hold of the one on the floor and stood him up. He took him to the door and shoved both of them out the door. When John went back behind the bar, he said, "I don't think this is your first time taking care of a problem."

Abby said, "I need another drink to settle my nerves."

John set a glass of whiskey in front of Abby and said, "This one is on me. It was worth that to see you go into action." They both laughed. Abby retired to her room.

The next morning, Abby got up early and picked up the puppy. They were on their way, headed back to Lariat. Abby had a blanket tied on the saddle. She knew this puppy was going to spring a leak once in a while. She put the blanket over her lap and on the saddle in front of her. The motion from Sally walking kept the puppy sleeping. She rode into Lariat late, but it was still daylight. Abby went to her house and fed the puppy and left him in a box, with a blanket for him to sleep on. Abby rode back to the saloon to tell Maggie about the puppy. Maggie was so excited about the puppy. She couldn't quit thanking Abby for going after the puppy for her.

Abby asked, "Where are we going to keep him so Billy won't find him?" Maggie decided to keep the puppy upstairs in one little room where she kept the clean sheets and pillowcases. Maggie had him all fixed up with a big fluffy blanket. She had some newspapers that Billy hadn't had time to take out to the trash yet. She covered the whole floor with the papers.

The next day was March 3. Dan, Billy, Arnold, and Sammi came rolling in with all the school desks and all the supplies that it takes to run a school. Dan, Billy, Arnold, and Sammi stopped in the saloon. After they ordered their drinks, Maggie brought them to the table. Maggie asked Dan if he would come with her.

Dan said, "Sure," and followed Maggie upstairs. When they got there, Maggie told Dan about the puppy. Dan asked, "Where is it?" Maggie took Dan by the hand and led him to the little room and opened the door. Dan said, "Maggie, that was a good idea. Billy's going to love that puppy. Okay, now when the puppy starts crying, you're going to be able to hear him down in the saloon. I know Billy's going to hear him."

"How loud can you hear him?"

"Just barely, but he is going to hear something he's never heard in here before. Okay, let me handle it, Maggie."

They went back down to the saloon. Dan went to the table and sat down and told Billy, "There is a rat upstairs. Do you think, Billy, you could go up and catch him and kill him?"

"No, Mr. Dan, I'm scared of rats. Don't you remember, Mr. Dan?"

Dan said, "Oh, that's right, I guess I forgot." You might know it wasn't five minutes before the puppy started crying.

Billy asked, "What's that noise?"

Dan said, "That's the rat."

Billy said, "I didn't know that rats made that kinda noise."

"When did you ever see a rat, Billy? You didn't stick around long enough to know what they sound like." It worked. Dan was completely assured that Billy wasn't going up those stairs under any circumstances. When Maggie brought another round of drinks. She smiled and patted Dan on the arm.

The morning of March 5, the people in Lariat were preparing for Billy's birthday party. Maggie asked Dan if he could keep Billy away from Abby's house until about six o'clock. Everybody should be there by then. Dan did that. When it was time, he and Billy rode over to Abby's new house. The closer they got, the more Billy noticed all the people. He said, "Wow, I hope nothing is wrong."

Dan and Billy tied their horses to the fence. As they were walking to the house, Dan asked Billy, "Do you know what day this is?"

Billy said, "I don't know, Mr. Dan."

"Well, Billy, this is March the fifth."

Billy looked at Dan and said, "This is my birthday, Mr. Dan?"

"That's right, Billy, this is your birthday. You are now thirteen years old."

Dan opened the door and let Billy go in first. If you talk about happy tears, Billy had an abundance of happy tears. The table in the middle of the floor was stacked with gifts and a big birthday cake that Abby had baked. Billy just couldn't stop those happy tears. Little Milly walked over to Billy and put her arms around him and said, "It's okay, Billy. It's okay."

Abby said, "Little Milly, those are happy tears. Billy is happy because it's his birthday, and he's happy with all the presents."

Billy started opening the presents, and the people were clapping every time he opened another present. He finally had opened all the presents that were on the table. Then Abby handed Billy her present. Billy opened it, and there was a brand-new, shiny .45 Colt. Billy just couldn't get rid of the happy tears. Dan handed Billy the present he had for him. Billy opened it, and there was a new shiny .44 Mag rifle and two boxes of shells. Billy was so excited. He couldn't get rid of those tears.

Maggie said, "Now, here's my present for you," as she gave him a big hug. Maggie opened the bedroom door. Out came the puppy. "Well, I guess you know." Everybody knew that everywhere Billy went, that puppy was going to be with him. Maggie asked, "Well, Billy, what are you going to name the puppy?"

As Billy held the puppy to his chest, he said, "I'm goin' to call him Buckshot."

The End

Get Published, Inc!
Thorofare, NJ 08086
15 October 2009
BA2009288